MW01098603

The Bridesmaid

By

Meg Gray

Meg Gray Edition 2013

Publisher Meg Gray

www.megcgray.com

For the newlyweds, Corrinne and Mike

Wishing you many years of wedded bliss.

Acknowledgements

First off, I would like to thank my husband for his incredible support and love. My children for their encouragement and interest in the stories I write. You are both an inspiration to me.

While I served as Oregon's Polled Hereford Queen in 1998, I have been removed from the beef industry for several years and want to thank Aunt Mary and Uncle Jim of Prather Ranch for sharing their wealth of knowledge about organic beef and farmers markets. Many thanks go to Corrinne for not only having a wedding this year which helped provide me with a great opportunity for research, but also for answering all questions related to Portland and the law. Allison, thanks for the help with the sorority details and I hope you were one of the nice girls!

And a very big thank you to the EZ Writers for their careful attention to detail and thoughtful critiques that have made my writing in general much better.

One

Everyone knows the color of envy is green and the color of love is red, but what is the color of deceit? Kate Michaels wondered this as she stepped over the streetcar tracks and onto the sidewalk in downtown Portland. If anyone asked her that question today, she would answer ivory. The simple, understated shade of the knee-length dress she wore screamed fraud—but it felt so good to wear something new and fashionable. She reached around and felt for the price tag, making sure it was still tucked beneath her wheat colored hair.

Kate didn't know when she'd started wearing deception so easily, but she was layering it on as if it were the new trend. The little white lies started out as small half-truths, but they'd grown, taking on a life of their own.

This dress, for instance, with its elegant crocheted overlay and silk lining that brushed against her skin like a whisper, let her hope for once that she wouldn't feel like the ugly stepsister among the tightly bonded sorority sisters—a group she'd been on the fringe of since freshman year at Oregon State University.

Kate lifted her chin and squared her shoulders, practicing her walk of confidence as she neared the restaurant where she was having lunch with the aforementioned sisters. The sun slipped behind a cloud as Kate stepped inside. A whiff of new paint rose and then sank under the wave of aromas that came from the kitchen. The interior was dark and sophisticated, gray walls, exposed brick and dark woods.

A young man dressed in black stood behind a podium and smiled at her. A flash of red stitching on his shirt read: Mike.

"Welcome to Alejandro's," he said with a big smile. "How may I help you?"

"I'm here for the Goodwich lunch," she told him. Mary Goodwich, her former roommate and life-saving friend, announced her engagement two days ago and dubbed Kate a bridesmaid. It was the only reason she was here subjecting herself to this lunch. He nodded and stepped toward the large opening of the black velvet curtains that led to the interior of the restaurant when the main door opened again. He froze. Kate looked over her shoulder and followed his gaze.

In the doorway, silhouetted by the radiant spring light, stood Olivia Fisher—the undisputed leader of the Fierce Four, sister of the groom, friend of the bride, and the queen of mean.

She wore a crisp black shirtdress, smartly tied at the waist. The silver zipper, starting at the dress's knee-length hemline, stopped short of her bosom, leaving a gape that exposed her impressive cleavage. The wind blew her long, straight, black hair in her face as the door closed behind her. Olivia pushed the hair back into place with her dark sunglasses, settling the frames on top of her head.

Olivia's eyes landed on Kate and she smiled apathetically, the toothless curve of her lips conveyed nothing more than tolerance. "Hi Kate," she said and followed up dryly with, "Great dress."

Kate felt the tug of a smile. It worked. She'd been noticed. And praised, not gushingly, but the dress had been acknowledged instead of rebuffed —the reaction her outfits usually invoked from the leader of the pack. As Olivia's espresso-colored eyes drew down the length of Kate's body, the heavy weight of her guilt washed away. Then Olivia's eyes reached her shoes and the tweakish pull of her beautifully glossed lips told Kate she'd failed inspection.

Kate shuffled her feet. She looked down and saw her comfortable black loafers through new eyes. The little scuff marks and the inside stitch coming loose sang a different song than the sophisticated dress she was wearing, but it's not like her closet was stocked full of choices. She had enough fashion sense not to wear her paper-thin flip-flops, running shoes, or even her manure-speckled boots she sometimes caught flack for. These were the most decent shoes she owned. Of course, she wished she could have bought the sandals on display at the boutique, the ones that matched the dress perfectly, but her credit card surely would have been declined with both purchases. Besides, the store's thirty-day return policy wouldn't apply after she wore them on the street. The dress was a different story.

Olivia dismissed Kate with her eyes, as if she no longer had time for her. Mike, still standing like a statue, watched as the goddess Olivia approached him.

"I'm here for the Goodwich party," Olivia said with all the grace and authority one would expect from a second year associate at one of Portland's largest law firms and a former Delta Gamma Sorority President.

"Ri—right this way," Mike instructed. His face bloomed into a full blush after his voice cracked on the words. Olivia seemed unfazed and Kate followed in her shadow. She kept her eyes down, drawn to the rustic, wide planked gray hardwood floor as they passed through the lunch crowd and into a private room, partitioned by more black velvet curtains.

The bride-to-be and Madison Richards, freshly tanned from her honeymoon in Florida, sat hunched over a three-inch notebook Kate instantly recognized.

Both women jumped from their seats and that's when round one of the squeals began. Olivia joined them, her own high-pitched trill pierced Kate's ear. Olivia bent her knees and extended her arms to receive Mary and Madison. The three of them linked together and bounced up and down in a three-way hug. Kate decided long ago that this was the ritual greeting of all sorority sisters whether they hadn't seen each other for ten minutes, ten months or ten years. Kate stepped to the side, clearly not a part of this reunion.

When the three broke formation Olivia reached out and snatched Mary's hand to look at the ring.

"Nice," she commented, holding Mary's hand by her fingertips. "I told Tony to go with the two carat diamond, but does he ever listen to me? He's too cheap for that, isn't he? But I guess this one does look pretty on your delicate fingers."

"Oh, I think it is just perfect." Mary the Good Witch, whose fair hair, permanent smile and propensity to wear pink earned her the nickname Glinda the good witch from the *Wizard of Oz*, let Olivia's snobbish words float right over her. Kate, from her sideline position, wished for the umpteenth time in her life that she could kick Olivia with her worn out loafer right where the sun don't shine. But before Kate finished her thought, Mary reached out and pulled her into a hug.

"Kathryn Michaels, it's so good to see you. It has been way too long." Mary squeezed her tight and Kate offered a sincere congratulations. Mary released Kate and held out her hand to show off the ring.

"Beautiful," Kate responded, but the word sank under a new round of squeals. Michelle, a fashion merchandiser for a kid's clothing shop—not her first choice, but she had big plans on moving up to Nordstrom or Saks Fifth Avenue any day—and Brandi, a former Miss Oregon contestant and certified aerobics instructor at The Downtown Gym, had just arrived. The Fierce Four, the name Kate gave to the four girls, Olivia, Brandi, Michelle and Madison, was now complete. Mary became a peripheral member of the group when she joined the Delta Gamma sorority house. It wasn't until she became seriously involved with Olivia's older brother that she was spliced in as one of them.

Kate took the opportunity to slide into a chair at the table next to Mary and the notebook. The first time Kate saw the notebook was in the dorm room she shared with Mary during freshman year. At that time, it was only a half-inch thick. Over the years, Mary collected pictures from bridal magazines, kept invitations and notes about weddings she attended and cataloged them for the day she would tie the knot. Mary had been planning her wedding since she was twelve.

Another round of oohs and aahs filled the room while Mary showed off the ring one more time. With shepherding arms, Mary guided everyone back to the table. Only Brandi, who took the chair next to Kate said hello.

"Okay, first things first," Mary said, flipping to a forward section of the notebook. Kate could see a hand drawn diagram with X's and O's, much like a football playbook. Mary's level of organization bordered on the edge of compulsive, but Kate imagined it served her well at the small women's business law firm where she worked.

All eyes were on Mary as she graced them with one of her most genuine smiles and said, "Thank you all for being here and thank you for agreeing to be part of my wedding." Tears sprang into her eyes and she pulled the black cloth napkin from the table to dab at them.

A moment later, with her emotions in check, Mary consulted the drawing in the notebook again. "Olivia has graciously accepted to be my maid of honor and my little brother Gabe will be the best man." Everyone smiled at Olivia who feigned humility with her own smile— she loved attention anyway she could get it.

"It's only for you, Mary, and my brother that I would walk down the aisle with a man so many years younger than me," Olivia said. Mary's brother, ten years their junior would be the only one in the wedding party not toasting with champagne, but Kate was glad her friend planned to include her brother.

"Well, you only walk out of the church together and then there's just one dance at the reception that you're obligated to dance with him," Mary said, trying to reassure her soon-to-be-sister-in-law. Olivia shrugged as though the effort may kill her but she would somehow bring herself to make the sacrifice in the name of matrimony.

"Bridesmaid Number One is Madison and she'll be paired with her lovely new husband Zackary." Madison smiled. Her wedding, which Kate had not been invited to, was held last month at a winery, The River's Gate. Mary described it as a romantic venue even though they were kept indoors by the torrential rain and winds coming off the Columbia River.

"Michelle and Leo will be next in line." Michelle rewarded herself with a tiny golf clap obviously pleased with the pairing. Rumor had it she and Leo had a little tête-à-tête after Zak and Madison's wedding, something she was probably hoping would continue.

"Brandi and Tyler are next in line," Mary said after another consultation of her diagram.

"He's on loan," Olivia said. Her sharp tone sliced through the light mood of the table and pulled all the attention back to her. Her brows were knit together in a scowl meant only for Brandi, who had an unfortunate habit of forgetting to keep her hands off unavailable men. Olivia and Tyler, an item for the last two years, had reached the status of serious and Kate was sure Olivia would be the next to wed as long as Brandi didn't get in her way.

The sharp lines of Olivia's face quickly faded to a smile as though her warning had been in good fun. Mary fastened a tight smile on her lips before she returned to the chart in front of her, sweeping Olivia's outburst under the table.

"And Kathryn and Alejandro will be the final bridesmaid and groomsman in line."

Alejandro, Kate thought as she searched her memory bank. The name was familiar, but she couldn't place it.

"He is a friend of Anthony's from USC," Mary continued for her. "They've stayed in touch over the years and now that he has just opened up this fabulous restaurant. We'll be seeing a lot more of him. He even offered to hold the reception here for us."

"That's wonderful," Kate replied, hoping she sounded like more of an eager bridesmaid than she felt.

"And you'll just love him," Mary gushed.

"He's not your type or anything," Olivia's voice shot out from across the table. "He's lived in California his whole life. Grown up around movie stars and everything. His mom is a makeup artist and works on the sets in Hollywood. He's used to dating models, you know, really high caliber women."

Got it, Kate thought, interpreting Olivia's words, *Alejandro prefers brainless bimbos to redneck country girls and she should keep her shitkickers in the closet.*

"Ooh, is he the one whose house we stayed at junior year for Spring Break? And his family is from like South America or something?" Brandi asked. The others nodded. "And he had a ponytail?" More nods. "And the adorable earring? And he dated that swimsuit model for a while?" More nods. "He is a super hottie. Can I switch with her? Kate can have Tyler and I'll take Alejandro." She drew out his name seductively.

"No, no, no," Mary said, taking on the schoolteacher voice she learned from her mother, a veteran elementary school teacher. "It is better this way. You and Tyler are closer in height. It would look unbalanced if Kate was with him for pictures and everything."

As cupcake sweet as Mary was, she was equally type A. If she had any reason for the strict order of bridesmaids and groomsmen, then she'd stick to it. Kate didn't care which self-absorbed frat boy she was paired with. As far as she was concerned, none of them were her type, especially not this Alejandro guy.

A waitress with a long black apron over her black leggings parted the curtains and stepped into the partitioned room. Kate noticed a smattering of freckles on the woman's nose and cheeks as she stood next to the table and asked to take their drink orders. Kate said she was fine with water and the waitress nodded. The others rattled off their requests; strawberry lemonade, no ice; iced tea with one artificial sweetener and lemon—a lemon slice, not a wedge. Next, a diet soda, again no ice, and finally a sparkling water with crushed ice if they had it otherwise no ice at all. Without batting an eyelash, the woman smiled and walked off with their orders committed to memory.

"So," Mary said, looking over her menu. "Alejandro is catering the wedding. I want a full review on whatever you order."

"Good idea," Olivia chimed in, taking up her menu. "Everybody order something different, so we can share."

Kate scanned the menu and the prices. Yikes! Everything sounded delicious, but an entrée alone was more than her weekly grocery bill. Couldn't she conjure some excuse for having already eaten? She, the master of white lies, had to be able to come up with something, anything.

Just then, her stomach growled, low and long.

Brandi heard the rumble and raised a perfectly plucked eyebrow at her.

"What are you getting?" Mary whispered as she leaned in from the other side of Kate.

"I don't know," Kate replied as their drinks arrived. Carly—the flash of red embroidery informed Kate—circled the table to make her deliveries. Tucking the circular tray under her arm, she started taking orders for lunch and Kate's eyes darted like mad across the menu searching for anything reasonable.

"A cup of vegetarian chili," Kate said when it was her turn. She returned her menu to Carly and nearly jumped out of her seat as a sharp gasp of air came from Olivia's mouth.

"Chili. Are you mad? Mary isn't going to serve chili at her wedding. This isn't some backwoods barbeque reception we're talking about. Mary's going for an upscale, classy event." Olivia shook her head and averted her eyes. The others joined her, all except Mary.

"Oh, you're smart," Mary said to Kate. "I should have ordered something small too. I mean I've got to fit into a wedding dress soon."

"You are so right, Mary." Olivia said and turned to Brandi. "Sign us up for extra classes." Of course, when she said *us* it didn't include Kate—she wasn't a member at their gym.

Brandi snapped her head in Olivia's direction. Her sleek black ponytail brushed Kate's shoulder. "You know I will," she said. "I'll get you all whipped into shape and looking good by the wedding day. How much time do I have?" she asked, looking back at Mary.

"The wedding is set for August twenty-fourth."

"Oh good, so we've got over a year to get everything pulled together," Madison said.

"Not exactly," Mary said. "We're getting married this summer."

Nobody moved. Nobody said anything. August twenty-fourth was three months away. That was insane. How could a wedding be pulled off that quickly in the city? And then another question slammed into Kate's brain. Why was the wedding happening so fast?

"I smell a shotgun," Brandi said, a devilish gleam in her eye.

Two

"Are you preggers?" Michelle whispered, while Olivia drove a heated stare in Mary's direction.

"Ooh," Madison tossed her head, making her blonde locks bounce. "Zak and I are going to start trying to have kids soon, too."

"You conniving, gold-digging, little hussy," Olivia spat. "Getting pregnant, just so my brother would finally…"

The shocked look on Mary's face was enough to tell Kate they had it all wrong. Of course they did, this was Mary the Good Witch they were talking about. The girl who had AAA and Nationwide Roadside Assistance just in case one company failed to come to her rescue. When it came to contraception, Kate was sure Mary employed triple if not quadruple protection, just in case. An unplanned pregnancy was not congruent with Miss Mary Goodwich. It was so preposterous it made Kate want to laugh.

And apparently, she did, because all the eyes at the table flipped from Mary to her. Kate laughed harder. One look at Mary's horror filled eyes had been enough to tell Kate that Mary's wedding date was not a by-product of an unplanned pregnancy. If any one of Mary's dear, self-absorbed friends took a moment to really think about it—if they really knew her at all—they would know this was not the case.

"I'm sorry Mary," Kate said and took a deep breath, calming the next round of giggles she felt coming on. "The thought of you getting knocked up is crazy."

"Right," Mary said with a twitch of a smile as she gathered her wits. She turned to address the others at the table, her gaze skimming over Olivia. "It just so happens the church had a cancellation that weekend and we decided there was no reason to wait. We love the idea of a summer wedding."

Good enough reasoning for me, Kate thought with a nod, but the steam billowing from Olivia's ears suggested she wasn't convinced. She sat, arms folded and a fiery scowl fixed on Mary.

"But, how in the world are you going to get everything done?" Madison asked.

"Oh, it won't be hard." Mary flipped the pages in her binder. "I've got my list right here." A number of boxes were already checked off on Mary's list. The girl optimized the word efficient. "We know what we want for the wedding, so all we have to do is make it happen." Only Mary could take a monumental event like her wedding and turn it into a simple step-by-step process.

"If you say so," Madison chimed with an unconvinced roll of her eyes.

"I know it's a lot to ask of you guys. Making this all happen in such a short amount of time. But it's going to be great. I just know it is." Mary took hold of Kate and Madison's hands. Brandi and Michelle joined the circle and waited for Olivia to decide if she was in or out.

After one more heated stare and a lift of her chin, she grabbed hands with Brandi and Michelle. "It will be incredible," she said with an artificial sweetness that left a bad taste in Kate's mouth.

* * *

Kate looked down at her lap.

Chili was a bad idea.

A very bad idea. After three tasty bites, Brandi's errant elbow knocked the cup from the table and directly into her lap, leaving behind a grapefruit size splotch. Thankfully, no one had noticed. All their girlie attention at the table had been focused on firing off ideas at Mary for wedding themes, hair dos, honeymoon destinations, and registry suggestions. Mary listened to it all, but never once entered a note or suggestion into her giant planning guide. Kate quietly scooped the beans from her lap into the napkin that was supposed to have caught the mess.

The whole episode had gone undetected thus far and Kate wanted to keep it that way. That's why she was the only one at the vacant table. Precisely seventeen minutes ago, Madison, Michelle, and Brandi escaped to the bathroom, where they were probably purging or popping laxatives to lose the pounds they gained over lunch. Mary and Olivia, who both suffered from a condition where calories never stuck to their thighs, left three minutes after them. They walked out arm in arm with the appearance of two happy soon-to-be-relatives.

Kate checked the face of her cell phone one more time. Eighteen minutes. It was time to head for the exit, to try to salvage this dress and get it returned before her credit card burst. Somehow, Olivia had orchestrated having the bill split six ways since they'd all shared "bitesies," and Kate didn't know how her little plastic card had handled the burden. Her next bill was not going to be pretty.

Kate stashed her cell phone in her little purse. The wedding time and date were entered into the automated calendar, along with the dress appointment Mary had scheduled for this Saturday at Bonita Bridal. The bride-to-be had insisted everyone lock those dates into their calendars immediately.

Kate freed her shoes and ruined dress from hiding. She walked to the opening in the black curtain. Cautiously she peered through the slight opening. Not a single member of the Fierce Four was in sight. It was time to make her getaway. She bee-lined it for the door, trying her best to hide the stain with her little purse. She was almost to the door when she spotted the Fierce Four and Mary outside on the sidewalk. Kate circled back. No way was she going out there to parade in front of that audience.

Kate took a seat at the bar beneath the long industrial metal tubing that ran the length of the ceiling. She'd wait them out here.

A man walked out of the kitchen carrying a rack of glasses. "Hello," he said as he slid the rack under the counter. "Can I get you something?" His smile revealed a small gap between his front teeth, but Kate barely noticed.

"No, no I'm fine," she replied with a dismissive wave and gripped the uneven edge of the thick concrete countertop as she stretched to look out the front windows. Still there.

"Are you waiting for someone?" he asked.

"No, more like avoiding a bunch of someones," Kate said as she turned away from the entrance.

The man, whose shirt flashed "AJ" and "Manager" at her in silky red letters, leaned over the counter to see what had her attention. In that same moment, Olivia stepped back, tossed her hair, and laughed in that everybody-look-at-me way she always did. "Oh," he said. "Friends of yours?"

"Sort of," she replied and turned away from the entrance.

"Can I at least get you a glass of water?"

"Why not?" Kate said as she leaned back again.

AJ grabbed a glass, poured a scoop of ice into it, and filled it with water. "Lemon?" he asked, setting the glass on a cocktail napkin in front of her.

"Yes, please," Kate said. AJ dropped a wedge in her glass. Kate leaned back to look out the window one more time, hoping against hope—but they were still there.

Resigned, Kate pulled the lemon wedge from her glass and sucked in a breath. *Here goes nothing.* She poured a stream of the ice water into her lap. She closed her eyes at the startling cold and put the glass back on the bar. Three ice cubes settled in the folds of her dress and she scooped them up before blotting at the puddle with the napkin.

"Oh, hey," AJ said. "We, um, usually drink from the glasses here."

Kate said nothing as she took the lemon wedge and squeezed the juice on top of her stain. She needed to soften the chili, keep it moist, if she ever wanted to get the stain out.

Oh, who was she kidding? She bought the dress the second the chili touched the crocheted threads. She couldn't return it now.

"Wow," AJ said. Kate glanced up at him as she reached for her water glass. Astonishment leapt from his eyes. "I've never seen that before. Is this some new self-hazing thing women do nowadays?"

"No," Kate said and poured more water into her lap to finish the treatment. She gasped at the cold. The water seeped between her firmly pressed together thighs—thighs that reminded her of tree trunks anytime she stood near one of the twiggy Fierce Four. "Big boned," that's what her mom called her whenever Kate bellyached about being the biggest girl in her class. She hated it when her mom said this, but right now, she would give anything to hear those two words in her mom's comforting tone.

"The sooner I get this stain soaked, the better chance I have of getting it out," she explained to AJ.

"Oh, well here," he said and handed her a stack of neatly folded bar rags.

"Thanks." She took one and dabbed at her lap. "God, I hope your boss isn't here."

"My boss?" AJ asked.

"Yeah, I hear he likes his women perfect. I can only imagine the impression I'd make on him right now. Wearing my lunch in my lap." She smiled sheepishly.

"I'm sorry. His women? You're one of his women?"

"Oh God, no. Not at all. I've just heard that your boss, Mr. Casanova—the great and obsessively hot Alejandro—has certain expectations about women. I know I don't live up to any of them—that was made perfectly clear to me earlier—but I don't want him to think I'm some slovenly chick he's going to have to put up with."

"I'm sorry," AJ said, gripping his side of the bar and leaning toward her. "I'm so confused. How do you know Alejandro?" The name rolled off his tongue with the slightest hint of an accent, which Kate found intriguing.

"Oh, he's going to be in this wedding with me in August. I guess your boss is a good friend of the groom or something."

"Are you talking about the Fisher-Goodwich Wedding?" AJ said, clarity coming to him. He stepped back to lean against the back counter and crossed his arms over his chest. The amber liquid in the bottles behind him, reflected off the mirrored shelves. His smile revealed that gap between his front teeth again and this time Kate did notice. It was very charming.

"Yes," Kate said, throwing a rag on the bar. The stain was as good as it was going to get until she got home. "So, is he here?" Kate asked again, looking over her shoulder.

"My boss?" AJ asked and smiled. "No. Not today. I pretty much run things around here. He's very hands off with this restaurant."

"I see. He keeps his hands off the business so they're free to manhandle the women in his life."

"Wow, you're quite the cynic, aren't you?" AJ asked.

Kate shrugged.

"You haven't even met the guy and already you have him pegged."

"It's not that hard to imagine. I know his type. I think the less time I have to spend with him the better."

AJ nodded. His face shifted and he opened his mouth before closing it again, as if he were trying to find the right words to respond to her, but couldn't. How could he? Kate knew exactly what this Alejandro guy was like—a guy who was so self-indulgent he named his own restaurant after himself. You couldn't get much more arrogant than that.

It occurred to Kate in the next moment that she was insulting this man's boss, his employer, and she was a little out of line berating

Alejandro's bad behavior in front of AJ. She was having a bad day, a really bad day, but taking her hunger and crankiness out on this innocent bystander wasn't going to change any of that.

"I'm sorry," she said. "I'm sure your boss is a very nice person. I'm just glad I didn't have to meet him today. It hasn't been one of my best days." Kate felt the cardboard tag scratch against her neck again. She reached around under her hair and pulled it free, ridding herself of the annoyance.

AJ's eyes grew to saucer size, the unspoken question of the dress's ownership hung in the air between them.

"Don't worry, it's paid for," she said. He nodded slowly, suspicion lurking in the creases of his forehead.

A short blonde waitress walked up to him carrying a plate with two sliders on it. Her eyes latched onto AJ and she smiled like a vixen at him when she handed him the plate.

"Bucky wants you to try these," she said, setting the plate next to him. She patted him on the chest and Kate wondered how long they'd been sleeping together.

AJ's indifference to her touch suggested never, but it was clear the little vixen was on a mission to change that. Kate couldn't blame her. The guy was good looking enough and he had a sweet smile. If she were in the mood, she might actually try to flirt with him, but she didn't feel up to it today. Kate held onto the bar and leaned back again. The coast was clear. She swiveled in her seat, ready to make her exit, when AJ placed the plate in front of her.

"Here you go," he said.

"What's this?" Kate asked.

"Some lunch. A napkin full of chili was brought into the kitchen. By the looks of it, I'm guessing you didn't get much to eat today. Maybe if you had a little food on your stomach you wouldn't be so hard on people you don't know." A twinkle came into AJ's eye.

"Very funny, but I can't," Kate said. "I've spent way too much today." She tapped the dress's tag in front of her.

"It's on the house," AJ said. "Our beef supplier is going belly-up, so we're trying out a few new retailers. Consider this a taste test. Let me know what you think." AJ grabbed a slider for himself.

Kate picked up the other bun, pinching it between her fingers. "What is it?" she asked.

"A Kobe beef slider."

"A Kobe beef slider?" She smiled. "So, you're going to have your meat flown in from Japan now, are you?" She smelled the meat before taking a small bite.

"No, it's a local Kobe producer," AJ explained. Kate raised her eyebrows and swallowed.

"It's not Kobe," she said.

"What? Sure it is." AJ studied her.

"No, for one it's not buttery enough and two, if it didn't come from Japan it's not Kobe, but some domesticated form. It's definitely grain-fed, you can taste that." She took another bite. "It's okay," she said as she put the last half of her slider back on the plate, then reached for an onion straw. "But I've had better. Do you know how long the beef was aged or where it was slaughtered and processed?"

"Uh, no I don't," AJ stammered and then a smile spread across his face as he looked across at her. "I wouldn't have taken you for a beef connoisseur." AJ turned his last bite over in his hand and smelled the meat. "I think it's great—the best we've tried so far."

"Well, I wouldn't sign on the dotted line yet, especially if they're feeding you that Kobe-beef line, who knows what else they're not telling you about their meat. You should definitely scope out the operation. See the slaughterhouse before you buy."

"Yeah, um, okay," AJ said. "Well, I still think it tastes good. Better than what's served in the Alejandro's restaurants in California."

"Well, here in the Pacific Northwest you're going to need more than good taste to win over some of your customers."

"What do you mean?" he asked, finishing off his slider and wiping his fingers on a napkin.

"People around here are a little fanatic about what they're eating. They are well educated and passionate about an organic, sustainable, and humanely raised product. I suggest you educate yourself about the customers you will be catering to."

AJ cocked an eyebrow at her.

Was she climbing onto her soapbox? Getting a little too preachy? Well, it didn't matter—quality beef was something she knew all about.

"That's right. I'm in tree hugger country. But it's not like I'm serving up the spotted owl. It's just a hamburger."

"Just a hamburger, huh? Well, Mr. AJ the manager. I wish you and your boss a lot of luck selling crap beef to the most environmentally-friendly crowd in America."

Amusement danced in AJ's eyes. "And just where did you, Ms.," he paused, waiting for her to fill in a name for him.

"Michaels. Kate Michaels."

"Where did you, Ms. Kate Michaels, learn so much about beef?"

"I'm a flesh peddler."

"A what?" AJ coughed out the words.

Kate smiled, she loved the reaction those words sparked. "It's what some of those uneducated tree huggers call people in my line of work. I sell beef at the Saturday Farmers Market. And I sell out every time."

"Interesting," AJ said at the same time Carly appeared next to him.

"We've had a request for the manager at table nine," she said, twisting her lips into a frown.

"What did you do this time, Carly?" AJ asked, a teasing grin on his face.

Carly's red corkscrew curls bounced, as she replied, "Absolutely nothing." She gestured toward a table where a man with a wreath of dark hair above his ears studied the menu while his companion, a rail thin woman in a cable knit sweater which looked like it'd been around since the 80s, leaned over the table whispering in earnest to him as he nodded complacently. "Baldy over there wants to know if the chicken is organic or free-range, or something like that."

A look of dismay crossed over AJ's face and he turned to Kate. She gave him a knowing smile as she slid off her seat.

"I hope for your sake it's free-range. Otherwise you've just lost yourself that sale and you're going to have to push the organic greens." With that, Kate left the restaurant, the wet stain partially concealed behind her bag.

Three

Some days Kate just woke up angry. The feeling coiled itself around her and squeezed, leaving her ready to fight anything that came her way.

Stomp. Stomp. Stomp, stomp, stomp. The spider was dead after the first stomp, the follow-ups were purely cathartic. Kate scraped the sole of her boot across the concrete floor, wiping away the spider guts.

Inside the dark and somewhat foul smelling basement of her Victorian duplex, Kate stood on guard, watching, waiting for the next eight-legged creature to try to cross her path. She'd exterminated six in the last ten minutes and she was ready for more. If she was going to move into this dungeon, the arachnid infestation had to be dealt with and the immediate solution was her boot. Besides, it was good therapy. After the dress debacle yesterday, she'd been in a dreadful mood that had yet to buck up.

She spent the morning studying for the bar exam, a mood souring activity if there ever was one, especially since she was making attempt number three at a passing score in two months. *Third time's a charm*, she kept telling herself, because this was becoming an expensive habit she desperately wanted to break—but for some stupid reason law firms insisted on passing bar scores from their new hires. She'd already lost her position at Lawson and Grizwald where she'd interned in the water rights division to some long-haired-bar-passing hippie.

The pressure was on with an influx of new grads hitting the job market soon. Kate's odds of being hired were about to plummet.

Stomp. Another spider down.

Kate hoped the approaching summer weather would entice her creepy crawly friends to move outdoors. Maybe, by fall she'd have the money to get the concrete walls covered in drywall, plugging any and all of their hidden entry points.

Who was she kidding? The small stash of drywall she'd collected up until now was barely enough to wall off the tiny bathroom, and there wasn't room in the budget for any more. So much for her grand plan of doing a cute one bed, one bath apartment for herself. It was more like a concrete studio with exposed pipes and electrical conduit decorating the walls. And not in that trendy way like at the restaurant—Alejandro's, but in the inexpensive I-can't-afford-to-put-up-walls sort of way. Big difference.

She was running out of time and money. The contractor she'd hired last month to re-do the electrical and drywall the ceiling had sent his first bill, which she couldn't exactly pay right now. If she didn't get her sorry behind out of that apartment upstairs and down here pronto, she would go belly up. Failure on the home front, or rather the duplex front, was not an option. She couldn't turn her father's pride into disappointment. The way he put his arm around her, in a rare show of affection, and praised her mature decision to forgo law school for a year to use the money he'd given her to invest in this rental property motivated her to keep at it. She couldn't—and she wouldn't—let him down. She was not going to find herself in the land of foreclosure and lose this god-forsaken-piece-of-shit-run-down-ugly-as-sin duplex to the bank.

Ooooh, there it was again—that anger squeezing tight. Kate scanned the floor, her twin braids skimmed her shoulders as she looked for another spindly spider to stomp.

Six months ago, Mary bailed on her to move in with Tony, taking her rent payment with her. It had left Kate with a major loss of income. This place needed to get finished and it wouldn't do that on its own.

Kate cinched the tool belt around the waist of her favorite faded jeans and grabbed a slab of drywall. God, it was heavy, not any heavier than the hay bales back home, but certainly more awkward. She dragged it to the interior of the bathroom and hoisted it onto the six-inch blocks of wood the contractor had shown her to use when installing the pieces. With her hip, she held the drywall in place and reached into her belt for a nail. She set it on the drywall, lined it up with the stud, and took a therapeutic thwack at it with her hammer. The contractor had suggested using a drill and screws, but her tool chest didn't boast a drill at this time. She'd grab one out of the barn when she went to the ranch tonight, but for now she could use her hammer and nails to set the pieces in place.

After she drove the first nail, she heard a door slam upstairs. Jake, her only remaining tenant that lived on the other side of the first floor, was home early. It must be another slow day at the record store. *What a surprise*, Kate thought, rolling her eyes and pulling out another nail. It seemed the store was having more and more slow days. Jake rarely pulled a full day's work anymore and Kate couldn't help but wonder when his rent checks might stop rolling in too.

From above, Jake's footsteps pounded and stopped directly overhead. With the nail poised in position, she listened to the sound of water being poured—wait that wasn't water. She was directly under Jake's bathroom. He was peeing in his toilet. *Lovely,* she thought, closing her eyes and wishing she could move out from under him just in case the plumbing from above sprang a leak, but she was trapped. Suddenly she wished she hadn't skimped on the insulation in the ceiling, she didn't need to know every time Jake went to relieve himself.

Kate heard the flush and then the sound of rushing water. She closed her eyes, hoping the aged pipes from above would hold in the sewage.

Jake's footsteps headed out of his bathroom and into his living room where he sat with a thud on the faded smelly blue couch that she loathed and flipped on the TV.

Was that Judge Judy? Kate shook her head, resumed her concentration and hammered the nail.

The unmistakable smell of cigarette smoke drifted down to her. *Oh, that stupid, stupid boy*. He knew he wasn't supposed to smoke inside. It was in his rental agreement and she'd jumped all over him the first time she saw him light up. Well, she didn't literally jump on him, because she was lying naked in his bed with a sheet pulled around her. But she let him know what she thought of his disgusting habit and how she could throw his ass out for breaching his contract. He'd smiled, a twinkle in his brown eyes, and marched stark naked to the window, blowing the smoke outside. Thank God, the cedar fence blocked his image from the neighbors. She thought it was cute at the time, but it infuriated her now. He was stinking up the carpets, walls—everything.

She'd have to redo all of it when he moved out. His little security deposit wouldn't cover half of it.

She should march up there and demand he put it out now, but she was stuck holding up this drywall. A couple more nails and she'd head up there—yes, she would. Give him a piece of her angry mind.

Kate's shoulders sagged at the thought. No, she wouldn't. If she went upstairs and knocked on his door, they would tumble into bed together. Because that's what they did. They dated, if you could call it that—he never once took her out to dinner or to the movies—it was always just hanging out and having sex at his place, for more months than she cared to admit. After they broke up, the sex continued.

All it took was a pinch of sadness, anger, or loneliness to send Kate knocking on his door. And if she knocked on his door today with all the anger twisted up inside of her she knew exactly what would happen. So, she let it go and hammered another nail. She set three more sheets of drywall, locked the door behind her, climbed into her old faded red pickup truck, and drove out of town.

Four

This was it. Bonita's Bridal Boutique.

Kate stepped inside the floral perfumed shop and shook the rain from her jacket. She was stomping her rain-covered boots on the floor mat when a sales clerk came up. "Can I help you?" she asked with barely a glance at Kate's wet, faded jeans.

Kate pushed the hood of her jacket back, letting her braided pigtails fall over her shoulders. "I'm here with Mary Goodwich." She shivered against the damp chill in her bones from the day's torrential downpour. Ever since Kate drove into the city this morning with her truck and trailer full of meat products for the market, she'd been dumped on by rain clouds. The downpour increased to a new level at the exact moment Kate took down her canopy and began to load her truck. Unlike the other vendors, she wasn't able to wait out the rains, because she was pressed to get to the bridal shop on time.

The sales clerk pointed beyond the racks, heavy with white satin dresses, to an archway. Kate walked through the delicate store feeling like a bull in a china shop. All the fragile tiaras, bracelets, fine tulle veils, and white dresses shielded themselves in garment bags and glass cases from her damp and dirty touch.

Through the archway, Kate found a series of curtained dressing rooms and walls of mirrors. Sales associates bustled around the dressing area, bagged gowns thrown over their shoulders. Kate stopped short at the sight of Mary up on a platform, contemplating a dress in the mirror. The Fierce Four, along with Mrs. Goodwich, and Mrs. Fisher were all in a row behind her.

"So beautiful," said Muriel Fisher, a dead ringer for Olivia, plus or minus thirty years, with her dark hair and olive toned skin. "Very high fashion, don't you think?" the woman asked, turning to her daughter before taking a nip from the champagne flute in her slender hand.

"Yes, I agree," Olivia said. "Very luxurious."

"Oh, you look gorgeous," Madison added, as she rested her flute of champagne on her knee.

Mary pressed her hands down her sides, smoothing the bodice which was pulled tight and secured in the back to show how the dress would fit in the correct size.

"This is a tulle petal skirt," the consultant told her. "Very trendy right now." Kate tried not to laugh as she stepped into the tiny square of space between Michelle's chair and a partitioning wall. The skirt looked like a bunch of feather dusters lifelessly hanging from the hip with a giant bow tied in the back. Her stifled laugh must have escaped on some level, because Mary's eyes found hers in the reflection of the mirror. Mary broke out in a giant smile. The joy of this experience was evident on her face.

"What do you think, Kathryn?" she asked and the rest of the party turned to look at her. Kate fixed the smile on her face to be less amused.

"Very pretty," Kate replied. "You look great and you'll sweep the aisle clean with that skirt. They'll have to give you a break on the cleaning deposit."

Mary brushed off her teasing with a laugh and stepped from her pedestal, dragging the layers of tulle petals with her as she went back into the dressing room. Her consultant scooped the rest of the train in behind her and closed the curtain. Now Kate understood why they didn't have doors on the dressing rooms, they'd never get them closed behind some of those trains.

Kate awkwardly leaned one shoulder against the corner of the wall and waited for Mary to show off dress number two.

"Kathryn, so lovely to see you, dear," Mrs. Goodwich called over the heads of the group from her end of the chairs. Kate gave her a wave. "Let's find you a chair," she said and stood.

"Oh, no, I'm fine," Kate said.

"Nonsense," Mrs. Goodwich said and flashed the same cheek-scrunching smile Mary inherited from her. Mrs. Goodwich spun around, tilting slightly, and looked for some assistance. She grabbed a girl overloaded with wedding dresses. "We need another chair," she told the girl, leaning in a little too close and tipping her almost empty champagne glass toward Kate. The overburdened girl looked at Kate and smiled.

"I'll be right back," she said and walked off.

"And more champagne too, please," Mrs. Goodwich called with one hand cupping the side of her mouth. She gave Kate a super happy grin and shrug before sitting back down. Kate wondered how many glasses the woman had already guzzled.

The curtains to the dressing room swished open and Mary stepped in front of the mirror, all smiles. The ruffled skirt looked like a generous swirling of white frosting on top of a cupcake, Mary's upper half a trinket on top.

The consultant pulled and arranged the train behind Mary while everyone else oohed and awed over the majestic quality of the dress. The overburdened girl returned, having traded in her load of gowns for an iron-scrolled chair.

"Thank you," Kate said, taking a seat next to Michelle who didn't scoot an inch to make room for Kate.

"More champagne, more champagne," Mrs. Goodwich's voice rang out as she held up her empty flute. Kate watched Mary's eyes through the mirror shoot to her mother in that pleading way that daughters ask their mothers not to embarrass them. Mrs. Goodwich was oblivious.

"Champagne or water?" the girl asked Kate, a slight tick of her head the only perceivable indication that Mrs. Goodwich's voice was grating on her nerves.

"Champagne," Kate answered, not needing anytime to consider the question. The girl walked away and gave Mrs. Goodwich a reassuring smile to let her know she was on her way to get more champagne.

"That looks like it could get kind of hot," Mrs. Goodwich said, turning her attention back to her daughter now that she knew champagne was on its way. "You don't want to be sweating buckets up there at the altar."

"It's not bad," Mary answered as she twisted and gauged her reflection in the mirror.

"And how much is that one?" Mrs. Goodwich asked.

Mary's eyes shot to her mother. "We don't have to worry about that right now, Mom." Mary answered with an edge to her voice that only surfaced when talking to her mother. A string of sadness tugged at

Kate's heart. She knew Mary was getting annoyed with her mother, but at least Mrs. Goodwich was here.

Kate looked again at Mary's god-awful dress when the champagne-delivery girl returned with her glass and a bottle for Mrs. Goodwich. Kate sipped from her glass and wondered why anyone would want to spend hundreds or even thousands, as she assumed was the case with this dress, for a gown they'd wear once. And all that fabric—albeit luxurious organza—what a waste. Kate knew when she got married, if she ever got married, the dress would be simple, no train, no frilly petals or cupcake-inspired skirts for her. The entire affair would focus on the love and bond between two people, not the length of the dress or train.

But she didn't need to worry about any of that for a while since her love life wasn't exactly flourishing, at this rate she'd probably never be anything more than Jake's call girl. At least until one of them moved on in their life. And it didn't look like that would happen anytime soon.

"Well, definitely keep it on the list," Olivia said. "You look fabulous in it. Truly."

"What do you think?" Mary asked, deferring to Kate who would rather sip her champagne than offer her true opinion.

"Scrumptious," Kate told her and took a swallow.

Mary beamed and turned from the mirror.

"I'm so glad you're here," she whispered and patted Kate on the knee as she swished by on her way to the dressing room.

"So ladies," Olivia said, addressing the bridesmaids who all sat to her left. "I'm working on the bridal shower. I've got calls out, but no luck yet on finding a locale with this short notice." Olivia's eye roll was not lost on Kate. "No worries, though," she continued, forcing her words to brighten. "I'll come up with something. In the meantime, everyone start thinking about themes and ideas. I'm leaving early tomorrow morning for the Boston office. I'll be gone all week, so let's powwow next Sunday. Say ten o'clock at the Starbucks by my building."

The whole line of them nodded as Mary stepped from the dressing room wearing yet another hideous dress.

"That is the one!" Olivia sang out as Mary awkwardly stepped up on the stage, the tight fit of the dress restricting the ease of her movements.

"Are you sure?" Mary asked, contorting her face as she considered the dress.

"Yes." Olivia handed her champagne to her mother and jumped up to stand next to Mary. "This is gorgeous." She swept Mary's hair up off her shoulders, twisted it and pressed it to the back of her head. "Look at that. Regal."

Mary tilted her head and twisted her shoulders still looking unconvinced.

"What do you think?" Olivia asked, appealing to the crowd. And, of course, everyone agreed except Kate who sat poker-faced. How could Olivia push this oversized mermaid fin on poor Mary, who obviously didn't like it?

"I liked it on the hanger, but not so much now that it's on," Mary said.

"Oh, don't be ridiculous," Olivia said to her own reflection in the mirror. "It shows off your figure. See how it hugs your hips and flares out so elegantly at the bottom."

It flared all right, like a mer-tail on steroids. It was completely disproportional and Mary could hardly move in the thing. It was a definite no.

"What do you think?" Mary asked and turned to look at Kate once more.

"It's…well…it's," Kate fumbled for words. "It's pretty. Very aqua-esque. You could put us all in sea foam green and we could play *Under the Sea.*"

Kate sipped her champagne, to save herself from any more descriptions while Mary smiled and Olivia scowled at her.

"It is gorgeous and Tony will just love it, I know he will," Olivia said, as if she had any authority over Tony's taste.

"Well, I don't have to decide today," Mary said in her usual placating way and turned from the stage. "That's it for me," Mary said over her shoulder. "You're up ladies."

Five

"Now, everybody turn around," Mary instructed, making a circular motion with her finger.

Kate felt like a cow on the auction block, standing on this stage with these other perfectly poised heifers. The five bridesmaids turned around so Mary could judge the back of all the dresses—Olivia in a floor length black chiffon number, Madison in a red satin tea-length, Michelle in a purple A-line dress, and Brandi in a black lace corset-style dress. Karma had granted Kate a teal crinkled chiffon dress with a mermaid fin. She held on for dear life to the top of the strapless dress so it didn't pool to the floor at her feet. Her dress was the only one that wouldn't fasten in the back. The sales girl, Candice, had clipped some elastic bands to the back, but Kate wasn't putting her faith in those things to keep this weighted dress in place.

"Oh well, they are all just beautiful," Mrs. Fisher gushed and fluttered her heavily mascaraed eyes.

"I know. I love them all," Mary agreed, giving her future mother-in-law a gentle pat on the arm. "What do you guys think?" She turned her attention back to the five on the stage.

"Well, I love Kate's," Olivia said. "It would be the perfect complement to that last dress you tried on. But I also love the flow of this one." Olivia swooned over her own image in the mirror.

"I'm a no on the strapless idea," Kate said and gave her dress another tug.

"You can always add straps to that one," Candice said as she stepped up next to Kate and placed a white ribbon over her shoulder to show the effect a strap would add to the dress. Kate made a face at Mary, which clearly communicated her distaste. It was a sign of their long friendship, these silent looks that did the talking for them.

"Well, you all look ravishing," Mary told them. "Go ahead and try on the next set, so we can see if there's anything else we like."

Kate held fast to the dress as Candice undid the bands in the back. When she was free, Kate ran sock footed into the dressing space she'd been forced into with Brandi who stood already stripped down to her underwear, if you could call that scrap of black lace underwear. Her matching push-up bra was one of those fancy ones where the straps could be manipulated for any type of dress, and she was crisscrossing them over her back for the next round. It was as if she'd known they would be trying on dresses today. Had Kate missed that memo or did Brandi always dress like that under her clothes?

Brandi shimmied into a short and glitzy number. Kate dropped her dress, exposing her braless chest and faded white full-coverage briefs. She snagged the bright yellow chiffon dress off the hanger, ready to cover herself up again when Brandi backed up to her.

"Zip me. Hurry, hurry." Brandi bounced like an impatient child.

"Um, okay," Kate said, draping the yellow dress over her arm. Brandi had backed her against the wall and she didn't have room to pull on her dress. Brandi held her long black hair in a pile on top of her head with one hand. She snuck a look over her shoulder and eyed Kate in the mirror.

"You really should think about joining my gym. Just a few classes and we could get that stomach washboard tight."

Just what every girl wants to hear, Kate thought while simultaneously sucking in her stomach and closing Brandi's zipper.

"Um, yeah I'll think about it," Kate said as tears pricked the back of her eyes. As soon as Brandi scooted out the curtain opening, Kate spun to face the mirror. She wasn't that overweight, maybe a couple of pounds, but all the women in her family were built this way. Small on top and wide through the hips. She was a pear-shape, always had been and always would be.

Kate sighed and pulled the yellow dress over her head. She looked at her reflection and groaned. The thick layers of chiffon on the short skirt, accentuated by her wide hips, made her look round—like a droplet of sunshine. This was awful.

"Do you need some help?" Candice asked, pulling the curtain back and stepping inside. She fastened the zipper and clipped the extra fabric together in the back. It was a small comfort to Kate that she wasn't bigger than the dress this time. Candice, who smelled oddly, but refreshingly of baby powder and spearmint, reached around Kate's waist to tie the black grosgrain ribbon in a loose bow. Ready for inspection Kate walked out of the dressing room.

All eyes, except for Brandi's who was busy flirting with her own reflection, fell on the vision of yellow. Their chattering ceased. Olivia brought a hand to her mouth to cover her laugh. Madison and Michelle just stared.

"Oh my, that's bright isn't it?" Mary said from her chair, looking like she might break out into hysterics.

But it was Mrs. Goodwich who couldn't hold her composure, another empty flute of champagne aiding her lack of self-control. She laughed a throw-your-head-back and slap-your-knee kind of laugh that instantly brought tears to her eyes. Mary shot her mother a pleading look, but it didn't do any good. The Fierce Four, including Brandi who had finally pulled her eyes off herself, joined in the laughter. Kate really couldn't blame them. The yellow was hideous, but it just so happened that she was the one wearing it. A tear slipped from her eye and she quickly brushed it away. Mary was immediately at her side and took both of her hands. She pulled Kate up onto the stage and stood next to her as they looked in the mirror.

"You know," Mary said, tilting her head to the side. "I actually kind of like it."

"You do?" Kate asked.

"Yeah." Mary dropped Kate's hands and circled around her. "It has great lines. Of course, I don't like the color." She made an icky face in the mirror at Kate, and then continued her inspection. "These covered buttons in the back are darling. And it has straps. I think this neckline would look good on everyone. What do you guys think?" Mary turned to look at the recovering foursome.

"Oh well, it's sort of…I don't know Mary," Olivia said as she walked over to join them in her dark green halter-top gown. "It doesn't match anything you tried on."

"No you're right it didn't," Mary agreed, still studying Kate's dress. "But, I don't know—there is just something about it that I really like. Try to imagine it in a soft pink." She turned to Olivia. "Like a petal. You would all look like a beautiful soft rose petal."

Pink ball of cotton candy was more like it, Kate thought.

"I…" Olivia's mouth opened, but Candice cut her off.

"I'm sorry ladies, but my next appointment is in fifteen minutes and I'd like to get your measurements before you leave."

"Of course," Mary said, not looking at Olivia. She tugged on one of Kate's braids. "You'll look beautiful in anything," she whispered and Kate gave her a tight smile because she knew that even if Mary dressed them all in burlap sacks the other four bridesmaids would still outshine her.

Kate headed for the dressing room where Candice waited, wielding a tape measure.

Six

Kate reached into a cooler under the table of her stand at the famers market, sticking her double-digit size behind in the air. She still cursed her friend Mary for thinking it a good idea to share their dress measurements in a text message. Kate's was the only one that rang up in the double digits, but it was her hips she'd wanted to explain. The rest of her body easily fell into a smaller size. It wasn't fair, if she were built bigger on top, no one would think twice of hassling her for having big boobs.

The follow-up text from Brandi, offering a free one-month trial membership at her gym and Madison's text with a link to the latest celebrity diet trends plunged her self-esteem into the toilet.

Thankfully, none of those wicked little witches were here now. It was just Kate and the morning sunshine. She locked the legs of her canopy into place to give her cover. The morning's blue-gray sky was dotted with clouds. She hoped the forecasted showers held off until this afternoon, otherwise, the market-goers would be slow in arriving and the day would drag on. With no wedding dress appointments scheduled today, Kate hoped she could sell out, pack it in, and head home early. On these days when she got up with the sun, she looked forward to a mid-day nap. Stifling a yawn, she layered the packages of frozen meat in her hands on the bed of ice at the front of her table.

"Hello, Gorgeous Girl," Alan called from the stand next to her and blew her a kiss.

"Mornin' Alan," she called back and then ducked down for another supply of meat. "Hey, where's your better half?" Kate asked when she noticed Alan was setting up all by himself this morning.

Alan kicked the legs of the table he was setting up into place before righting it, and then leaned onto the tabletop with one hand.

"He's under the weather this morning," he said with a flap of his hand and flutter of his eyes. "Caught a little sniffle this week, so I told him to sit this one out."

"Well, I'll set aside a package of stew meat for you. Nothing like a little comfort food when you're feeling sick."

"Thanks," Alan said and carried two baguettes over to Kate. He gave her a cheek-to-cheek kiss before returning to his stand and unrolling "The Dough Boys" banner. He and his partner Liam started the bread baking business five years ago and they'd been stationed next to Kate since she started selling at the market three years ago. She loved their position at the end of the Portland State University buildings, Starbucks only a few paces away. They were on a flat stretch of concrete near the music stage and a stand of tall trees created a protective umbrella over the grassy center.

Kate looked up as Raine of Raine Water Farms walked past her booth, carrying two boxes full of her organic lavender oatmeal soap and skin care products.

Last month when Raine first joined the market, she was stationed on the other side of The Dough Boys. Alan, Liam, and Kate took the time to introduce themselves and while Liam asked about Raine's organic practices Kate smelled one of the purple wrapped soaps. The scent immediately transported her back to her childhood. Vibrant tufts of purple growing outside the front door sprang into her mind. And so did her mom, clipping off bunches of the fragrant flowers that she would hang upside down in her makeshift art studio until they dried.

Kate lusted over the smell all morning, wanting the fragrance near her again. She consciously held back a one-pound package of ground meat and when there was a lull in the customer traffic Kate dashed to Raine's booth, hoping to strike up a trade.

One look at the meat resting on her table sent Raine's hand straight to her mouth. Her other hand waved Kate off.

"I think she's a vegan," Liam had said as she returned to her stand. The very next Saturday Raine steered clear of Kate's table and set up shop on the opposite side of the market, the tall window covered building as her backdrop now.

Kate still yearned for the lavender products, but fear of another vomit-inducing reaction from Raine kept her from approaching the table again, even with cash in her hand.

"You still want some of that?" Alan asked, watching Kate salivate as Raine disappeared into the crowd on the other side of the market.

Kate nodded. "Yeah, I was thinking a nice basket of soaps would be a great gift for my friend's bridal shower. But I'm afraid the sight of me will make the woman want to throw up again."

Alan chuckled as he set out his lawn chair.

Kate ducked down for another supply of meat. When she stood up again her first customer was waiting for her.

Minnie, a blue-eyed girl with short blonde curls, was a regular and always arrived early. She worked for three local families as a raw food chef and did her weekly prep on Saturdays. According to Minnie, the families that employed her preferred the Michaels beef because it was more lean and flavorful than others they'd tried. Kate was just going to have to take Minnie's word on that, because she had no desire to whip up some raw beef recipes. Even if Minnie assured her that a little citrus or salt, pepper and cheese mixed with the beef made for a delectable meal.

The line in front of Kate's stand was growing and she worked quickly to package the two fillets for the couple in front of her. *A romantic night in*, she assumed. The flowers, wine, and fresh greens brimming from their arms along with that sappy intertwining look of being in love they shared gave them away.

She filed their cash away in her box and looked up to find a good-looking guy standing in front of her. She notched up her smile by a couple of degrees as she drank in his appealing qualities. *Wait*—there was something familiar about him. That gap-tooth smile, the dark cropped hair that showed signs of a subtle wave, and deep blue eyes—an intoxicating cobalt blue. How had she missed those eyes the other day?

"What a surprise," she said to AJ when she finally found her voice. "What are you doing here?"

"Looking for you," he answered. "This is the third market I've been to this morning. And now I have finally found you."

"Why would you be looking for me?"

"Because I have a few questions for you," he answered and reached into the pocket of his dark blue jeans. Kate's heart skipped a beat as he pulled out a folded piece of paper. His shy smile brought an unexpected warmth to her heart, causing her cheeks to flush.

"What breed are your cattle?" AJ asked, reading straight from the paper.

"Hereford," she replied as he glanced up and then back down at the paper.

"Is that a cross breed?" he asked, confusion written all over his face.

A giggle bubbled inside her but she held it back. "No, we're a purebred operation."

"Oh, okay." He looked down at his sheet again. "What is the cattle's basic diet?"

"Ahem," came from the next person in line.

Kate leaned to the left to look at the next customer. "Just a minute, Stuart," she said to another one of her regulars who lacked in patience. "I've got your order on ice. No need to get pushy back there."

The sight of this delicious man standing in front of her like a nine-year-old boy giving a book report was a huge day-brightener. Kate wished she could entertain his forced questions a little longer, but for the sake of her other customers she needed to move him along.

"The cattle are one hundred percent grass fed, and we don't use any growth hormones or antibiotics. Our cattle are naturally raised on our ranch in Hayden Valley, Oregon." AJ's relieved smile assured her she was providing the exact information he was after. And that smile brought out a little something in her she hadn't felt in a while—*giddy?* She put her hands on the table in front of her and leaned forward. "Why the sudden interest in my meat, Mr. Manager?"

"Because you were right and I was wrong," he said, and if she wasn't mistaken his voice matched the flirtation in her own.

"Oooh," she said, sounding uncharacteristically like one of the Fierce Four. She stood back from the table. "I like being right. So, what was I right about?"

"Let's just say, that my chef was trying to pull a fast one on me and if I hadn't talked to you last week I'd have made a very bad business mistake. One that probably wouldn't have gone over well with my…you know."

"Your boss?"

AJ nodded. "Yeah, I could have really screwed this whole thing up. The restaurant's taking a big chance on me and I don't want to let any of them down. It was a rookie mistake, not being more involved in finding a new meat vendor. And unfortunately right now, I'm looking for meat and a new chef."

"Well, if it's meat you're looking for. I've got that. Would you like me to put together a sampling for you?"

"That would be great," AJ said and watched as she gathered four steaks and six pounds of ground beef from the beds of ice on the table. She put the meat in a bag for him along with a brochure and the ranch's business card.

Kate handed him the bag as he pulled out his credit card. "Sorry, we're sort of a cash and check only operation."

"Of course," AJ said, his beautiful eyes landing on the big sign in front of him, clearly stating *cash and check only*. He opened his wallet wider. "Um, all I've got is a twenty," he said weakly.

"Don't worry about it." She lowered her voice. "Consider it a sample."

"I'll settle up with you later. I promise," he said as Stuart elbowed his way to the front. Kate smiled and waved to AJ as he walked off, and then she grabbed Stuart's steaks and the container of puppy meat cakes he ordered every week for his Cocker Spaniel.

Seven

"Tall coffee," Kate ordered.

"Room for cream?" the barista asked, holding a white paper cup in hand. It was tempting but with the Fierce Four all whispers and giggles at a table behind her, she was reminded that her indulgence would not go unnoticed.

"Black is fine," Kate said as she counted out the nickels, quarters, and dimes she'd scrounged her apartment for before coming to the powwow today.

With her coffee cup in hand, Kate walked around the tree-slab bar that divided the coffee shop in half. She sank down into the last available seat of the five-chair semicircle.

"Okay, well now that we're all finally here, let's get started." Olivia's gaze swept to Kate before she pulled her laptop out of her leather bag and set it on the coffee table. "Did everyone get my text about the date and place?" Olivia's eyes ran the line of them and they all nodded. "Great, so we've only got three weeks to plan, which isn't much time. My building was the only place I could find with an opening between now and the wedding. It's not ideal—I wanted to book the country club, but of course that was taken."

Olivia reached for her cup and saucer, taking a dainty drink from her beautifully foamed latte. "So, does anyone have any theme ideas?" She asked as she returned her cup to the table and switched her laptop on. "Well," she continued when nobody else spoke up. "I was thinking we should do a Breakfast at Tiffany's inspired brunch. What do all of you think about that?" Olivia waited for an answer as her laptop purred to life.

Enthusiastic nods bobbed down the line and Olivia's delicately penciled lips cracked into a smile.

"I can't do a brunch," Kate quietly announced.

Olivia looked at her in disgust, "Why not?"

"Because I work on Saturday mornings."

"Oh right, you and your little market. Well, in that case what time works for you?" she asked with a condescending tilt to her head.

"I'm usually done by two, but…"

"Great. Two o'clock it is then. We don't want to do it any later than that. Otherwise the guests will expect a full dinner, and we want to keep this a light affair."

"Right," Kate agreed, keeping the rest of her statement to herself about how she sometimes didn't get out of the market until two-thirty or three and then she'd have to go home and change before driving back to the shower. She'd figure it out on her own—do the anti-rain dance or something in the morning and hope she could sell out early.

"All right." Olivia clicked around on the screen in front of her. "Since we can't do a brunch," Olivia shot Kate a look before continuing. "Are there any other ideas for a theme?"

"How about a lingerie party?" Brandi asked.

"Oh, I like that idea, but why don't we do that for the bachelorette party. My great aunt Millie will be there and I don't want her having a heart attack."

"Okay," Brandi said with a toss of her head.

"So…"

"I think an English tea party might be a nice idea for an afternoon shower," Kate said.

"Oooh, what a cute idea," Olivia said, her voice going all high and pitchy. "But *I* was thinking we should do an LBD shower."

"Great idea," Michelle said, beaming. "Yes, let's do that."

"Love it. Love it," Brandi said.

"Super great idea." Madison's pink cheeks puckered with her smile.

"What's an LBD?" Kate asked.

"Little. Black. Dress." Olivia rolled her eyes as she pulled up a page on her laptop covered with party ideas.

A serious debate began about whether polka dots, stripes, damask or a herringbone pattern should be used for the invitations.

"It sets the tone for the whole shower," is the last thing Kate heard before tuning the Fierce Four out.

Soft bluegrass music played over the speakers, the sound of the syrup pumps and the frothing machine overlapped the music every so often. Kate looked out the front window to see a handful of people gathered at the bus stop. The day was gray but dry.

The harsh grind of a blender shifted Kate's attention to the counter as ice cubes turned to slush. The display of local ales next to the menu board caught her eye and she wondered if maybe she should have opted for one of those instead of this scalding cup of coffee. She took a sip of her heavily concentrated coffee and immediately felt the caffeine rush into her veins.

Kate pressed her thumbnail into the hole of her paper cup lid. She idly wondered how much the guy who invented this lid with a hole in it made. It was such a simple design and now millions, no probably billions, of cup lids were used every day and some guy out there was just sitting back raking in the cash—because he put a hole in a lid. Why couldn't she come up with something as equally brainless and brilliant and make oodles of money?

A low, gravelly voice ordering a mocha caught Kate's attention at the barista stand. The black slouch beanie, flip-flops, cargo shorts, and tight Henley registered like a cymbal.

Jake. What was he doing here? On this side of the city?

Kate tried to melt into the seat, keeping her eyes on the cup in her hands. If she played it cool and kept her head down, he'd be out of here soon. She tried to listen for his drink to be called, aurally tracking his movements, but Olivia's impatient shriek brought her head up abruptly.

"Kate, are you at all interested in this party for Mary, because…" Kate didn't hear anymore. She'd been spotted. Jake came around the bar and was headed straight for her.

No, no. Do not approach, she silently warned him.

Do. Not. Approach. The message wasn't getting through. Panic set in. Kate instantly felt pearls of sweat on her lip. *Where was a sinkhole when she needed one?*

"Hi, Kate," Jake said with all the ease and swagger of a man approaching a group of beautiful women.

"Hi," Kate said, ducking her head and sweeping a loose strand of hair from her face. Jake's gaze travelled around the group. *There is no way I'm introducing you to these vultures*, she tried to communicate.

"Hi, I'm Brandi," the boy toy shopper of the group said, reaching across Olivia to offer her hand. Jake smiled as he took it.

"Jake," he replied and then turned back to Kate. "I haven't seen you around much lately."

"Yeah, I've been busy," she said, daring not to look at him.

"Okay, well maybe I'll see you later today," which was code for come on over and let's get it on when you're done here.

"Yeah, maybe," Kate answered, forcing her voice to be light and airy. He turned to leave without so much as a goodbye.

"Who was that?" Brandi asked, eyes popping.

"My neighbor."

"That's not the dead-beat loser Mary's always harping on you about, is it?" Olivia asked, agog.

"No, no, no," Kate lied. When had Mary mentioned Jake to Olivia?

"But he's your neighbor and his name is Jake." Sometimes Kate wished Olivia hadn't been top of her class in law school, but somewhere closer to the middle like she had been, then it might be a whole lot easier to slip these little lies past her.

"Coincidence."

"You have more than one neighbor named Jake?" Olivia was on to her.

"Yep. It's a whole neighborhood of Jakes. I'm thinking about petitioning the city to rename the street Jake Avenue." *Stop! Too much information. Any good liar knows to say as little as possible. Do not create long explanations.*

Olivia's eyebrows arched into two perfectly inverted v's.

"Well, I'd do him in a heartbeat," Brandi announced from her seat.

"You'd do anything with a d…" Madison camouflaged the last word with her cup as she took another drink.

"How about showing us the place you've got picked out for the shower? I'd love to see it," Kate said with the fakest bright smile ever invented.

"Oh yes, let's see it," Madison squealed, and just like that the attention of the group had been returned to Mary's bridal shower.

*   *   *

"Thank you Byron," Olivia said to the door attendant of her building.

"Certainly, Ms. Fisher," he replied and gave her a face-splitting smile.

The lobby was all bright white with sleek and modern lines. Pendant lighting hung down from the tall ceiling. Beyond a wall of mailboxes was a bank of elevators. Olivia pressed the button and they waited in front of a straight lined navy blue sofa.

Madison leapt into the elevator when it arrived. "Oh, this is so fun. Tell me you guys had this much fun planning my shower."

"Of course, we did," Olivia said, stepping in behind her. "And you will have just as much fun planning mine."

Madison beamed. "What? You and Tyler are getting engaged?"

"Of course we are," Olivia said and turned around as the door slid closed.

"What? When?" Brandi chimed in.

Olivia shrugged. "I'm working on it," she said with a nonchalant toss of her head, as the elevator rose to the fifth floor.

The doors opened and they all followed Olivia to a double set of doors. She pulled them open and showed off a very nondescript rectangle of a room—three brown walls, brown carpet, and a wall of windows. Clearly, this room was missed when the upgrades were applied to the rest of the building. The defining feature of the room was the beautiful green foliage that screened the view from the windows. Three sets of French doors allowed access to the outdoor space. Kate went for the nearest one while Olivia led her followers to the center of the banquet room. Outside Kate followed a concrete path toward a sitting area filled with four tables and two barbeque stands. She walked to the railing and looked over at the cars below. The afternoon breeze carried the smell of garlic on it, from the deli down the street.

Kate turned and leaned her back against the railing. This is where she would have held the shower. The terraced grass landscaping and potted trees were beautiful. Olivia was doing this her way, though, her over-the-top and to-the-nines kind of way. Kate was just along for the ride. She pushed off the railing and walked back inside.

"So, the guest list is at about sixty people right now," Olivia said. "It will be a little tight, but the building has round tables we can use and the caterers will set up over here." She walked to the empty corner directly outside of the swinging kitchen door. "Oooh." She tiptoe ran back to the group in her nude heels. "Did I mention that Alejandro's is doing the catering for us?"

Ugh, Kate felt a nauseating twist in her stomach at the mention of the illustrious Alejandro, while everyone else squealed with delight.

"Okay, okay, okay," Olivia said, simmering everyone down. "So we covered a lot today and I think we've got a really solid start on the planning. I will go ahead and take it from here. We'll just divide the expenses in the end. That way it will be from all of us, okay?" Olivia asked with a smile that looked gracious, but clearly said "this is my show now."

The group was all nods.

"Great, any questions?"

"How much do you think it's going to cost?" Kate asked and four heads whipped in her direction.

"Well, I don't know," Olivia replied with a disgusted and impatient shake of her head. "We've only started planning, but it's for our Mary, so it really doesn't matter now, does it?"

"Guess not," Kate mumbled, wondering if Olivia accepted credit cards for payment, because she had a feeling the forty-seven dollars and sixty-two cents in her checking account wasn't going to cover her share of this event.

Eight

Kate's finger froze in front of the doorbell. She knew she shouldn't do it. She really shouldn't ring Jake's doorbell, but she had to. He was the only person around who could help her. She'd be okay. Nothing would happen. She was strong. In control of her life.

Hadn't she walked right past his door only three days ago after his public invitation at Starbucks? She didn't run home to him. No, she walked seven blocks to the Pottery Shack and painted pottery for three hours in hopes that Kitten could sell some of her pieces to help her fund the ridiculous bridal shower.

She was building up her immunity to Jake. He was a habit, a horrible habit, that she was trying to kick and today would *not* be her undoing.

It was purely for safety sake that she was here, recruiting Jake for help. If there was any other way, she would do it, but she was not going to let the salvaged ice blue toilet in the back of her truck be the end of her. Navigating the ten-dollar find, from the old warehouse redistribution center on the east side of the river, down her dark stairs to the basement could prove to be treacherous. One little misstep and she might tumble to the bottom, a toilet bowl landing on top of her, crushing her. Death by a toilet was not the way she planned to leave this world and so she simply needed a little help.

She didn't give herself the time to rethink her actions and pressed the small circular button. This request for help would not lead to anything more than a firm handshake. She needed Jake to help her unload the toilet and then she would send him on his way. She'd been doing so well, avoiding him, resisting the temptation—she could handle this.

But then Temptation opened the door in nothing but his cargo shorts. Kate's mouth went dry. Why was he only half-dressed? The sight of his bare chest, with the dark wiry curls of hair that led to his stomach and down to…*oh no, don't go there*, she thought clearing her head as Jake said, "Hey."

"Hi," Kate said, hooking her thumbs in her back pockets and pulling her gaze to meet his. "Um," she hesitated. There was no way to back out now. "You got a minute?" she asked, tossing her head. "I could use some help unloading some stuff."

"Sure." Jake shrugged and slipped into a pair of flip-flops. He pulled a hooded sweatshirt off the hook by the door and put it on before he followed her around back.

Jake pulled his hood up, to cover his head, and dug his hands into the front pocket of his sweatshirt.

"I got this toilet for the basement apartment," she explained and Jake said nothing, looking like he couldn't care less.

Kate lifted the bowl from the tailgate as Jake leaned against the side of the truck.

"So, what do you want me to do?" he asked, as she started for the basement.

Follow me with the other piece, she thought, halting in the yard. But when she turned and saw him huddled against the mild cold of the day, she changed her request. He was probably more at risk to get hurt than she was.

"Just make sure I don't die," she yelled and headed for the stairs.

When she came back up, Jake was standing in the same place and she wondered if he'd be able to hear her scream from all the way over there. What did it matter? The guy was a jerk. A first-rate jerk at that and she wondered what had ever possessed her to ask him for help. She grabbed the toilet tank and took off for the basement again.

Kate set the tank next to the bowl and surveyed the basement. Over the last week, she'd succeeded in getting the rest of the drywall put up around the bathroom. The drill she'd brought back from the ranch had sped up the process, and she had to admit her cutouts around the outlets and light switches looked good. Maybe if she didn't pass the bar again, she'd give up her attorney dream and start applying for contracting positions. Although, the economy hadn't done much for their industry either.

Kate carefully realigned the chestnuts she'd kicked out of the way when she came through the door. She'd read that these were good for getting rid of spiders. So far, so good. She hadn't seen a spider in the basement for a few days.

Kate jogged up the stairs, thinking she'd get the lawn mower out before heading downstairs to install the toilet. Her pace slowed when she saw Jake still standing next to the truck. Why hadn't he gone back inside? Kate knew why and now she had to deal with the urge he always brought to her. How was she going to deal with this?

She walked over to close the tailgate and kept her eyes on the ground.

"Thanks again for your help," she said, trying not to look at him. If she made eye contact, it might send the message she was looking for something else from him and she was trying hard not to want anything from him.

"So," he said and stepped closer. She looked up into his lust-filled eyes and felt the muscles south of her navel clench with desire. She was weak. So very weak. Where was her self-control?

A text message came through on her phone. The beep tugged Kate out of her moment with Jake. Thankful for the save, she pulled the phone from her pocket and read the message. It was from Mary:

`Wedding Emergency. Meet me in front of my office in one hour, please.`

Kate typed back.

`Ok`

She hoped the break in her attention toward Jake would help her loose her desire for an afternoon sex snack. She had to meet Mary in an hour. She didn't have time for him right now, but when she looked up at his scruffy beard and suggestive half smile, she lost her nerve. She had an hour, which was more than enough time for what they were going to do.

* * *

An hour and ten minutes later Kate found Mary outside The Law Office of Rose Patterson in downtown Portland.

"There you are." Mary smiled and held out her hands to Kate. "Come on. I only have an hour for lunch, so we've got to hurry."

"Okay," Kate said thankful Mary hadn't questioned her tardiness. Two blocks later, they were climbing the stairs to a bridal store. Mary talked non-stop on the way over which gave Kate time to forget about the quickie she and Jake had performed on the floor of her living room, not even taking the time to go somewhere more comfortable.

"The invitations will be here in four weeks," Mary explained and Kate nodded as they walked through the glass doors. "Olivia and Muriel have agreed to help me stuff them, but I'd love it if you could too."

Kate smiled at her friend noncommittally. Olivia was a force on her own, but Olivia plus her mother was ten times more challenging to stomach. So when the time came, Kate would conjure up some excuse to decline the invitation.

Right now, the best course of action was to change the subject. "Is everybody else meeting us here?" Kate asked meaning the other bridesmaids.

"Um…no they all had to work." Mary's eyes shifted from left to right, the way they always did when she was hiding something. Kate didn't press her friend. Mary could have her secrets and so could Kate.

Kate did a quick visual appraisal of the store. It was about half the size of Bonita's. Two women stood behind the counter discussing the pages of a catalogue. Neither woman approached to offer a greeting nor a glass of champagne as Mary browsed the gowns hanging on the metal racks. Kate quickly surmised that this wasn't the kind of shop Olivia and her following would approve of. Maybe that's why Mary had only invited Kate.

"What are we doing here?" Kate whispered.

"Looking for a dress," Mary answered.

"But I thought you liked that poufy one at Bonita."

"Well, yes I did," Mary whispered back. "But it was outrageously expensive and it takes six months to order it. So, I figured I'd check this place out. They're having a—rack sale." Mary mouthed the final two words as if they were obscenities.

Kate stepped in next to Mary and helped shuffle through the dresses.

"How's the bridal shower planning going?" Mary asked, giving the once over to a cap-sleeve beaded dress, before flipping past it.

"Fine."

"Olivia said it's going to be at her building."

Kate nodded.

"Well, it's so sweet of you guys to put on a shower for me, especially considering the time table I've put you on."

Kate half-smiled, the bridal shower was something she tried not to think about. The last email from Olivia stated the staggering cost of the catering and room rental. And Kate knew this was just the beginning. She tried to block the numbers from her brain, because whenever she did think about it, she felt herself falling short of breath.

Finally, one of the salesclerks approached. "How can I help you?" the woman asked in a thick accent. Russian, maybe?

"I'm looking for a wedding dress," Mary explained.

The woman nodded. "You know we have sale today," she added, her chiseled features never cracking to show a smile. "Sixty to eighty percent off dress."

"Yes, I know," Mary said, pulling a dress from the rack. "I'd like to try on this one." The woman, who'd failed to offer her name, took the dress and Mary shuffled through the remaining dresses. Mary selected three others and Kate helped her carry them all back to the small bedroom sized dressing room.

"Come on, we've got to do this fast," Mary said, dragging Kate back into the room when she tried to leave. Kate took a seat on the padded bench and waited.

Mary pulled a strapless bra from her purse and changed out of her work clothes—a gray pant suit with a pale pink blouse and black patent leather heels.

"So, I was wondering," Mary said as she stepped into the wedding gown that very much resembled the cupcake style dress from the other store. "Are you bringing anyone with you to the wedding? I'm addressing your invitation to you and a guest, but I'm trying to get a head count early on."

"Oh, I don't know," Kate said as her thoughts pitifully jumped to Jake. He'd been a jerk today, but there was some undeniable animal attraction between them. Some quality about him kept sending her back for more, even if she felt ashamed after the "more." Maybe she would bring him to the wedding. It beat suffering through the night alone.

"You're not thinking about bringing Jake are you?" Mary's face turned sour as she slipped her arms through the straps of the dress. "I wish you'd just throw him out of that place. He's bad for you. He's junk food. You need to find someone you can have a healthy relationship with."

"I know," Kate said, hating how Mary could read her thoughts sometimes.

Mary turned, so Kate could run the zipper up her back. "I don't think Alejandro is bringing a date, so you can spend time with him."

Great, more talk of the narcissistic Alejandro.

"Did you like the restaurant?" Mary continued, not waiting for an answer. "I just love it. I think it's so great he's doing the reception for us there. He's just such a sweetheart."

Before Kate could answer the stone-faced salesclerk burst in with a handful of clips and went to work cinching the bodice around Mary's midsection.

Mary walked out to look at herself in the tall three-way mirrors. Kate didn't follow. She knew her opinion of the dress. And the next dress—marshmallow pudding, and the next—a puddle of whip cream, and the final one—a bird's nest with loose feathers falling from the skirt. Seriously, what were these designers thinking? Who wanted to look like a dessert or an animal—marine or feathered—on her wedding day? Whatever happened to simple and classic?

As Kate helped a discouraged looking Mary out of the feathered dress, the salesclerk barged in again, another gown draped over her arm.

"Try this," she said, handing it over to Mary. Mary checked her watch, their hour was nearly over. "It eighty percent off," the woman reminded her.

Mary checked the tag and smiled. "Okay, one more," she said and pulled the spaghetti straps from the hanger.

The salesclerk pulled the zipper closed and they all paused, because it fit like a glove, no clips and no gapes. Rhinestones nestled in the embroidered threads glimmered off the bodice.

"This design matches the invitations perfectly," Mary said with a squeal as she studied the embroidery. She took off to the mirrors and stepped on the pedestal. She gasped and clasped her hands together, "I look like a princess. Don't I look like a princess?"

The salesclerk grabbed a tiara and an elbow length veil. Mary settled her hands where the bodice meets the skirt as the tiara and veil were placed on her head, magically transforming her into the leading lady of a fairytale.

Kate smiled. "Yes, Mary you look like a princess."

Layers of tulle circled Mary's legs and while Kate could never image wearing anything that full, it was the perfect dress for Mary. And so, they walked out of the store with a discount dress made for Mary.

Nine

That was *him*. That had to be him.

Kate stood in the doorway of the now very descript room of Olivia's building. White lights twinkled off one wall, beneath white sheer paneling and bursts of white roses teemed from black vases on the dozen or so white clothed tables in the room. A black and white damask bag hung from the back of every chair and black paper lanterns dangled from the ceiling.

But it was the man across the room tangled in a conversation with Brandi that had her captivated. He was tall with long dark hair pulled into a ponytail. He wore the standard uniform of all employees at Alejandro's and held an empty tray. Brandi with a flute of champagne in hand swayed girlishly while she twisted a lock of hair around a finger. She stared up at the man's dazzling white smile—yes, even from all the way over here, Kate could tell he had perfectly white teeth and a dazzling smile.

Brandi took her hair twisting hand and laid it on his chest as he said something. She slithered her hand down his front as she laughed at his words, probably something dull witted like, "Hey baby, can I get your digits, 'cuz I just lost mine?"

She looked like a seductress over there in her black lacy baby doll. The mini layers of tulle skirting barely covered her hind assets.

Not that Brandi couldn't afford to show off those assets, but seriously hadn't the whole lingerie party idea been nixed from the get go.

Mr. Perfect Nose and Perfectly Bronzed Glowing Skin Man had to be Alejandro. He looked like the swimsuit-model-dating kind of fellow. He was definitely Brandi-material and she could have him. Kate would keep her distance and bury herself in the background.

Sidestepping along the back wall, to keep Alejandro in view, she reached the gift table and set her present down. Not a sampling of Raine Water Farms' finest lavender soaps, but hopefully a close second.

"This is great." Mary came out of nowhere and sideswiped Kate into a hug. "This is wonderful. You guys are amazing. Amazing."

The Good Witch let out a squeal as Olivia, Madison and Michelle joined them. Kate winced as Mary dragged her into a hug with the other three and they bounced like a handful of black jellybeans.

Kate stumbled back as they broke out of the hug and her eyes searched the room for Alejandro. Where was he? Brandi was talking to some vaguely familiar, perfectly put together brunette, but Alejandro had disappeared.

"If you'll excuse us Mary we have a few details to settle," Olivia said, turning her hundred-watt smile on the guest of honor.

"Of course," Mary said, adjusting the petal pink belt of her black dress. "I'll leave you to it." She scurried off and waved down her hard-of-hearing Aunt Vera.

The kitchen door flew open and out walked Alejandro with a tray full of champagne. Kate's gaze stuck to him like a magnet.

"Kate." Olivia's voice broke the pull of her attention away.

"Yes?" Kate replied, missing the once over Olivia gave her attire. She was more concerned about the whereabouts of one tall, dark, and mildly handsome stranger.

"You're all helping with the games. So, when it's time join me up front and just follow my lead. Also, you have to make the bow bouquet. Got it?"

"Okay, sure," Kate nodded, but her eyes were back to tracking Alejandro. He was headed in their direction! Kate's pulse quickened and her palms began to sweat.

"And what about my…" The annoying sound of Olivia's voice interfered with her tracking process again.

"Oh yeah," Kate said as Alejandro was stopped by Mrs. Goodwich, seeking a drink. Kate let out a grateful breath mixed with a muddled prayer of forgiveness as she handed over the money that had been soaking up the perspiration from her palm.

"What am I supposed to do with this?" Olivia asked, obviously put out.

Alejandro was on the move again. *Escape. Escape*, was all Kate could think.

"Dunno." Kate shrugged as the three classic beauties stared dumb-faced at the wad of fives, tens and twenties she'd handed Olivia.

Kate sidled out of the makeshift trap the three had put her in and headed for—oh no, where could she go—candy! The white clothed table with the black skirting up ahead was just where she needed to go.

From the tall glass containers Kate scooped out enough treats to fill a pint size bag and didn't bother to tie off the top. She inhaled, letting the chocolate fumes calm her nerves. From the silver tray at the front of the table, she grabbed a black and white cookie. *Mmmm, it was delicious.*

Alejandro was a safe distance away, across the room in the far corner. He was being fawned over by a gaggle of middle-aged women and soaking up every bit of attention.

Kate wondered why she was so nervous about meeting this guy as she let the sugary goodness soothe her rattled nerves.

He was just a guy. *Who dated supermodels*! Kate took another bite of her cookie. Maybe it was because she was feeling a little frazzled around the edges today—what with having to rush out of the market, committing a small act of thievery to collect enough money to pay off Olivia, and then showing up here in her casual knit dress and flip-flops while everyone else wore silk and lace and shiny high heels which, of course, made them look amazing.

Kate looked at the four-foot tall vase she was standing next to. Its hourglass shape was wrapped in black satin and belted with glitzy silver. *Awesome, the decorations were better dressed than she was.*

Kate grabbed another cookie.

* * *

Kate started to take a drink as she looked at the wall of black and white portraits depicting Mary and Tony's journey through life from infancy to engagement. She stopped herself right before the glass touched her lips, remembering it wasn't hers. She'd swiped the abandoned glass when it looked like Alejandro was about to strut his long, tall masculine form in her direction. Thankfully, a glass in hand had been enough to signal him away. And she'd kept a tight hold on it as her deflector ever since. Alejandro slipped into the kitchen a few minutes ago. She was keeping the swinging kitchen door well within her peripheral view as she stood here staring at an awkward middle school picture of Mary with her curly frizzed hair and a mouthful of tinny braces.

The unmistakable ping of Olivia's squeal chimed behind her.

"Oh, Dee." Aha, that's who Brandi had been talking to earlier. The perfectly pieced together woman was Dee Carlson of Perfect Daze—she co-owned an event planning business with her BFF Cara Dillon. The business owners were Delta Gamma sisters who graduated two years ahead of Olivia and Company. "I can't thank you enough for pulling this whole thing together on such short notice and still giving us the sisterly discount."

Discount? Dee wouldn't be giving anyone a discount unless they were paying her for something and there was no way Olivia had used *their* money to pay Dee, an incredibly expensive and highly professional event planner to do this, would she?

"Anything for my sisters," Dee said with that high-pitched giggle of a sorority sister, although it wasn't one of the most annoying ones Kate had ever heard. "I'm just glad you had flexibility in your budget so we could rush all the suppliers."

Flexibility? Nobody said anything about flexibility to Kate. When had there ever been talk of a budget? All Kate got was a mandating text subtly filled with the legalese she'd expect from an attorney like Olivia demanding prompt payment, or else. Kate never would have flexed if there had been an option. Was there an option? Could she un-flex now and get some of her money back? Because outsourcing this event had never been cleared with her.

The kitchen door swung open, and Kate very obviously flipped her head in that direction, but pulled it back as soon as she saw Carly delivering a tray of food to the buffet table.

"Well, you know, anything for our Mary," Olivia said and Kate's ears joined the conversation behind her again.

Our Mary. She was not Olivia's Mary. She was Kate's Mary. If Olivia knew one ounce about Mary she would know that a picnic in the park would have been sufficient. Kate felt the words on the tip of her tongue wanting to be yelled out.

"It's too bad the others weren't on board with an afternoon tea party. We could have incorporated the outdoor garden into the decorating—maybe even saved a little on decorations."

Saved? Yes, Kate wanted that option. Why hadn't she been consulted? Why had Olivia masterminded this whole thing without any input?

"I know, but they were all so set on this LBD idea. I couldn't disappoint them."

Not everybody. Kate turned ready to share her thought when the kitchen door swung open and Mr. You Know Who came out balancing a tray of food. In her moment of distraction, Olivia and Dee had moved into a conversation with Mrs. Fisher and two other guests. Her moment was gone and in surrender, Kate tipped back the glass of champagne not caring in the least that her lips weren't the first to touch this rim.

*   *   *

"These are soooo good," Mrs. Goodwich said from the chair next to Kate. The woman tipped up her glass and drained the rest of the champagne punch. She whipped her head in both directions before coming back to center and swaying to a halt. "Where is that dear girl? The one with all the drinks."

Kate pointed to the left and Mrs. Goodwich's face lit up. "Over here. Over here," she called to the petite blonde waitress. The one Kate distinctly remembered from the restaurant that was invested in getting AJ's attention. The waitress made her way to Mrs. Goodwich and exchanged her empty glass for a full one. Kate also traded in her half glass of orphaned champagne for a new one. She figured she better get a refill now, before Alejandro showed up again toting his drink tray.

Speaking of Alejandro, he'd been missing for nearly fifteen minutes. Once the food was laid out at the buffet tables, he disappeared.

Kate looked down at her plate, piled high with crab cakes, and shrimp kabobs. Even with the Fierce Four's eyes directly in front of her in line, she had stacked her plate, fully determined to get her money's worth. She poked at one of the stunning crab cakes. It smelled delicious, but she was so on edge, awaiting the next appearance of Mr. Tall, Dark and Handsome that her appetite had vanished.

But if she didn't eat, and the food was wasted then so was the money she'd borrowed-without-asking-for today. So Kate took a bite, chewed, and forced the food down.

"Are you going to eat that, sweetie?" Mrs. Goodwich asked, pointing with her fork at a shrimp kabob on Kate's plate.

Kate shook her head and Mrs. Goodwich speared the middle shrimp with a fork and pulled the entire kabob over to her plate.

Well, at least Mrs. Goodwich was getting her fill today. The woman had been like a mother to Kate during her undergrad years, taking both she and Mary by the arm on Mom's weekends when they would go to the fashion show or out to dinner. The year Mary participated in SING, the musical showcase put on by the fraternities and sororities, Kate sat alone in the bleachers with Mrs. Goodwich and they talked effortlessly about classes and boys. Kate admitted there were no serious boys in her life, but she didn't admit to the boys that actually were in her life. She wouldn't confess those one-night stands and drunken hook-ups to Mrs. Goodwich, just like she wouldn't have told her own mother if she'd been there.

"Oh my," Mrs. Goodwich hiccupped. Kate turned and saw the woman digging around inside the front of her black dress. Searching. "Where did that little booger go? It just jumped right in." The entire table watched as Mrs. Goodwich pulled out a wayward cherry tomato and popped it in her mouth. The guests at their table all laughed except Aunt Vera on the other side of Kate who had nodded off some time ago.

"Well, I'll just take care of that little problem," Mrs. Goodwich said, tucking her napkin around her neckline like a bib.

"Oh. My. God." Olivia's voice tolled from the neighboring table. Kate's back was to her, but she knew Olivia's lip-curling, eye-popping face by heart.

An ember of fury flamed inside Kate. Olivia had no business dropping her catty judgments on Mrs. Goodwich like that. The woman, a bit uncouth at times, was still a fountain of goodness, just like Mary. And in an act to align herself with Mrs. Goodwich, Kate raised her napkin to her chest ready to tuck the corner in her neckline when the kitchen door flew open.

Ten

"Game time!" Olivia stood at the front of the room, using her voice to bring everyone's attention to her. "Look into your tote bags. Get out the notebook, pen and blindfold."

Kate lifted the beautiful bag from the back of her chair and set it in her lap. The soft satin straps fell open and exposed a glut of goodies. Mrs. Goodwich giggled with delight as she pulled out a monogramed black notebook with the letters M and A intertwined on the cover.

Kate stared bewildered. Slowly, she sorted through the contents of the bag, completely tuning out the instructions Olivia was shouting. Besides the notebook, there was also a black feathered pen, a satin sleeping mask, a bottle of bubble bath, a personalized pot of lip-gloss—again monogrammed with the bride and grooms' initials—a charm bracelet with a dozen sparkling black flowers, a box of twin heart shaped soaps, a tiny manicure set, and a tube of personalized chocolates.

"Blindfolds, please. Blindfolds," Olivia chanted. Kate dug around and pulled out the black satin sleeping mask, her notebook, and the feathered pen. She dropped the bag on the floor and flipped open the notebook. She pulled the blindfold into place as Olivia gave the next instructions, "Now, do your best sketch of a dress for Mary. Be as creative as you can, but remember—no peeking." *No peeking? You mean she had to do this blindfolded.*

The wispy feather tickled Kate's wrist as she tried to focus on drawing, but numbers and dollar signs crowded her brain. How much had that little bag at her feet cost? She pulled up the corner of her mask and did a quick count of the tables then multiplied it by the chairs. There were easily sixty bags in the room and the gifts inside had to cost, oh God, Kate had no idea how much all of that could have cost, maybe…

"That's it. Time's up," Olivia called. "Bridesmaids, please collect the papers."

Kate stood, forgetting about the calculations. She circled the room to collect the waving pieces of paper. She fell into step behind Madison and handed her stack of obscure drawings to Olivia.

"Okay, now Mary will look through these while everybody starts the next game. We, the bridesmaids, are your team captains. We will divide into teams and…" Out of a box, Olivia pulled a six-roll package of toilet paper. "You will dress us in toilet paper. Mary will be our judge, selecting her favorite. So, off you go ladies."

Kate, the last in line to get her hands on a package of toilet paper, headed for the only open space in the room—the corner near the kitchen door. She waited as a group of women funneled toward her, led by Mrs. Goodwich and her glass of champagne punch.

Kate couldn't think of another time when she'd felt so ridiculous. Women pawed over her and tucked strips of toilet paper under her arms. They were down to their last roll, which had been saved for the veil. Kate turned, facing the kitchen door, so the group could work their magic when the door swung open. Kate's heart stopped, fearing the famed Alejandro would get an eyeful of her standing there, draped in two-ply.

Her heart restarted when Carly came out and before the door completely shut behind her Kate caught a glimpse of AJ talking to a man with salt and pepper hair. The man, whose profile Kate barely glimpsed, was uncovering a plate of food. *Health inspector,* Kate caught herself wondering. AJ looked serious, arms folded over his chest and eyes watching the man study his food. Briefly, his eyes left the inspector and found Kate's, his lips curved into a half-smile just as the door closed.

But no sighting of Alejandro. Kate didn't like being at a disadvantage, not knowing his whereabouts. Where could the man have gone?

"Times up," Olivia called.

Mary's cousin Amelia grabbed Kate by the elbow, detaining her as the other white-wrapped bridesmaids made their way to the center of the room. "Wait!" Amelia hissed as she tied on one more bow.

"Times up, ladies!" Olivia sang out, an impatient edge to her voice. "Everyone to your seats." Olivia of course was stunning, mummy wrapped in her floor length tissue dress, complete with a bouquet of tissue flowers. *How had they had enough rolls for that?* Kate wondered.

Kate took a step forward when a tipsy Mrs. Goodwich stumbled onto her train, tearing the entire backside off the dress.

"Oooops," Mrs. Goodwich giggled as Kate walked away, leaving half her dress in the corner along with a dozen crestfallen faces of those that had worked so hard to doll up Kate.

"Ladies you've done a fabulous job. If Mary doesn't hurry up and pick a dress for herself we may have to wrap her in toilet paper just to get her down the aisle." Olivia laughed and Mary's head shot up. Her eyes connected with Kate's. *Why doesn't Olivia know you picked out a dress?* Kate silently asked her.

Mary responded with a slight shake to her head.

"So which is it Mary?" Olivia prompted and Mary returned her attention to her tp-models.

"I like this one." Mary pointed to Olivia's dress.

"Yay. We win, we win," Olivia called out and a small round of applause circulated the tables. "And which dress design did you pick?"

Mary held up an elegantly drawn full-length figure. *No way was the person who drew that blindfolded*, Kate thought.

"Oh, that's mine. That's mine." Olivia jumped up and down. Mary's face turned pink. "Yay, it's time for prizes!" The kitchen door pushed open. A serving cart topped with two-tier kitchen towel cakes decorated with stainless steel utensils and black ribbons was rolled to the center of the room. "My team come on up and pick your prize," Olivia called while Kate striped out of her two-ply dress which left behind tiny white pills. *Why didn't Olivia skimp on the tp? One-ply wouldn't leave a lint trail like this*, Kate thought.

Kate picked another tp-fuzz off her dress as she sat dutifully next to Mary and assembled her bow bouquet. Mrs. Goodwich let out a whoop as Mary broke another ribbon on her gift and passed it to Kate. "I want oodles of grandbabies," Mrs. Goodwich squawked as Kate finagled the new ribbon onto the paper plate bouquet. "Break me another one, Sweetikins."

Kate could feel Olivia's stiff reproach from the other side of Mary as she twisted her head away, keeping Mrs. Goodwich out of her line of vision.

The pile of place settings, towels, sheets and silverware were growing. Next, Mary pulled a lacy French maid teddy out of a box.

"Oh my heavens," a frail voice shook on the words. *Great Aunt Millie*, Kate presumed as Olivia shot Brandi a death glare. Mrs. Fisher popped up and brought a glass of water over to the gaping woman. Mary balled the negligée back into the box and sent an embarrassed thank you in Brandi's direction.

Kate's was the final gift to be opened. Mary pulled the tissue out of the bag and then the jelly jars—one at a time and read the labels aloud, "Vanilla sugar scrub." Mary passed the jar to Olivia. "Brown sugar scrub," she said, reading the next label and then, "Lemon sugar scrub. Thank you, these are great."

"What are those?" asked Madison, the one in charge of scribing the gift list.

Olivia opened the lemon scrub and took a whiff.

No, not that one, Kate thought.

"Is this toilet scrub?" Olivia coughed out, not attempting to lower her voice.

Why did Olivia have to open that one? The lemon juice was too strong. Kate knew it, but she'd only had enough supplies for the three batches. She hoped the lemon scent would settle over time, but judging by Olivia's reaction it was still too strong.

Mary quickly rewrapped the jars and tucked them in the bag. "Those were really thoughtful," she added.

"Yeah, you're so good at those homey crafty things," Olivia said, but the weight of her toilet scrub words drowned any complement she might try to pass off now.

As the guests began to move from their chairs, a cart carrying six tiers of cupcakes rolled out of the kitchen. The tops were decorated with a swirl of pink frosting. Kate didn't think she could ever look at a cupcake again without picturing Mary on top of it.

The wait staff, sans Alejandro—*where could he be?*—circled the room, heavily armed with trays of champagne. How could the man have simply disappeared?

While the sugar-hungry guests swarmed the cake cart, Kate stepped out of the room in search of the restroom. She found it down a quiet hall.

She flipped the latch on her corner stall when she heard the door open again.

"I'm telling you Mads," Olivia's unmistakable voice ranted. "She hasn't touched the champagne. I've been watching."

"Do you really think she is pregnant? Because it would really suck if they got pregnant before us."

"Yeah, I do," Olivia said, ignoring the obvious distress in Madison's voice. "Tony was taking too long to propose. I know it. She did this just to nudge him along. It's a shame, because he could do so much better than her."

Oooh, Kate felt her back stiffen as Olivia took a jab at her dearest friend. What did that girl know about Mary? Mary was plenty good enough for Tony. He was the one who had to strive to equal Mary, because his sister counted for many strikes against him. Why was Mary marrying into this family? Didn't she realize what she was getting into?

"Yeah," Madison agreed. Kate heard the sound of their purses snapping shut and then they were gone. Out the door.

* * *

Back in the banquet room, Kate searched for Mary. She needed to tell her what Olivia was saying about her, help her put this pregnancy rumor to rest. Poor, sweet, defenseless Mary, who always looked for the good in others was about to marry into a family with a wicked witch as a sister-in-law.

As Kate walked past the cupcake cart, she picked up a plate and carried it toward the wall of windows when she finally spotted Mary coming inside from the gardens. Michelle and a panting Brandi were with her.

"Oh my God," Brandi fanned herself. "He is simply gorgeous." Her words slurred together as she waved her champagne in front of her face. Kate wondered if she was already one up on Mrs. Goodwich's drink total.

Mary, holding a glass of water not champagne, stopped when she saw Kate. "Have you met Alejandro yet?"

Kate shook her head. "I have to talk to you."

"Okay," Mary smiled. "Let's go outside. I'll introduce you and then we can talk." Mary let go of Brandi's arm, who shifted all of her weight onto Michelle.

Outside. Of course, why hadn't she thought of that? He must have been hiding outside.

"He is a god in his own right," Brandi breathed out each word.

"Let's get you some coffee," Michelle said with a disgusted sigh and dragged Brandi away.

Mary shook her head.

"Oh Mary, there you are," Muriel Fisher said, walking over with her arms outstretched. "Come dear, I want you to meet the Wickham's. Dear, dear old friends of ours."

Mary moved to join her future-mother-in-law, but not before turning back to Kate. "Go on out there and say hello. I'll come find you." She pointed toward the door and Kate sucked in her breath, preparing to meet the divine Alejandro.

Instead of the tall, lean, sculpted Alejandro, she found AJ, in his long black apron and black shirt, sleeves rolled to his elbows. He was replacing the chairs at the garden tables. Black lanterns globes were tied beneath the sun umbrellas and more tote bags—completely unused, *what a waste*—hung on the back of every chair.

A flood of relief came over Kate at the sight of him.

"Well, hi," he said, looking up at Kate.

"Hi. I was sent out here to meet your boss. But I guess I must have missed him."

"Um, yeah." AJ looked at her sideways. "My boss already left. It's just me out here."

Another flood of relief swept over Kate as the stress of having to avoid the man handler evaporated, "My loss, huh? He sent Brandi back inside drooling all over herself."

AJ smiled and shook his head. "Here have a seat," he offered, pulling out a chair and she obliged. She was glad when he took the seat across from her. This was the best company she'd been in since she got here.

"They're perfect for each other."

"Who?"

"Your boss and Brandi. They would make a very good couple. Two of a kind you know?"

"I don't think so," AJ said very seriously. Kate cocked her head.

"Well, they were practically all over each other in there earlier." Kate gestured toward the banquet room. She knew what she saw—those two would have been tearing each other's clothes off if they could.

"They were together? Inside?"

"Yeah, him and his golden tan. And sporty ponytail. Offering up his trays of champagne like some love potion. He had every woman over the age of forty hanging on his every word," Kate said with an emphatic nod and peeled back the paper from her chocolate cupcake.

"Oh, that's…" AJ trailed off as Kate's cupcake flipped upside down and landed frosting side down in her lap.

"Oh, no," she yelped, scooping the cake off her lap and leaving behind the heap of pink frosting. God, what was it with her and food falling in her lap all the time now.

AJ dashed for the kitchen access door off the patio. He returned with a stack of napkins and a wet rag.

"Thanks," she said, taking the rag and wiping up the buttercream puddle.

"Do you want me to get you a lemon so you can do your stain removing thing?"

"No," Kate said with a resigned shake of her head. "I can wash this out when I get home."

Just then, the kitchen door opened and Carly walked out holding a plate with a new cupcake.

"Thanks," Kate said as Carly set it down in front of her and took away the crumbled one. Kate stared at the cupcake wondering if she had the stomach for it now. "Seems as though food and I don't have a very good relationship right now," Kate said, trying to make a joke.

"What do you mean?"

"I mean, everything I eat keeps falling in my lap. Maybe I should take it as some sign to lay-off. Drop a few pounds. Skinny up, so I can be a size two bridesmaid like the rest of the girls."

"You don't strike me as someone who needs to lose a few pounds," AJ said with a trace of shyness.

"Maybe not," she said, feeling a bit shy herself. She wasn't the kind of girl to go on about her weight in front of a guy, but AJ was just so easy to talk to. Words came out of her mouth in front of him that she usually kept to herself.

AJ face turned grim. "Why is it women are so caught up in dress sizes anyway?" he asked, a crease indenting his forehead.

Kate looked at him and he held her gaze. *Who did care? And when had she become so concerned about her dress size? Only when it had been broadcasted,* she remembered. But there was a societal attachment to a woman's image too.

"Society." She shrugged.

AJ shook his head.

"Men like your boss don't help either," Kate continued. "Guys like that who objectify women are really a part of the problem too, you know."

"I see your opinion has yet to be altered," AJ smirked at her.

"Until I have been proven otherwise, I reserve the right to stick to my opinion," Kate answered, picking up the fork Carly had thoughtfully brought her. She broke off a piece of the cupcake and took a bite.

AJ smiled. "How is that cupcake?"

"Good," Kate said. "But I think I'd like it better with a side of ice cream."

His smile deepened, "Some would say you're saving on calories." He winked at her.

"Are you saying I should be watching my calories now?" she joked back at him.

"Nope. I said *some* would say you're saving on calories without the ice cream."

"You're right. Skinny bitches, who think food is the enemy, would say that."

"So, food isn't your enemy?"

Kate shrugged and nodded, her mouth chewing another bite of cupcake. "Only when it falls square in my lap." She pinched a crumb off her plate and popped it in her mouth.

AJ chuckled and watched her take another bite. "I'm glad you came out here," he finally said.

"Really?" she asked, feeling the same way.

"Yeah. I had our new chef prepare your meat yesterday. I read over all your ranch information and visited the website. I'd like to put in an order."

"So, did thee ole Alejandro get to try it?"

AJ smiled, his eyes twinkled. "Yeah, he did and he loved it. So what's the best way to go about putting in an order?"

Kate sat back. "Well, if you're serious about wanting to purchase meat from us, my dad will insist on you visiting the ranch. He's an old school face-to-face, seal the deal with a handshake kind of guy."

"Okay," AJ said. "When does he come to the city? Maybe I could meet up with him then?"

"He doesn't come to the city. I suggest you take a trip out to the ranch. See the whole operation. The herd. The slaughterhouse. It's sort of a requirement my dad has anyway. He won't draw up a contract unless he feels his buyer is one-hundred percent informed about the product."

"Okay," AJ nodded. "So where is the ranch exactly?"

"Hayden Valley," Kate reminded him.

AJ shook his head.

"It's about three hours east of the city."

"Is there an airport I can fly into?"

"No," Kate laughed. "Our town is much too small for that. Unless Alejandro has a private plane. There's a little airstrip out in the Buford's field."

AJ shook his head again. "Does a bus line run through there?"

"No. Car or truck is the only other way in or out of the valley. Do you not have a car?"

"Not anymore," AJ said, leaning forward and setting his elbows on his knees. He clasped his hands together. "My girlfriend sort of totaled it."

"Girlfriend?" Kate asked, folding her arms over her chest.

"*Ex*-girlfriend," he said and Kate's defenses relaxed. "After, she more or less stole my car while heavily intoxicated I decided to get out of the relationship." He unclasped his hands turning them upward.

Kate gave a little laugh. "Sounds like we have similar taste in relationship partners."

"Oh yeah?" AJ smiled. "You have a drunk, bulimic, car crashing boyfriend in your past too?"

"No. More like a chain smoking, barely employed neighbor of an ex-boyfriend that I still sleep with from time to time," Kate said matter-of-factly.

Kate caught the glimmer of shock that passed over his face. "Interesting," AJ said before he dropped his gaze to the ground.

"I can take you."

AJ's head popped up. "Excuse me?"

"I can take you to the ranch. I go every Friday night to pick up meat for the farmers market. Can you get next Friday night off? I'd have you back plenty early on Saturday."

"Are you asking me on an overnight getaway, Miss Kate? 'Cuz I just don' know that that'd be proper 'n all," AJ said in an old western accent.

"What is that?" Kate asked, running her finger through the frosting on her cupcake.

"It's my John Wayne impression, not bad, yeah?"

"Terrible," she said and paused with her finger full of frosting in front of her mouth. "So do you want my meat or not?" she asked and then licked the frosting from her finger.

AJ smiled. "Yes, I would love to get my hands on your meat," he said, raising his eyebrows at her.

Eleven

Kate lifted and lowered the ice blue toilet seat lid. No squeaks, no wiggles.

Next, she sat down fully clothed on the seat and rocked back and forth. Side-to-side. Again, no squeaks. No wiggles. She'd done good. The toilet install was complete and she did it solo in less time than the online how-to video had suggested.

On either side of the toilet were two more plumbing openings—plugged and waiting. On one side would be a sink. A simple pedestal is what Kate imagined, but it depended entirely on what reclaimed beauty she could find at the warehouse. A glorious soaking tub on the other side would be nice too, but in the end, Kate knew she'd have to settle for a single stand up shower. A tub shower combo wouldn't fit down the stairs or into her budget.

So much for the twenty-four bottles of bubble bath she took off with after the bridal shower. Kate looked over at the pile of damask bags abandoned in her bare living room. She snagged the unused bags off the backs of the garden terrace chairs before she left on Saturday. The thought of those ridiculous favors being dumped in the trash or worse yet going home with Olivia, the cash cow, made her tense with rage and so she simply slipped the straps over her arms and headed for the door. It was too bad she couldn't trade those bags with the contractor whose third statement requesting immediate payment arrived today along with her monstrous credit card bill.

Kate stood up. She couldn't let her unpaid bills get her down. Everything would be paid off one day.

Right now, she had to focus on finishing her current task. Kate studied her reclaimed prize, feeling doggone proud of herself. She was really getting the hang of this renovation work. She laid the spud gasket, set the tank, and tightened all the bolts. This commode was good to go. All she had to do was turn on the water line.

With a twist of the valve, she heard the rush of water as the tank filled. Kate watched and waited, looking for leaks. Not a one. She stood and let the tank finish filling.

Shouldn't it be full by now? Why was the water still running? Kate lifted the toilet lid. It seemed at the right level, but she could still hear water running. She lifted the top of the tank and was met with a blast of cold water. Right between the eyes.

Kate bent down, toilet water raining over her, and twisted the shut off valve. The water ceased and she stood. Beads of water dripped down her chin. What just happened?

Kate calmly set the toilet lid back in place and turned on her heels. She needed to walk away now. If she stayed, the toilet might be met with the wrath of her wrench and that ultimately would solve nothing. Her feet slipped and slid off her flip-flops as she stalked to the door and headed for the stairs. She held tight to the railing and stomped up the stairs into the afternoon sun. Her wet t-shirt stuck to her skin and Kate peeled it away, balling it up in front of her belly button. She gave it a squeeze and water dripped on the grass in front of her as she pounded around the side of the house.

"Hey," Jake said, brightly as he sauntered up the sidewalk. "You wanna…"

She marched up the front steps, blatantly ignoring him. *Did she wanna what? Didn't the boy have eyes? Couldn't he see that she was drenched? In toilet water!*

No, she didn't wanna do anything with him and she let him know it by slamming the door behind her.

* * *

Freshly showered, and feeling cozy in her gray sweats and black Oregon State t-shirt Kate walked up the sidewalk of Portland's Alphabet district in her sanitized flip-flops—so what if the toilet water had been clean, it was still toilet water.

The evening hour had brought loads of people to the street. Long lines stretched out of the eclectic eateries. Kate twisted her body to steer through the heavy foot traffic. The cardboard box of pizza in one hand led the way, and the six-pack of cream soda—bottles, not cans—trailed behind in the other. The smell of the rich tomato sauce and garlic from the peperoni pizza wafted out of the box.

Mary had put in a call this afternoon for a throwback night, something they hadn't done in a long time, at least not since Mary moved out.

The pizza and cream soda were reminders of their first months of college, pure innocence and optimism. And then, after Kate's life-altering event, pizza, cream soda, and made for TV movies had been her lifeline—all with Mary by her side.

So when Mary's call came, Kate was on the move in no time flat. Mary needed comfort and Kate was here to deliver, even if it meant pirating a bit more cash for the pizza and soda.

The idea that this call for indulgence might have something to do with an unplanned pregnancy itched in the back of Kate's mind like an irritating rash. She hadn't gotten the chance to talk to Mary at the bridal shower. Kate left immediately following her act of klepto.

But as she waited on the corner of Twenty-Third and Marshall, Olivia's irritating words came back to her, *She did this just to nudge him along. He could do so much better...*

The streetcar rumbled past and Kate crossed in a mob of walkers. On the other side of the street, she turned away from the group and the hopping energy of Twenty-Third Street. Three blocks later Kate found herself in a sleepy residential strip of the city. The historic brownstone where Mary and Tony lived came into view. Kate slapped up the stairs in her flip-flops and rang the buzzer.

"I'll be right down." Mary's bubble filled voice said, not a weary, stressed-out-because-I'm-unexpectedly-pregnant voice. Score one for Team Not Pregnant. See Kate knew it. There was no way Mary had a secret bun in the oven.

Within seconds, Mary was at the door in her pink Benny Beaver t-shirt, the old school one with the smiling bucktooth beaver. The angry beaver face had never been Mary's style.

Mary reached for the pizza box, "Mmmm." She inhaled, closing her eyes. "Just what I need tonight." She pulled Kate inside and the two climbed up the stairs to Mary and Tony's second floor apartment.

Mary headed straight for the tiny, max capacity of one, kitchen. She pulled two plates out of the blonde wood cupboards and set them next to the pizza box while Kate popped the tops of two cream sodas.

She sat at the bar on a stool and watched as Mary pulled a big salad and six bakery boxes from the fridge.

"I made a salad to go with our pizza and I've got dessert." Her eyes sparkled as she opened the first box. A slice of chocolate cake with mousse filling.

"That looks yummy," Kate said as Mary opened another similar box, showing her a slice of white cake with a cream filling. "So does that."

Mary nodded. "Yeah. And we have to sample all of them. Tonight. Okay?" Mary opened the other boxes, showing off two more chocolate cakes and two more white cakes.

"What are you doing with all this cake?" The words pregnancy and cravings reared in the back of Kate's mind.

"These are my samples for the wedding cake. I know I want a chocolate layer and a white layer. I just need to pick which bakery to go with and get my order in tomorrow."

Phew. Pregnancy suspicion averted. "Is Tony going to help us sample?"

"No, he's in L.A. for a couple of weeks," Mary said with a look of longing in her eyes. "I can't wait until he gets back to make this decision. So, I need your help."

"You got it," Kate said.

"Okay, let's get started." Mary slid open a drawer, pulled out two forks, and handed one to Kate.

Six cake tastings later, they had made a decision. Hands down, the cakes from Water Street Bakery were the best.

"Yay, I'll put my order in tomorrow." Mary flipped open her wedding notebook and checked off a box.

"How are you going to have them decorate it?" Kate asked, reaching for a slice of pizza.

Mary flipped ahead several pages before turning the notebook for Kate to see. "Like this." She pointed to a frosted white three-tier cake, decorated with lines and swirls. A cascade of pink flowers trailed from the top to the bottom layer. Mary leaned over the counter and pointed to the sides of the cake. "I'm going to bring in a picture of the dress, so they can match the designs. Don't you think it will be great?"

"Yes, I do," Kate said, passing the notebook back to Mary. "So, you still like the dress?"

"Of course, why wouldn't I?" Mary asked, leaning her hip into the counter. They had shared a number of meals like this back in the duplex apartment. Neither had invested in a dining room set so they either stood around in the kitchen leaned up against the counters or on the couch balancing plates on their knees.

"At the shower Olivia didn't know about the dress. I thought maybe you'd changed your mind."

"Oh no." Mary smiled and waved her off. "I just forgot to tell her about it." *Forgot?* How does one forget to mention her wedding dress, one of the most important elements in a wedding, to her maid of honor?

Mary scooped salad onto both of their plates and they ate in silence for a few minutes.

"How's the job hunt going?" Mary asked.

Kate shrugged. Mary, along with everyone else in her life, was under the impression Kate had passed the bar exam the first time around. The job hunt as far as they were all concerned was just a run of bad timing. It was just one of those things Kate had "forgotten" to clarify for everyone.

"There might be an opening at the office in a few months," Mary said. Kate looked up at her friend, was she serious? Mary's eyes were vacant. What was she thinking about, Kate wondered. *Hmmm*, was this a starry-eyed, I'm-about-to-be-a-mother look or was it an I-miss-my-fiancé look? Kate couldn't tell and she feared Team I'm Pregnant was about to get a point.

"Is somebody leaving the office?" Kate asked. The Law Office of Rose Patterson was a small but mighty force of three women fighting for the rights of other women in employment, family, and business law.

"Oh," Mary said, shaking her head, like she was trying to clear her thoughts. "It's just talk right now, but I'll let you know if anything comes of it."

"Wouldn't it be great if we could work together?" Kate asked Mary, thinking about the possibility of employment. But Mary looked away and stared down at her salad.

"Yeah, it would," her friend said, her eyes glued to the lettuce. Kate thought she saw Mary force a swallow, but when she looked up she was all bright eyed and smiley.

Mary's phone rang on the counter next to her. She grabbed it and quickly picked up the call.

"Hey Baby," she said, her face lighting into a smile. Her free hand drifted to her stomach and Kate was reminded of the way she had done the same thing at the discount bridal store. It didn't register with her then, but it did now. Isn't that what expectant mothers did? Make that a two point score for Team I'm Pregnant.

"How was your day?" Mary asked into the phone as she snuck into the bedroom for a little privacy.

Kate stood and cleared the mountain of grease soaked napkins from the counter. With Mary out of the way, Kate easily moved around the tiny kitchen and washed their plates. She was putting the leftover pizza in the refrigerator when Mary resurfaced from the bedroom.

"How's Tony?" Kate asked.

"He's good," Mary replied, smiling, but that distant look was back in her eyes. Point for pregnant? "He's working like crazy down there. I can't wait till he's home."

"I bet," Kate said and handed Mary her bottle of cream soda.

"You ready to check out what's on HBO?" Mary asked.

Kate nodded, wondering how much longer she could go without confronting Mary.

"Let's finish off this cake too." Mary piled the boxes into her arms and carried them to the coffee table. Kate who felt ready to bust couldn't help but wonder where Mary's sudden appetite for cake had come from. She'd picked at her salad and single piece of pizza. Was this a craving? *Crap,* one more point for Team I'm Pregnant.

Sitting down on the soft black couch Kate picked at the label on her cream soda bottle wondering how best to broach the subject of Mary's suspected pregnancy. There were too many signs to ignore. She had to know. Something was definitely up.

"Is everything going okay?" Kate asked.

"Of course," Mary said, reopening all the boxes of cake.

"Some of the girls," Kate said, hating the fact that she now placed herself in this group. "Think that maybe you are pregnant."

"What?" Mary's eyes were horror-filled again and Kate instantly regretted having asked the question. "You said so yourself. That would be crazy."

"I know what I said, but if you are. It would be okay. You could admit it and no one would think badly of you."

"Really, you think I am pregnant?"

Well, look at all this cake you want to eat. "I think there is something you're not telling me," Kate challenged.

Mary opened her mouth like she was about to spill the truth, but then clamped it shut and shook her head. "It's nothing," she said with a wave of her hand, but her eyes did that shifty left to right thing again. "I've just got a lot on my plate trying to get the wedding pulled together." Mary tried to paste on her usual smile, but it was a bit fractured and whatever she had been about to say was lost. All happy pretenses were back in the air.

"Is there anything I can do to help?" Kate asked.

"Not right now."

"What about Muriel and Olivia. Are they being helpful?"

Kate sensed the way Mary carefully chose her words. "Oh yes. They'd probably be happy to take over all the planning, if I let them. But I want to do this my way. They'll have to wait for Olivia's turn to have total control."

"Well, they probably won't have to wait long," Kate said.

"Why? What do you mean?" Mary blurted out.

"I don't know," Kate said, treading lightly. "I just got the impression a proposal was coming soon, but it was probably just Olivia being dramatic. You know how she loves drama?"

"Yes, I do." Mary's smile was still fixed in place, but there was a look in her eye that turned the wheels in Kate's mind. "Well, that's really exciting," she said.

"Yeah," Kate agreed and debated how to press this Olivia situation. "So, you and Olivia are going to be sisters pretty soon, huh?"

"I guess so," Mary said a little whimsically.

"And you get to spend all the holidays together."

Mary nodded.

"She's quite a force."

"Yes, she is," Mary agreed and then smiled. "Sometimes I can hardly believe she and Anthony are related. I tease him sometimes and ask him if he's adopted. But he's just like his dad and Olivia well, she's just like Muriel." Mary shrugged.

"And you're okay with all of that. I mean she can get pretty nasty sometimes."

Mary nodded and Kate wondered what exactly she was agreeing with. "But I'm not marrying Olivia. I'm marrying her brother and he's perfect for me," Mary finally answered. "Everything will be fine." There was a choke to Mary's voice and Kate reached out to squeeze her friend's hand. Tony was a good guy, but Kate still hoped Mary wasn't joining his family because she felt she had to.

"So, what's next on your wedding list?" Kate asked, trying to return the subject to Mary and her wedding and away from her own agenda.

"Well, I have to finalize the guest list this week. The invitations will be here soon and Muriel keeps texting me with new people and addresses every day. I have to meet with Alejandro tomorrow on my lunch break. We're going to finalize the menu for the reception." Mary forked a piece of chocolate cake into her mouth. "You got to meet him on Saturday, didn't you?" she asked.

Kate half-shrugged and half-smiled. She made all the acquaintance she needed to through her observations of the man at the bridal shower.

"He's been so great to work with on this whole wedding thing." Mary was back to her euphoric self, talking about her wedding. "I'm going to pick out the bridesmaids dresses this week too. Any input?"

"No." Kate shook her head. "Whatever you choose is fine with me." And it was the truth. This was Mary's show. If she wanted Kate to look like a fish or a bead of sunshine in front of hundreds of people she would do it. She would do anything for her nearest and dearest friend. Just like Mary would for her. That's what true friendship was all about.

And it was believing she wasn't pregnant when Team Pregnant was ahead by two.

Twelve

The soccer mom in the gray minivan, with its stupid five person stick figure family and "Baby on Board" sign, was about to see nothing but grill in the rearview mirror if she didn't pull over, pronto!

Kate felt AJ suck the air out of the cab of the truck as she eased her bumper at sixty miles per hour closer to the minivan's taillights. Soccer Mom finally signaled and pulled into the right lane. Kate jammed the truck into fifth gear. The trailer she pulled hiccupped with the transition as the old Ford passed the minivan. AJ's white knuckled grip on the door handle had yet to relax since Kate pulled away from Alejandro's and into traffic.

Portland's afternoon traffic rarely brought out Kate's best driving. The wedding message she received today had only served to intensify her road rage.

It wasn't until she was idly cruising on Interstate 84 that the hostility left her driving and AJ released his death grip.

"So, how's your day going?" he asked, like he'd just slid into the seat next to her.

Kate rolled her lips between her teeth, trying not to smile. "Shitty," she replied with a sideways glance.

"Boyfriend troubles?"

"No." She flipped her head toward AJ. The tail end of one braid nearly smacked her in the eye before she turned back to the road. "I don't have a boyfriend."

"Right." A smile edged its way into his words. "Then are there problems with your friends-with-benefits neighbor?"

"No." Thanks to that healthy dousing of toilet water, she had dodged her only possible hookup moment with Jake this week.

"Then is there some other reason I've been watching my life flash before my eyes since I got in this truck?"

Kate grabbed her cell phone out of the cup holder and drove one-handed while she searched for her latest text from Mary. AJ resumed his grip on the handle.

Kate passed the phone to him and he scrolled through the images on the screen.

"So, let me guess," AJ said. An adorable involuntary twitch pulled his lips into a half-smile. "You don't like pink, is that it?"

"No, that's not it." Kate retrieved her phone from his hands. "I mean no, I don't like pink, but that's not what I'm upset about. It's that she's asking me to pay over three hundred dollars for the dress. And that's not even factoring in the shoes." The glittery silver pumps cost as much as the dress and while they were to-die-for beautiful, Kate would rather die than pay for them. It was ridiculous. "I don't want to pay hundreds of dollars to dress up like a pink flamingo. I mean, really. Why is it my responsibility to pay for this godforsaken dress? If I had that kind of money to spend willy-nilly, I would *not* buy a Pepto-pink dress to wear only once. What am I going to do with a dress like that?" Induct it into the Expensive-Dress-Never-To-Be-Worn-Again Club in the back of her closet, right next to Ivory Chili-stain.

AJ said nothing, so Kate continued with her rant.

"Mary's the one who asked me to be in her wedding. It wasn't the other way around. I didn't go begging for a place at the alter next to her. So, not only has she invited me to be in her wedding, but now she's telling me I have to wear this hideous pink dress. And she expects me to pay for it. Seriously, what the fuzz is that all about?"

AJ cracked up at her question. His laughter filled the cab and Kate tried to act irritated, but the sound of his voice was intoxicatingly rich with humor.

She thought she presented a solid argument, really drove her point home, but he was laughing, hysterically. What was so funny?

"Why are you laughing?" she asked, putting enough vinegar in her voice to give the impression she may come unhinged again.

"Did you just say fuzz?"

"Yeah, so?" Kate shrugged.

"Who says fuzz?"

Kate smiled. It was a silly thing to say. "Someone who has lived with Mary Goodwich for too many years." She joined AJ and laughed. Fuzz, fudge, son-of-a-biscuit, these were all Mary-isms she'd picked up over the years.

She sighed the laughter out of her body. "But don't you agree that it's wrong to ask someone to be in your wedding and then to ask them to pay for an ugly dress they'll never wear again?"

"If it wasn't an ugly dress, would you be okay with it?" AJ asked.

"Well, no. I would never spend over three hundred dollars on a dress." Fleetingly Ivory Chili-stain flashed through her mind, but she never actually intended to pay for that dress. "This whole wedding thing is a load of crap. Every time I turn around, I have to plunk down more money for something. I'm strapped for cash as it is and I don't appreciate going farther into debt for someone else's wedding. Even if it is for Mary."

AJ nodded. Finally, she was getting her point across.

"All I know," Kate said. "Is that if I get married I will not ask my bridesmaids to pay for their dresses. It's just bad manners."

AJ smiled and turned to look out his window. The lush green on green scenery of the valley flickered past the window. He turned back to her, "You know I think it's a pretty common practice for the bridesmaids to pay for their dresses. A lot of times the guys have to pay for their tuxes too."

"What?" Kate was shocked. "I thought the groom's family always took care of that expense."

"No." AJ shook his head again. "The last wedding I went to was in Nebraska. I was one of the groomsmen. I paid for my own airfare, my hotel room, part of the bachelor party, the tux, and a gift. I easily spent close to three, maybe four, grand on everything."

Kate's jaw dropped. "No way."

"Yeah. You had better start saving. Once your other friends start getting married you're going to be plunking down a whole lot more money."

"What friends?"

"The friends that you're in the wedding with?"

"Those girls are not my friends. The Fierce Four are a clan all their own."

"Then why do you hang out with them?"

"It's not like I do it willingly," Kate said with a shake of her head. "I tolerate them strictly out of loyalty to Mary. If it wasn't for her my life would be very different than it is today." Kate's voice turned thoughtful and she was glad when AJ didn't press her further. She didn't like to talk about those dark days during her freshman year.

Silence filled the cab once more as the dense green of the valley opened up. The distant brown swells of the hillsides, burnt and brittle from the summer sun, decorated the landscape. The power-generating winds off the Columbia River pushed against the truck and Kate used both hands to keep the old faded Ford between the lines. AJ's cell phone rang and he became immersed in a conversation. Something about the restaurant, of that Kate was sure, the words reservations, staff and stock kept coming up. Kate gave him his privacy by diving into her own thoughts and trying to think of some way to plead with Mary to rethink this dress situation.

Kate was still wrestling with what to say to Mary when AJ hung up his phone, done putting out fires at the restaurant.

"Is everything okay at the restaurant?" Kate asked as she signaled and took the exit off the interstate.

"Yeah," AJ said with a distracted look in his eye and dropped his phone in his lap.

Kate turned onto highway 197. "You aren't very convincing."

"Just a little short staffed. A couple of employees called in sick at the last minute."

"How do you call in sick at the last minute when you have an evening shift?" Kate asked.

"Exactly," AJ replied. "Makes you think they aren't very sick, doesn't it?"

"Ooooh, are they going to get fired?"

"I don't know yet," AJ said, rubbing his temples. "I really don't like to fire people."

"You fired your chef. The one who cooked up those crappy Kobe beef sliders."

AJ chuckled. "Bucky?"

"Yeah, that guy. What made you fire him?"

"I didn't exactly fire him. I gave him the choice to convince me to keep him or let him go without any further questions about the scheme he was trying to run behind my back. And he chose to leave."

"Guilty, huh?"

"That's my guess."

"So what was he doing?"

"Well, after I talked to you and you questioned the meat, I asked him about it. Where it was processed and if it was grain fed?" AJ cocked a smile in her direction. "Those were the only things I could remember you saying. He stuttered out a couple of responses. But then I asked him when I could go visit the slaughterhouse and his face went blank. Almost scared. So, I did a little digging, went through receipts and emails. I even looked up the ranch on the internet. It's somewhere in Idaho and the ranch manager has the same last name as Bucky. I googled the guy and he has the ranch listed under three different names, all listing different practices in raising the animals. One claimed to be an organic ranch, another natural, and then of course the Kobe producer."

"Did you ask him about it?"

"Sort of. I told him what I found out and asked if he wanted to leave before I asked any more questions or face my questions and risk being fired. He chose to leave."

"Wow, quite the hard nose, aren't you?" Kate teased, as the truck climbed and twisted around another curve in the road.

"Ha, ha," AJ said. "Personnel is the worst part of my job sometimes."

"Do you fire people a lot?"

"I didn't fire Bucky, technically he quit. But no I don't fire people often. Everybody makes mistakes and as long as my employees are willing to admit to those mistakes and learn from them, then I'm all about second chances."

"Is that what they teach you in Intro to Restaurant Management?"

"No, it's more of a personal philosophy." AJ smiled at Kate as she turned the truck onto the next road, which led to Hayden Valley.

The narrow two-lane road snaked toward the Deschutes River and before long they rolled into the ghost town of Hayden Valley with its boarded up storefronts and single pump gas station. The neon sign of Uncle Willy's Tavern flickered across from the Pump and Go. What newcomers didn't see was the bank, post office, market, and hardware store hidden on the backside of the main street, along with Mac Dee's Diner. The town's only church sat perched on the hillside, its steeple reaching toward the heavens.

The town stood today, as Kate had always known it. The old timers talked of the good old days when the shops were full and business was booming. That was before the terrible floods in the sixties and the decline of both the lumber and agriculture industries. Kate took comfort in the sameness of the old town while AJ, she assumed, was wondering how they had dropped into this foreign land. His eyes hadn't left the scenery since they pulled into town.

"Do you need to stop for anything?" Kate asked, looking for a reaction from the city boy next to her. "We'll be at the ranch in about ten minutes."

"What would you suggest I stop for?" AJ asked, that endearing twitch of a smile escaping again.

"Oh I don't know. The Pump and Go has a new fancy espresso-makin' machine or we could swing into the hardware store. Hardy's has the best line of dog food in the county and you're certain to find a rare treasure at Thrifty Treats." It was the so-called antique shop run out of the garage side of The Pump and Go.

"I think I'll pass," AJ said with a laugh as the town spit them out on the other side.

Kate accelerated, picking up speed as they passed the gravel driveways of her family's long time neighbors. At the trellised bridge that stretched across the river, she sucked in a breath and held it until they reached the other side.

Up ahead on the right an eighteen-wheeler was pulled off to the side of the road. The driver was on his back, under the engine. Kate slowed down and came to a stop on the shoulder in front of the semi.

"I'll be right back," she said to AJ's confused face.

The afternoon air was dry and stale. Her brown scuffed boots tapped quietly along the ribbon of asphalt. She pulled the loose hairs that had escaped from her braids back behind her ears.

She tapped the boot of the driver with her toe. "Hey Mac, you need a hand?"

Mac slid out from behind the front tire. He sat up and wiped his hands on a rag all without one look at Kate. His sun baked arms and hands were covered in grease and dirt. The old flannel shirt he wore was thin and streaked with grease. He stood and waved Kate off. She took a step back as he climbed the steps into the cab, his slight frame moved with ease into the seat. The engine coughed and choked before a giant cloud of black smoke burst from beneath the hood.

* * *

Kate opened her door of the pick-up. "Scoot over," she said to AJ. His head whipped toward her and then back to his open window where Mac's smoke covered face and beady brown eyes stared at him. The man's gray stubble covered his once young face. His unsmiling lips and eyes reflected a hard life, his story backed up by his crooked nose, broken many years ago and badly reset.

"Come on," Kate said, patting the seat next to her.

AJ slid to the center seat. *Are you crazy*, screamed from his eyes as Mac climbed in the truck. AJ's petrified body sat stiff as a board next to her and his alarm seized the air in the cab. Two miles down the road, Kate pulled off and into a gravel driveway.

"Stop. Here." Mac's voice was as rough as sandpaper. AJ's body inched closer to hers.

The pickup truck's tires skidded to a stop on the loose rocks. "I can drive you all the way," Kate offered.

Mac shook his head and reached for the door handle.

"How is Danny?" she asked, leaning forward on her steering wheel.

The old man's whisper of a headshake answered her question.

"He's in our prayers every day," Kate said, catching a flash of white from the old man's eyes, a scant acknowledgment of the terrible way fate had tied them together. Without a word, the old man slapped a hand on the door and headed down the long driveway, favoring his right leg with each step.

Thirteen

AJ slid across the seat and turned back to Kate. She ignored the inaudible questions he flung her way as she pulled back onto the road. A mile down the road she turned into the gravel driveway of The Michaels Hereford Ranch. Weathered wood beams framed the entrance and wire fencing stretched between posts of the same dilapidated era. The truck shuddered over the ribs of the metal cattle guard. Kate drove slowly along the dirt road, careful not to kick up dust and sprinkle it inside the open cab. Trees dotted the front pastures and then the old house came into view, a tall towering box.

The house was as simple as a house could get. A cube stacked on top of another cube. No dormers, no gables, no porches wrapped the faces of the home—nothing to fill its character.

Kate saw the screen door on the front of the house swing open as gravel crunched beneath the truck's tires on the driveway. Out walked her daddy, fitting his black Stetson on his head. His long wiry legs carried him swiftly across the driveway and he was there to greet Kate when she stepped out of the truck.

"Hi Daddy," she said, stretching up on her tiptoes to reach her arms around his neck for a hug that he returned with a light pat on her back.

"Hi Kate." The deep lines of grief around his eyes made him look years older than he really was. Kate's heart ached just like it always did, wishing she could wash away that grief.

Both Kate and her father looked up when they heard AJ's footsteps on the loose gravel. He came around the front of the truck, his hands deep inside his pockets.

"Daddy, this is AJ." Kate tipped her head to the side trying to remember if she knew his last name or not, but nothing came to her.

AJ stepped forward, pulling his hands from his pockets and extending one for a handshake.

"Hello, Mr. Michaels," AJ said with a bright and confident voice. "It is very nice to meet you." His hand was accepted into a hearty handshake. Kate followed her father's gaze as it dropped to AJ's designer leather shoes, dark jeans, and short sleeve button down shirt. It hung loosely, un-tucked. In the city, he'd be pulling off a casual Northwest vibe, but out here against the dust and dried hills, he was way overdressed.

"We'll take my rig," Mr. Michaels said, jerking his head toward the white Ford parked next to the old converted garage. AJ followed, only looking back to Kate once before climbing into the truck. Her daddy's truck rumbled down the worn grass alleyway to the back pasture where the stock was kept.

Kate turned away and caught sight of Aunt Val in the doorframe, her figure masked behind the screen door. Kate suddenly became conscious of the huge grin on her face. She wiped it away and grabbed her duffel from the bed of the truck before heading to the house.

* * *

Kate's eyes traveled to the window as she peeled another potato from the garden. Her hands moved like an unconscious agent beneath her thoughts, wondering how AJ was faring in the company of her daddy. She hoped he wasn't talking too much. Daddy didn't like that. And Daddy didn't like any of the city folk who tried too hard to sound important. Maybe she should have prepared AJ more. But something told her it would all be okay. It's not like AJ was a chauvinist pig like his boss. No, Alejandro would have floundered out here, but AJ could handle it.

"Your friend seems awful nice," Aunt Val said, breaking into her thoughts.

"Yeah, he is, but he's not really my friend. I met him at a restaurant owned by one of Mary's fiancé's friends." Kate transferred the peeled potato onto the cutting board in front of Val and picked up another scrubbed tater, her hands peeling again.

"Leave it to sweet Mary to bring something nice into your life." Aunt Val smiled. "How's the wedding stuff going?"

"You know Mary. She's got it all falling right into place." Kate paused, detaching her peeler from the potato. "Do you know if it's okay for the bride to ask the bridesmaids to pay for their dresses?"

"I don't know darling. Is that what Mary's doing?"

"Yeah. And it ain't cheap."

"I'm sure Mary wouldn't ask you to do anything that wasn't proper. If that's the way it's done, then I guess that's the way it's done."

Kate nodded in defeat at the potato in her hand and started peeling again.

"You still seeing that other fella?" Aunt Val, twelve years younger than her daddy, was like the big sister Kate never had. When Val's bum of an ex-husband split on her after a scant year of marriage, she moved back to the Michaels Ranch and into Kate's room. They'd double bunked until Kate left for college.

Kate set the next potato on Val's cutting board with a ragged shake of her head. "I'm trying so hard to quit him. I know he's not good for me, but then I just…I don't know. I'm pathetic." Kate reached for the last potato in the pile.

"You are not pathetic." Aunt Val set her knife on the cutting board and turned to face Kate head on. "I don't ever want to hear you say those words. Who got herself through four years of college with a degree in Ag Business?"

"I did." Kate muttered with less than a fraction of the enthusiasm she knew her aunt expected.

"And who bought herself a house and put herself through law school?"

"I did."

"Don't sell yourself short beautiful girl. You've done a lot of things right. We all make mistakes. It's how we move on from those mistakes that defines us. You'll get over this fella. I know you will. And the sooner you do, the sooner you can make room for someone else." Aunt Val's eyes flicked to the window and Kate looked out to see the white Ford cruising down the driveway in a cloud of dust. Kate abandoned her project and burst through the screen door, letting it squeal and crash closed.

AJ's tan arm rested on the window edge, but dust smoked out his face. When the cloud settled, Kate felt a wash of relief as she saw his smile. Daddy hopped out of the truck and headed straight for the barn. Kate started after him, but stopped and cupped her hands to her mouth. "Dinner's in twenty minutes, Daddy."

He waved to show her he heard, but didn't turn around.

AJ was out of the truck and headed toward Kate's red Ford where he pulled his own bag from the bed.

"Hey," he said as he approached.

"Hi," she replied, glad to see he made it back in one piece.

"Is there somewhere I could freshen up?" he asked, glancing down at his pants and shoes that were coated in a film of dirt.

"Of course," she said, reaching for a stick of hay stuck in his hair. And for a moment, their eyes locked.

* * *

Dinner was coming to an end when Kate's father looked her way. "Kate did you make a deposit last week?"

Crap. Kate couldn't look at him. She plowed her fork through her mashed potatoes. "Um, no. I didn't have time after the market. I was late for Mary's bridal shower. And this week has been really busy. I'm sorry. It slipped my mind." *Lie. Lie. Lie.*

"It's all right, but I need to pay on my accounts by the end of the month."

"I'll make the deposit tomorrow Daddy. Right after the market. I promise."

"I know you will. Hope you got all that money somewhere safe."

"Oh, I do," Kate said, thinking of the wad Olivia stashed in her purse and the rest of the money locked away in her cash box. "And I'm sorry Daddy. I'll put it all in the bank tomorrow."

"You're a good girl, Kate. I trust you." Kate was already red in the face from lying to her father and she was sure she just darkened a shade when he called her a "good girl," like she was twelve. Especially with AJ's eyes turned on her.

Daddy's chair scraped against the hardwood floor as he pushed back from the table. "Son," he said in his deep throaty voice. AJ looked up at him. "We have some business to wrap up. If you're finished we can head to my office."

AJ dropped his gaze to Kate, but she wouldn't look his way. "Yes sir, I am finished." He stood and followed Daddy into the office.

Fourteen

Kate stomped across the yard to the detached garage. She turned the rusted knob and yanked the old wooden door with enough force she thought for a moment she may have broken the hinges. She paused and then slowly opened the door the rest of the way. The hinges were fine.

The incandescent light of the evening sun lit the interior. Dust particles danced in the stream of light that accompanied her through the door. If Daddy ever found out what she had really done with that money she'd lose her reign as Daughter of the Year faster than a round of small town gossip.

Kate walked across the powdery white dust on the floor, the soles of her boots sanded by the sharp grains of clay. She really should sweep the place, clean it up a bit—give it the respect it deserved. Sadness punctured her heart.

She hardly came out here anymore. Her trips on Friday nights were getting shorter and shorter. She did most of her throwing these days in the backroom at the Pottery Shack. It's where she worked that first year she moved to Portland after buying the duplex. Kitten, the owner, had put her on full-time, teaching classes, throwing pottery and creating work to be sold. It had been a dream job. A lot of hours, but it was a lot of hours doing something she loved. When law school started up Kitten let her stay on part-time to help with classes and she still consigned her projects in the shop.

Just last week Kitten had called. Another one of Kate's tea sets and a deep ceramic bowl had sold. The proceeds couldn't have come at a better time. Those tiny profits were going right into the bank tomorrow, along with the two weeks' worth of earnings from the market—tomorrow's and the remainder of last week's. By this time tomorrow, her debt to her father would be repaid and there just might be a little left over for Kate. Very little.

Kate picked up the lop-sided pot sitting on the windowsill, and broke it free from the cobweb net. It was her first project, thrown at the age of eight. She worked this clay from beginning to end. The words "I Love Mom," were painted on the side. She'd used a brush entirely too big for the application and the o's looked more like big dots than letters, but her mom had loved it just the same.

Kate dipped her fingers inside, swept out the cobwebs and dumped the dead fly carcass decomposing at the bottom into the sink before returning it to the sill. Through the dust-speckled glass, she saw Aunt Val enticing the chicken flock back into the coop with a handful of leftover greens. The hens followed her in a zigzag line, heads thrusting forward and back.

Kate turned away from the window and leaned against the smooth wooden edge of the countered workbench. She eyed the pottery wheel in the center of the room and walked toward it. If it were any other night she'd pull out a lump of clay and get lost in the process of creation, but not tonight—AJ could be done meeting with Daddy any minute.

Kate straddled the old picnic bench set up in front of the wheel and ran her hands over the cool stone. She picked at a flake of dried clay, crusted to the edge of the wheel. She loved the feel of the clay beneath her hands, relinquishing control to her and her instincts to turn it into a piece of art. It had taken years of practice. Years of dedication, but she had the best teacher. Anytime she ruined a pot, her mom would look over and say, "You're doing great. Just try again."

Kate would reform the clay and try again and again until she got it right. That's what she wished she could do with her life right now, bring everything back together and try again. Try again.

"Hey." AJ's voice slipped gently into her thoughts and she turned to find him standing in the doorway.

"Hey," Kate said back. "Did you and Daddy come to an agreement?"

"Yeah, we did."

AJ's feet slowly treaded across the floor toward her and she felt a slight twinge of anticipation.

"He's very proud of his meat, isn't he?" he asked, sitting on the bench behind her.

Kate swung her leg over the side so they were sitting shoulder to shoulder. The smell of his cologne awakened her senses, making her ultra-aware of his proximity. She tensed briefly when his arm brushed hers and then she smiled. "Yes. It was his and my mom's dream to run an operation like this. It's taken a lot of time and hard work to get here."

A beat of silence passed between them. "So, what's this place out here?" AJ circled his finger in the air.

"This used to be my mom's studio. She was a potter."

"And do you pot?" AJ's brow furrowed as he used the unconventional verb.

Kate giggled. "Yeah, I pot a little. It's just a hobby, though."

"Really? Well, I'd love to see some of your work."

"I don't think I have anything here that I've done recently," she said, looking around the studio. "I do most of my work at the Pottery Shack back in the city. The owner lets me sell my stuff there and I help with classes sometimes. It's just a little side project I have going."

"Aah, and yet another secret layer of Ms. Kate Michaels is revealed," AJ said, playfully.

"Yeah," Kate deadpanned. "I have many secrets."

AJ's eyes turned serious, "Like where your father's money is?"

"What do you mean?" Kate asked sharply, leaning away from him. "You heard me say I forgot to put it in the bank. That's all."

"He may have believed you, but…"

"But what? You don't. Is that it? You think I would steal from my own family?"

"Hey, nobody said anything about stealing…"

"That's right because I didn't. I said I'd have it in the bank tomorrow and I meant it. Why is this any of your business anyway? Who made you the lie detector?"

AJ threw his hands up in surrender. "Just trying to be a friend, that's all."

On the verge of tears, Kate stood and stormed out of the studio. She marched down the dirt path, thunder in her steps as she headed away from the house. AJ's footfalls approached from behind her as he ran to catch up.

"Kate, I'm sorry." He grabbed her elbow and she stopped, drawing in a deep breath of evening air. A chorus of crickets chirped their lullabies in the undisturbed field behind them.

"I know." Her words were carried out on the breath of her exhale. She fixed her gaze on the distant flat-topped mountains, unable to bring herself to look at AJ. "I did take the money," she said softly. She looked down, fighting off the tears that begged to escape her eyes. A thin cloud of dust swirled around her ankles as she scuffed her boot on the path.

AJ dug his hands into his pockets and said nothing. When she looked up, she was met with the most kind and compassionate eyes she'd ever seen.

"I know it was wrong." She continued walking down the path and AJ fell into step beside her. "But I had to pay Olivia for the bridal shower and it was the only cash I could come up with, so I took it without asking." Shame seeped in again.

"I'm sorry," AJ said. "I didn't know. I shouldn't have brought it up."

"It's okay," Kate said.

"Is there anything I can do to help? I might be looking for someone to cover a couple of shifts at the restaurant waiting tables." He winked at her.

"Thanks," Kate said, unable to resist the smile that sprang to her lips. "I think I'll be okay though. This wedding is just really bringing me down. But everything will turn around once I pass the bar exam next month. I'll be able to start soliciting firms again." Kate hoped her voice sounded more believable than she felt, because her faith that anything was about to change was waning just like the summer sun in the sky.

"You're taking the bar next month?" The surprise in AJ's voice alerted her to the secret she let slip.

"Yes, but please don't tell anyone," Kate begged. "Everybody thinks I already passed it."

"So, you've taken it before?"

"Yes."

"I wouldn't sweat it too much. Think of the first time as a practice run. I'm sure you'll do better the second time around."

"Third."

"What did you say?"

"I said, third. This is the third time I'm taking it." Kate stopped and threw her hands over her face in embarrassment. "If anybody else finds out they'll think I'm a loser," Kate said between her fingers.

AJ gently tugged her hands away from her face, "I don't think you're a loser."

"Maybe you should. I mean what kind of a person bombs a test like that? Twice."

"Lots of people probably do. I hear it's a really hard test."

Kate lifted her eyes in a minor eye roll. "Some days I wonder why I'm even going to try again. Maybe I'm not meant to be a lawyer." Kate turned and started walking again.

"Yeah, maybe not."

"That was helpful."

AJ shrugged. "What do you want me to say? You might be right. There might be a better job out there for you that you haven't thought about yet. If you weren't on this lawyer track what do you think you'd be doing?"

Kate thought about it. She didn't know. She had been so blinded by her need to finish this task of passing the bar she hadn't seriously considered any other possibilities. Yeah, she could swing a hammer, but she didn't want to be a contractor. She didn't mind selling meat at the market. It was actually kind of fun, but then again it wasn't a career. Working at the Pottery Shack was great too. It would be incredible if she could live off selling her artwork, but she wasn't that good. And it would take her a lifetime to pay off the humongous student loans she'd racked up selling one pot at a time. "I don't know," she finally answered. "What about you? What would be your dream job?"

"A year ago I would have said living by the ocean and surfing all day."

"And now?"

AJ smiled. "Can you keep a secret?"

"Of course."

"If I could. I would buy Alejandro's outright and run it myself. Be the boss. Call all the shots on my own."

"Why Alejandro's? Why not open your own place?"

"I guess I feel like it is my place, since I've been there from the beginning. It's like my baby and I have a vision for her. One that I think differs from the owner's."

"So, Alejandro is pretty much a control freak."

"No. Don't get me wrong," AJ said, smiling. "I love my boss. I think he is great. I've learned a lot from him. I just wish he trusted me to make more decisions on my own."

"Maybe once he sees how great your new beef sells out he'll start passing you more responsibilities."

AJ gave his ridiculously sweet smile to her again. "Yeah, no more crap beef equals points with management."

They walked on, neither one of them saying anything. "Thanks for sharing your secret," Kate said and looked across AJ catching sight of the large lone elm tree set in the flattened pasture, it's form silhouetted in the evening light. A cow bawled from beneath its branches and a spritely red calf answered, running to its mother and latching onto her udder for an evening snack. "Do you want to know another secret about me?"

"Absolutely," AJ said with eagerness.

"When I was fourteen I kissed my first boy under that tree over there." She pointed to the elm. "It's where I imagined said boy would propose to me when we were older."

"And whatever happened to said boy?"

"He never talked to me again after that night." She smiled at the memory. "When his hands got a little curious and he wanted to do more than a little kissing, I told him to back off or I'd have Daddy come after him with the shotgun."

AJ laughed. "I get the feeling your dad would have followed through on that threat. He looks tough on the outside, but I get nothing but love and respect for his daughter underneath. He thinks the world of you. The only time his eyes light up are when he talks about you."

Kate's smile was tight. "He used to smile a lot more." A small picket fenced square of land was only a few steps away and she thought about turning around, but daylight was about to slip away. Kate knew this land like the back of her hand day or night, but that didn't mean she wanted to come back out here without the sun's company if she didn't have to. She rested her hands on the splintery slats, and stared at the graves inside. Four wooden crosses marked the resting places of her grandparents and great-grandparents. Two carved stones delivered from The Dalles marked the other two graves. "My mom and brother died seven years ago. I'm all he has left."

AJ stood next to her as quiet and strong as the granite stones he studied. Nothing more than names and dates were listed. It didn't give anyone a picture of the people that were lost, simply their names. "How did they die?" His voice was soft and rough.

"Car accident." She swallowed the lump in her throat. "I was a freshman in college. I came home a couple of weeks before the end of fall term to go to the sports award banquet at the high school. My brother, Gavin, had lettered in football. He was only a sophomore. Daddy and I didn't stay for the whole thing. We had a cow about to calve and didn't want to leave her alone for too long. Mom and Gavin stayed until the end. They were only about an hour behind us. It was cold that night and the bridge gets icy in the winter. Our neighbor drives an eighteen-wheeler…"

"Mac?"

"No, his son Danny. He crossed the bridge at the same time. Hit a patch of ice. And…" Kate stopped. She couldn't explain the rest to him. The images of the crushed metal of their family's Bronco still burned in her mind, along with the vision of the jack-knifed eighteen-wheeler. She and her dad had waited and watched as crews cleared the wreckage before they could cross the bridge and get to the hospital. When they arrived, they were told both bodies had expired. That was the first and only time Kate ever saw her father crumble into pieces as he hit his knees in that sterile unfamiliar hallway. He buried his face in his hands and made the mournful sounds of a grief-stricken soul.

"Is that why you hold your breath when you drive over the bridge?" AJ asked.

She let out a laugh that mixed with her impending emotion. The breeze blew back her fallen wisps of hair. "You noticed?"

"Yes, I did."

"I prefer to close my eyes and picture them instead, but it doesn't seem like a good idea when I'm driving."

"You're probably right," AJ said with just the right amount of teasing in his voice.

Kate smiled. "If it wasn't for my friend Mary, the one getting married." AJ nodded and she continued, "I never would have survived that year. Daddy brought me back to school that next Monday. He knew I'd never make it if I drove myself. When he dropped me off, he told me to focus on my education because that's what would make Gavin and Mom proud, seeing me graduate. Neither he nor mom went to college, so it was a pretty big deal to them that I was going. But I didn't want to be there. I wanted to drop out. I wanted to come home. But he wouldn't let me. He dropped me off in front of my dorm and drove away. Somehow, Mary got me to every class. When Thanksgiving rolled around there was a terrible snowstorm on this side of the mountain and Daddy couldn't come get me. Mary took me home with her and then when we went back to school she dragged me to the library. Forced me to eat and study and I got through finals. I hardly remember those days, but I do remember Mary." Kate smiled, recalling her roommate's sunny disposition. "She threw the curtains open every morning and would sing to me to get me out of bed. She was my life saver in those days."

"What about your neighbor? The other driver." AJ's voice was as gentle as the summer's breeze. She couldn't see his eyes anymore, the light from the sky was gone, but she could imagine them looking at her, she'd memorized their dramatic cobalt color.

"Danny walked away," she said as they turned back toward the house. "But the guilt of surviving the accident was too much for him. He turned to alcohol and hasn't found his way out of the bottle yet. It was awful having Mom and Gavin taken from us, but his family has to stand back and watch him suffer and torture himself every day for something that was an accident."

"It's very kind of you and your family to pray for him."

"It's the only thing we can do. Like Daddy says it was a terrible accident where we lost two lives, but it would be a tragedy to lose another."

"He's a wise man."

Kate nodded even though she knew AJ couldn't see her through the darkness.

Up ahead the kitchen light burned. The other windows were dark. Aunt Val met them in the kitchen.

"I've got the couch set up for you in the den," she said to AJ. "And you're bunking with me, missy." She pointed to Kate. "Now don't you two stay up too late. Your daddy started cleaning his gun as soon as he saw you take off on that walk. If you know what's good for you keep your good nights quick." She eyed Kate and then disappeared up the stairs.

"Sorry about that," Kate said, hooking her thumbs in her back pockets. "My family's a little unrefined."

"I think they're great." AJ pushed his hands into his pockets and casually shrugged his shoulders.

In the dim light of the farmhouse, Kate was struck by how AJ didn't look as out of place to her as when he first arrived at the ranch. "Well, good night then," she said, stepping backward toward the stairs.

"Good night." AJ smiled—an endearing smile that burned like midnight oil in her mind as she drifted off to sleep on the sliver of the lumpy old mattress Val spared for her.

Fifteen

"Please tell me there's a Starbucks on the way out of town," AJ said, climbing into the truck, bleary eyed. It was four a.m., the sun hadn't even glinted the horizon yet.

"We won't be in Starbucks territory for at least an hour. Hopefully, this will tide you over." Kate passed him a stainless steel travel mug filled with fresh coffee. "Is black okay?"

"Black's fine." AJ took a tentative sip.

"Aunt Val packed us some breakfast burritos too. Egg and sausage I think." She handed him the paper bag from the center seat.

AJ opened it and took a big whiff. "Mmm. That smells good." He pulled out one foil wrapped burrito and offered it to Kate.

"No, thanks," she said, firing up the engine. "I'm not hungry yet."

AJ rolled the top of the bag down again and opened the foil wrapper. "So, talk to me about what I'm eating here."

"What do you mean?" Kate asked, throwing him a sideways glance. "It's scrambled egg, some cheese, and sausage rolled into a tortilla."

"No, I mean is it all organic? Were these eggs humanely treated? Because I live in an environmentally friendly area and am passionate about where my food comes from."

Kate laughed as she pressed the truck forward. The trailer her daddy and Aunt Val had loaded with the meat for today's market resisted the forward motion before surrendering to the pull. "The chickens are free-range." She pointed out her window at the coop. "And they are fed an organic diet. The sausage is a family recipe, using only the finest ground beef Michaels Hereford Ranch has to offer. I assume you got that spiel yesterday," Kate glanced at AJ and saw him nod against the pre-dawn light. "As for the tortillas and cheese, they probably came from Hayden Market, which has a surprisingly large selection of organic products. Does that meet your standards?"

AJ took a bite and nodded. He dug for a napkin in the bag and wiped the corner of his mouth. Kate could hear the scratch of the napkin over his dark stubble. "I'd eat it no matter where it came from because I'm so hungry right now. I just like to hear you talk about food."

Kate shook her head and laughed as she pulled the truck and trailer onto the road. The eyes of a coyote reflected in the headlights, and then disappeared as the animal scampered to safety in the ditch.

AJ tipped back his coffee mug as she shifted gears. Kate made the transition as smoothly as possible, but AJ still came up sputtering as the coffee rushed down his throat.

"Sorry," Kate giggled.

"Yeah, I bet you are," AJ said as he reached for the cup holder and set the mug inside. With the back of his hand, he wiped his chin. "Why do I get the feeling you did that on purpose?"

"I didn't, I promise. But I'll try not to shift the next time you take a drink," she said, effortlessly sliding the truck into fourth gear.

The arched trellises of the bridge loomed ahead and the easy-going atmosphere inside the cab withered. Kate gripped the steering wheel with both hands and took a deep breath as the tires rolled beneath the steel beams. From the corner of her eye, she caught AJ setting his burrito in his lap and forming the sign of the cross. With his eyes closed, he folded his hands together. On the other side, he performed another cross and then resumed his breakfast. Kate was touched that he joined in her homage and didn't know the appropriate words to thank him.

AJ crumpled his foil into a ball and put it back in the bag. "You ready for your breakfast yet?" he asked, in such an ordinary way, as if praying as he crossed over a bridge was as routine as fastening his seatbelt.

"Yeah." She smiled at him graciously as she took the unwrapped burrito. The egg and sausage hit the spot. She was hungrier than she'd realized.

AJ folded his jacket into a tiny square and propped it up against the window. "I'm going to rest my eyes for a few minutes," he said to Kate and she nodded because her mouth was full.

A few minutes passed and then an hour. AJ's head dropped from his makeshift pillow and he jerked it back, somehow remaining wrapped in his cocoon of sleep. He looked adorable in that uncomfortable, folded position. The rising sun reflected off the waters of the Columbia River outside AJ's window, bringing new light to the day.

Kate loved having AJ with her. His presence made the trip go faster. Not as fast as the trip to the ranch when they'd talked, but still it was nice to know she wasn't alone. She looked again at his sleeping face and thought about her deepest secrets that he now held. It was scary to think someone she hardly knew was her new confidant.

She'd never slept with AJ, never seen the skin beneath his shirt, and yet she felt more connected and secure around him than any other man she'd ever been in contact with and she'd been in contact with more than a few over the years.

In an effort to fill the void that had been carved into her heart during her freshman year Kate had sought comfort from the opposite sex. She didn't need a shrink to tell her why she'd done it, she knew. And she thought in time, as the pain lessened, she'd be able to resist the pull of the male species. Her lack of self-respect had added on more layers of pain and caused her recovery to take longer than she imagined. After graduation, when she moved to Portland, she vowed to change her ways and succeeded during that first year. But, when the anniversary of her mother and brother's deaths arrived and Mary was away for the weekend, Jake's sultry brown eyes had been her undoing.

Kate looked over at AJ again and smiled, marveling at what a kind and respectful soul he was. Aunt Val was right, Mary and her ridiculous wedding had brought a good friend into her life and boy was he going to have one nasty kink in his neck when they arrived.

Kate sailed effortlessly into the city, the traffic as light as a busy day on the country roads. She pulled up next to Alejandro's and nudged AJ. "We're here," she said with a little singsong in her voice.

"Already?" AJ opened his eyes and sat up. He reached for the back of his neck and rubbed before looking out his window, "Yep, I guess we've made it." He turned to Kate and shook the drowsiness from his head. "Sorry I slept the whole way."

"It's okay. I'm used to taking the drive by myself."

"Still," he said and stretched, adding a yawn. "It wasn't very polite of me. I missed out on hours of stimulating conversation with you."

"Well, we'll just have to have a stimulating conversation some other time."

"Maybe over dinner and drinks?"

"Maybe," she replied, her face lighting into a smile.

AJ's smile matched hers as he reached for the door handle. "Okay then," he said and climbed out, letting the door fall closed behind him. He grabbed his duffel from the bed and walked around the front of the truck.

Kate rolled down her window.

"Thanks for the memorable experience," AJ said, laying his hands on the edge of her window.

"You're welcome," she said, her eyes suddenly drawn to his lips, but then he pushed away from her, stepped onto the sidewalk, and waved.

The truck growled as she pulled away from the curb, but her heart sang when she looked in her rearview mirror and saw AJ still watching her.

* * *

"That girl is sappy, happy." Kate turned to see Liam resting an elbow on Alan's shoulder. Both Dough Boys watched her as she pulled a selection of shrink-wrapped beef cuts out of the cooler.

"You gettin' some action, girl?" Alan asked.

Kate's cheeks flamed. "No," she said and looked away. But the perma-grin on her face wouldn't budge. AJ's suggestion for dinner, an actual date proposition, had put her on cloud nine and she was going to stay on this ride for as long as she could.

Sixteen

Slam-dunk for Team Not Pregnant.

Midol. A box of Voo-Doo donuts. The raggedy plaid pajama pants. Acne cream dabbed around Mary's jaw line put an end to the pregnancy scuttlebutt in Kate's mind.

"Cramps?" Kate asked Mary as she walked into her friend's apartment.

"Like the worst case ever," Mary said, picking up a half-eaten chocolate-chocolate donut. She took one bite, looked at it with disgust, and dropped it back in the box. "Come on. I've got everything set up in here."

Kate followed Mary into the living room where four floral etched boxes sat on the coffee table. The giant wedding notebook lay open on the center couch cushion. Mary sat crisscross on the floor between the table and couch. Kate slipped out of her flip-flops and tossed her keys and purse next to them, before taking a seat next to her friend.

"If you work on putting the stamps on the response envelopes, I'll keep putting names on these," Mary said, lifting a large stack of envelopes.

"So, Olivia and Muriel bailed on you?" Kate asked, as she looked inside the boxes for the tiny response envelopes with Mary and Tony's address printed on the front.

"Yeah," Mary said with a single shoulder shrug. "Tyler suddenly whisked Olivia off for a surprise getaway." Mary's lack of enthusiasm for such a romantic gesture surprised Kate.

"Where did they go?" Kate lined the stamp up in the corner of the envelope before looking up at Mary, who gave another half shrug.

"New York."

"New York City?"

"Yeah," Mary looked from the envelope she was writing on to her notebook and back again. "It's like her favorite place in the world. Anthony's sure she's going to come back with a ring on her finger." Again, with the lack of enthusiasm.

"Really?"

"Yeah, you said so yourself. She's got it in her head that it's time to get engaged. I think that's why Muriel backed out too."

"Because Olivia's gone?"

"Because she wants to be home when the call comes in from Olivia."

"Oh."

Mary moved on to her next envelope while Kate tried to gauge her friend's reaction to Olivia's potential engagement.

"Does Tony not like Tyler or something? You don't seem very excited that they might be getting engaged."

Mary smiled, slightly chagrined. "We are happy for them. It just figures."

"How does it figure?" *Where did negative Mary come from?* Kate wondered. This was a side of her friend she wasn't used to seeing. Maybe this really was the worst case of cramps ever.

"I just wish she'd waited instead of stealing the attention of her parents away from Anthony. It'll be better when we're gone." Mary's hand kept the pen moving across the envelope.

"Gone?"

Mary hesitated for a moment before she flipped to the next envelope. "Yeah, you know. The honeymoon. A two week vacation from everything." An anxious smile crossed Mary's face as she looked up, her eyes darted left then right. "Are you hungry?"

"Um, no." Kate hadn't had much of an appetite since she'd left AJ at the restaurant.

She hadn't dared to let the idea of a guy like him being interested in her jump into her mind until he'd proposed the idea of having dinner together. Now, the possibility of a new love entering her life was constantly in the forefront of her thoughts. So much so, she forgot to eat breakfast this morning and refused to ask Jake for help when she pulled behind the duplex yesterday—a sink from the salvation warehouse loaded in the back. She risked death by a kitchen sink over knocking on that boy's door. He wasn't worth ruining what might be on the horizon of her life.

Mary hopped up and returned with a bowl of pretzels and two waters. "Well, you're going to need sustenance. We've got a lot of work ahead of us tonight."

"You're right," Kate said, taking a pretzel and looking at the pile of two hundred and forty-seven envelopes she had to finish stamping.

"So what did you think about the dress?" Mary asked as she sat down again and picked up her pen. "I never heard back from you after I sent the text last week. All the other girls love it."

"Oh, yeah it's great."

"Michelle and Olivia came over and combed the web with me. Michelle said it would be better to go with a department store dress, because their shipping timetable would be much faster. It took hours of searching, but when Olivia showed it to me on the screen, I just knew it was the perfect dress for all of you to wear. It's long and flowing like mine. And has the same neckline. I think it will be just gorgeous on all of you."

"Yeah, it's great, but the dress is kind of expensive, don't you think?" Kate said.

"Not really." Mary shook her head. "It costs about the same as what you'd pay at a bridal store."

"Right, but with the shoes too…"

"I know, aren't they fantastic." Mary let out a tiny squeal as she glanced up from her scribing. "Michelle said they are the best brand on the market and will really save your feet, wearing them all day. I bought myself a pair too, so we'll all be matching!"

"Great," Kate said unable to catch onto Mary's enthusiasm. She tried to make her appeal again. "So, you're set on this dress. No way we could go back to that discount store and find some dresses."

Mary puffed out a laugh, "Olivia would die if she had to wear a discount dress for my wedding."

"Yeah, I guess she would," Kate said.

Mary must have caught the lackluster in her voice because her pen froze and her head popped up. "What's wrong? I thought you said whatever I picked out was okay. Do you not like the dress? It has straps. I made sure it had straps."

"No," Kate rushed to assure her friend who looked like she might spiral into a panic. "I like the dress." Mary's eyes were still trained on her, the worry heavy within them. "I mean I love the dress. It's just that I don't exactly have that kind of cash on me."

"Oh." Mary twitched her lips, replacing the worry with puzzlement. "Well, didn't Jake just pay his rent?"

"Yes, but there's not much left over from that," Kate answered. *Or rather, none at all*, but she didn't need to admit that to her friend.

Mary nodded. "Well, just pay me when you can. I had to put them all on my credit card, which gave me an incredible number of airline miles, but I'd like to get it paid off as soon as I can. Do you know what kind of interest rates those companies charge?"

Yes, Kate thought, *I'm all too familiar with what they charge.* "I'll get it to you as soon as I can," she said, thinking the contractor may have to go another month without receiving a payment.

"Ooooh, one tiny snafu though," Mary said, shaking her pen at Kate.

"What's that?" Kate asked, worried that the price had unexpectedly gone up.

"Well, yours is on backorder." Mary's face showed a hint of anxiety. "Everyone else's will be here next week, which leaves them plenty of time for alterations."

"When will mine arrive?" Kate asked.

"Not until two weeks before the wedding."

"That should be enough time," Kate said.

"I guess. Do you want to call about the alterations and see if there is someone who could turn the dress around that quickly?"

"That's okay. Aunt Val can do any alterations that I need." Val along with half the other women in Hayden Valley could thread a needle and rip out a seam better than any big city alterations professional. And it wouldn't cost her a cent.

"Are you sure? I mean I know she can sew, but this is a pretty expensive piece of clothing we're talking about."

Fully aware of the price, Kate wanted to say, but held back. "It will be fine. Val has years of experience. I trust her." Kate could see this wasn't going to satisfy Mary. "But, I'll make some calls just in case. It is probably a good idea to have a backup plan."

Mary's face brightened, "That's what I was thinking." She turned back to her envelopes while Kate thought to herself, *No one but Val is touching that dress.*

It was almost eleven o'clock when Kate threw in the towel. "I've got to go," she said, tucking the last invitation ensemble into the inner envelope. The time it took Mary to carefully script each name in beautiful elegant handwriting had slowed the process to a crawl.

"This isn't going as fast as I'd hoped." Mary's weary face almost persuaded Kate to stay, but she couldn't. She had to go home. She could barely keep her eyes open and tomorrow she was teaching the Tiny-pots class at the Pottery Shack before heading to the ranch to pick up the first order of meat for Alejandro's.

"Want me to come back on Saturday?" Kate offered. "I'm free after the market." She reached for Mary's hand and pulled her to her feet.

"Oh gosh, don't be silly," Mary said with her usual smile. "You've done enough already. I'll get these done by then. And if not, then my sweet husband-to-be can help." A sparkle shined in Mary's eye at the mention of her fiancé.

"Are you sure?" Kate asked as they walked to the door, even though she knew very well that she'd done everything she could to help. It was down to Mary carefully addressing each envelope now, something Kate didn't have the patience or finesse for.

"Positive. Thank you again for all your help." Mary pulled her into a tight hug. "You're such a good friend. I'm going to miss you." The sound of a teary sniff punctuated the end of Mary's sentence.

Miss me? "I guess I could stay if you need me to. If you're lonely without Tony around…"

"No, no. I'm fine. Fine. Fine. Fine."

Uh-oh, too many fines.

Mary pulled out of the hug, looking her happy and perky self—minus the subtle sniffle swipe. What was eating at this girl? With the knocked up theory tossed out the window, Kate was at a loss for what the source of Mary's emotional ways could be. Pre-wedding stress? Or too many nights away from Tony? It was anyone's guess.

Seventeen

The golden glow of morning light softened the cold and desolate feeling of the city. The air was cool and crisp, the sun not yet having had the chance to infuse its heat on the land below. Kate hopped from her truck and knocked on the metal service door of Alejandro's. Her heart thrummed with anticipation as she waited.

Disappointment dripped to her toes when an unfamiliar man opened the door, the white chef's jacket a drastic contrast to his dark skin and short black hair. He was as thick as he was tall and didn't offer anything this side of a personality—no smile, no words.

"Hi, I'm Kate Michaels," she offered. "I have your order of meat." She pulled one hand from her back pocket and motioned toward the parked truck. She hoped this would produce AJ, but the chef bellowed another name. "Car-leeee."

Another dousing of disappointment.

"Meat's here," he said, his voice roughing up the words as the curly haired waitress Kate was becoming oh, so, familiar with appeared.

"Hi," Carly greeted with way more warmth than the chef who was bent over, propping the door open. The three of them formed a chain. Kate pulled out the boxes and handed them to Carly who passed them off to the chef in the doorway. The chef delivered them inside.

Each time Carly came back for another box, Kate refused the temptation to question her on AJ's whereabouts.

When the last box was unloaded, Carly followed the chef inside and Kate strained to look through the doorway, hoping Carly was off to get AJ. But the helpful waitress returned with only a check that she waved in the air.

"AJ made me promise not to let you leave without this," Carly said. "He's out on a shellfish emergency." Sudden relief swam through Kate's body as she took the check. Even though, she had no idea what a shellfish emergency involved it meant AJ's absence wasn't necessarily voluntary. Kate wanted to believe AJ would have been here if he could.

"Well, thank you," Kate said before she climbed back into her truck.

Exactly one week later, on a bright and intoxicatingly cheerful summer morning, Kate knocked on the metal door again. The bulky personality-deprived chef opened the door and Carly was right behind him. The three resumed their human chain from last week and unloaded all the boxes. Payment was presented by Carly again along with the excuse that AJ was out on an employee emergency.

Kate wondered, how many emergencies one restaurant manager could have and hoped to see AJ again before the end of the summer. The glimmering promise of a potential dinner date was losing its luster.

Kate tried to shake off the disappointment as she drove away and headed straight for the bank. She had a deposit to make before she found a quiet place in the city to sit down and study.

* * *

Kate sat at the round table in the back of the Pottery Shack. Her thick bar exam prep book lay open on the table next to her. The small classroom wouldn't be used again until this evening and Kate thought it an ideal place to study, except she hadn't even glanced at the pages yet. The intention to study was there, but the desire to paint was stronger.

The teapot, saucers, and cups she'd been working on over the last week were ready to be painted. She was keeping the background neutral and painting a series of delicate pink flowers from the base to the rim of a teacup. The saucers were complete and next she'd move on to the pot itself. The other two sets she had created like this—one in blue and one in lavender—both sold quickly and Kate hoped this set would go just as fast.

Kate tipped the teacup right side up and studied her handiwork. The front door jingled and Kitten's vivacious greeting sounded from the front of the store. The girl was a complete contrast to her name with her pixie blonde hair, and multitude of facial piercings—we're talking nose, lips, eyebrows, that little place above the bridge of the nose, but below the eyebrow junction, and of course, the ears with a path of stones that climbed from her lobe to the root of the helix.

A moment later, footsteps approached and Kate looked up.

AJ? "What are you doing here?" she asked.

"Stalking you," he replied with a smile so deep she knew he was kidding.

"I'm pretty sure the first rule in stalking is to not tell the person you're doing it."

"You're right," he said, taking the seat next to her. "Maybe I should give up this new hobby of mine?"

"Maybe," she agreed, although she liked the idea of him being interested enough to find her.

"Actually, I was walking by. I didn't realize this place was so close to the restaurant…"

Kate on the other hand was fully aware of the restaurant's location. And it may have even played a role in her decision to study here, not that she ever dreamed it would have brought AJ to her, but maybe she'd been thinking about taking a casual study break walk. In the general direction of the restaurant, maybe?

"I remembered you said you worked here sometimes. So I thought I'd take a chance that you were here today." He smiled. "Looks like chance was in my favor."

Kate's cheeks beamed as his blue eyes watched her.

"Sorry I missed you at the restaurant. Were Earl and Carly helpful?"

Earl? Why did that name not seem to fit the big brick of a man she'd met? "Yes they were. I'm guessing Earl is your new chef?"

"Yeah."

"Not much of a morning person is he?"

AJ smiled. "No, I guess not. But the food he plates is exceptional. You should taste the new hamburger he's created. The beef, of course, is sublime and then he adds a black bean spread and has this incredible new slaw of cabbage and peppers that are sliced so thin. It's amazing."

Kate leaned into the table and set her chin in her hand as she took a turn watching AJ talk about food.

"And he has an idea about doing something with a sirloin and potatoes and corn that sounds out of this world. You'll have to come by and try it."

"I'd love to."

"Yeah?"

"Yeah."

A moment of contented silence passed between them before AJ spoke again, "So, what are you doing here?" He pointed to Kate's project on the table and eyed her test prep book.

"Well, I'm supposed to be studying, but painting is more fun."

"That's right. The bar exam," he said, widening his eyes like the test was something to fear.

"Yeah, but as you can see I'm not so good at the studying part."

"Well, I wouldn't worry about it too much. If this lawyering thing doesn't pan out you've got plenty of talent to fall back on."

"I wish I could agree," Kate said as she dipped her brush into the green paint. "I'd be willing to give up on this whole legal avenue, if I could." Kate steadied her hand and painted a gently curving thin line from the center of the saucer to the outer edge. "I loved law school and I find the law fascinating." She looked to AJ before dipping her brush again. "But when I look at the hours new lawyers spend in an office behind a desk I start to worry that I wouldn't make it. Being buried in paperwork for the next twenty years isn't all that appealing. But I owe it to my father now."

"You owe it to yourself first to find something that inspires you. I'm sure your father would understand that."

"Maybe." Kate held her paintbrush mid-stroke. "But I'd rather not find out if I don't have to," she said and resumed her painting. "He's more fragile than he looks."

"I don't know. I think he might be stronger than you think."

"You don't understand." Kate picked up a different paintbrush, ready to start on the pink petals. "When I told him I was thinking about going to law school he smiled. His real smile. It was the first time I'd seen him smile like that since the accident, and then a week later he brought me a check." Kate paused as she dotted two petals on the side of her cup. "It was the sum from Gavin's life insurance policy and college fund." Kate took a ragged breath. She'd never told anyone this, not even Mary. "He said that since Gavin wouldn't be going to college he wanted me to use it. To make my dreams come true. And do you know what I did with all that money?"

"Used it for law school?"

"Not exactly." Kate shook her head. "I bought a rundown old duplex on the other side of town, thinking it would be a good investment. A great way to grow my money and help pay for law school. So, I sunk most of the money into the down payment. Stashed the rest in savings and worked here for the next year. Between the rent payments and my wages I was doing pretty good, so I applied for student loans and started law school. The money slipped away toward tuition and books. By the time I graduated, I was broke. I wasn't too worried, because the firm I interned for was going to hire me. But then, I didn't pass the bar. Good-bye job. Then, Mary moved out and it was good-bye steady income."

"That's some heavy stuff," AJ said.

Kate set her paintbrush down. For a moment she worried, she had just completely undersold herself. Shown off all her pathetic scars, but to her relief AJ didn't jump out of his chair and head for the door. Instead, he reached across the table for her book. "Then, I guess we'd better get to studying." He turned the page and read the words. His eyes squinted as they crossed the page. "I don't have the first clue about what this says," AJ confessed. "How am I supposed to formulate a question out of this? I have no idea what to ask you."

"There are practice questions in the back." Kate set her teacup to the side to dry and sat back folding her arms over her chest.

AJ flipped through the pages and read over a question while Kate watched him.

"You ready for me to ask you a question?"

"Sure," Kate said with a smile and a shrug. A little study partner help couldn't hurt. AJ looked back at the book and read aloud the half page hypothetical question about a pizza delivery person who was texting while driving and hit a pedestrian. AJ read the two targeted questions at the end. Kate knew this one, she rattled off the tort claims the pedestrian may have against the pizza delivery driver and the claims the pedestrian may have against the pizza delivery driver's employer. Kate padded her answer with the appropriate legal terms expected in her response and AJ looked up when she was finished.

"That's pretty much exactly what the answer says," he told her.

"I know. I've been studying this stuff for a while you know."

"Well, then let's try another." AJ flipped forward in the book and read a multiple-choice question about when an oral contract is enforceable. This was an easy one and Kate quickly regurgitated the answer.

"Okay," AJ said, closing the book. "Looks like you've got this down, so no more worrying and stressing about studying."

"Yeah right?" Kate said with a little laugh. Just because she knew the answer to two questions didn't mean she was going to sail through the exam in a few weeks. She still had oodles of preparation to do. But his vote of confidence didn't go unappreciated.

"Are you going to give these to Mary as a wedding gift?" he asked, in a deliberate move to change the subject.

"No way," Kate laughed and picked up the last teacup in the bunch that hadn't been painted yet. "Mary doesn't even know I make these."

AJ narrowed his eyes on her.

"She knows I used to work here, obviously, and that I like to do crafty things. But I've never shown her any of my work or told her that I sell it."

"Why not?"

Kate shrugged. "I don't know. It's probably that crowd she runs with. They're into really trendy and modern things. I don't want Mary to suffer any putdowns from those girls on my account," she said, remembering the embarrassed way Mary tucked away her hand scrubs after Olivia's comment at the bridal shower.

"Well, I think you should be very proud of your work. They're incredibly professional looking to me."

"Thanks," Kate said. "That's sweet of you to say, but I'll leave these for Kitten to sell."

"Your choice," AJ said as Kate refilled her palette with green and pink paint. "I've got to get going, but there's something I have to ask for before I go." AJ leaned forward onto the closed book.

Kate flipped the lid of the paint closed and looked up. *Oh God. He was so close. And those eyes. Beautiful blue. What did he want? Did he want to kiss her, because the answer would be yes, yes, yes. Like a hundred times over yes…*

"Can I get your number?"

"My number?" Kate squeaked out, eyes locked on those cobalt jewels.

"Yeah," AJ said with his adorable half-smile. "I really want to call you, but every time I go to do it I realize I don't have your number."

Kate turned away from him and dug through her purse for a pen. She found a black ballpoint, tugged the cap off, and stuck it on the other end. Across the thigh of her jeans, she rubbed away the grainy residue of the ceramics paint and lifted AJ's arm, letting his wrist roll over in her hand.

She tightened her grip when his palm faced upward, the warmth of his skin sent a tantalizing quiver down her spine. With an impish grin, she scribbled her ten-digit number across his hand, from pinky to thumb.

"There. Now you have it," she said as she unwillingly released her grip.

AJ smiled and closed his fingers around the number. "Yes, I do. And I'll be using it." He stood up, rested a hand on her shoulder for a moment, then grabbed her book, and started to walk away.

"Hey, my book," she called after him.

"Don't worry, you'll get it back." He held up his hand, showing her his palm as a reminder that he'd be calling. And then he was gone, out of sight and Kate was back on cloud nine.

* * *

Tucked inside her mailbox when she got home was the wedding invitation. With an excitement that Kate hadn't anticipated, she opened the envelopes and thumbed through the pieces looking for the response card. She knew right where it was—sandwiched in the middle with the envelope she had stamped.

The number two danced through her brain as she stared down at the "guests attending" line. She knew exactly who she wanted to accompany her to this wedding.

Eighteen

The next morning Kate stepped onto the porch of her duplex after a two hour cram session of bar exam flash cards—AJ may have snagged her book, but he had no idea about the flashcards and outlines she had piled in her bedroom. She dropped the wedding invitation into the outgoing mail slot, a number one for the guest count and a checked box for the chicken dinner. Kate tsked her friend Mary for not offering a beef entrée, especially now that Alejandro's was supplied with the finest selection of beef in all of Oregon. But, she decided to let her friend off the hook. Alejandro had probably failed to mention this detail in their planning.

Last night Kate put herself to sleep fantasizing about bringing a date to Mary's wedding. She pictured herself walking into the reception on AJ's arm in her long flowing, ridiculously expensive pink dress. And having him, as her confirmed dance partner after her one wedding party dance with Alejandro that Mary had ordered, would turn the wedding into an anticipated rather than dreaded event.

Kate sealed the envelope knowing AJ would be at the reception, just not as her date. With his boss as a member of the wedding party, he'd have to be the one in charge behind the scenes. And Kate decided she wouldn't mind hanging out behind the scenes with him. She would do her one requisite dance with his sleazy boss, sit at the bridal table eating her chicken, and then slip backstage. Perhaps, donning an apron over her flamingo-pink dress and offering to help in the kitchen. She'd wash the dishes or sweep the floor in her sparkling silver shoes, just to be near AJ.

At the sound of Jake's deadbolt releasing, Kate hurried down the stairs and around to the back of the duplex. The thought of greeting Jake this morning turned her stomach and she didn't want to sour the semi-happy mood she was experiencing. As soon as she hit the basement steps her phone rang, an unfamiliar number lit up the screen. But a very familiar voice came through from the other end and Kate spent the next hour talking to AJ.

*   *   *

Kate set the level on the bracket she had just secured to the wall. Level as could be. Next step, install faucet and drain. Kate was lost in her task as phrases from her call with AJ floated in the back of her mind. He asked her four more bar exam questions and admitted to Kate that he was actually learning a thing or two about the law. He joked that he might even join her on exam day, just to see how he would do. She laughed so easily at his jokes and it was a great way to start her day.

From a squatting position, Kate lifted the porcelain sink and set it on the bracket, keeping it snug against the wall. She looked down at the ugly metal legs that came with the sink and thought about forgoing them. They would throw off the aesthetics in a big way. But, then she looked around and laughed to herself. The aesthetics of this place were thrown off a long time ago. A couple of support legs beneath her wall sink were the least of her worries. It was better to be safe and keep the basin supported than risk having the drywall ripped from the studs.

Supply lines and drainpipe came next and then it was time to check for leaks. Water filled the sink and then Kate let it all wash out. Success. No leaks. No sprays. Another job done in the duplex dungeon. Now it was time to go slay the dragon—the Fierce Four led by a recently returned Olivia and Mary at the Shabby Chic Salon.

*   *   *

"It was amazing," Olivia said. A huge square diamond ring shined off her left hand in front of an awed crowd.

"Tell it again. Tell it again," Madison begged even though Kate could safely assume she had heard the tale a hundred times since Olivia's return.

"Okay," Olivia said. "First, Tyler surprised me by showing up at the office on Tuesday which was the two year anniversary of our first date. He had two dozen roses and a couple of first class tickets. He conspired with my mom. She arranged for me to take the week off and had a packed bag ready and waiting. Right there in the office."

Perks of working at the same firm as your mother, Kate thought.

"The first night we were there we had a romantic dinner at my favorite restaurant in Manhattan. It would have been the perfect place for him to propose with the dim lights and expensive wine list, but he didn't." Olivia rolled her eyes as she twirled a strand of hair around her perfectly manicured French-tipped fingers. Kate flipped the page of the *Vogue* magazine she was perusing.

"We did every romantic thing the city has to offer," Olivia continued. "We went for a carriage ride in Central Park. No proposal. We spent the day at Coney Island. No proposal, thank God, because that would have been tacky. Proposing on a carnival ride instead of a horse-drawn carriage." Three heads bobbed in agreement. "The next night we had dinner at the Boathouse in Central Park and Tyler had rented a gondola for afterward, but still he didn't propose. So, I figured he must have something really big planned if he hadn't proposed yet." Olivia gave a bubbly giggle. "The next night when we went to the top of the Empire State Building and looked down on the twinkling lights of the city. I thought for sure that's what he'd been saving up for, but *no*. He didn't propose again." Olivia crossed one leg over the other and Madison clapped her hands in anticipation of the climax to the story. "I knew we were leaving the next day and couldn't understand why he'd dragged me all the way across the country without the intent to propose. I mean it was *time*. We've been talking about it for months and then to go all the way to New York City only to come back home and have him propose in the living room of my condo was not going to cut it." Olivia tossed her hair over her shoulder and leaned forward, three pairs of ears fixed on her words. "So, I let him know how I was feeling." She shrugged. "You know, gave him a little distance."

Kate could image that by a little distance Olivia meant the Ice Queen had come out in full force. She could picture Olivia's nettled posture, glaring eyes, and a vexed purse to her lips. Tyler surely would have known he was in the doghouse.

"By the time we got to the airport we were hardly speaking." Olivia laughed. "We boarded and he insisted I take the window seat. I figured he was trying to make it up to me, because he usually prefers the window, but whatever. So, I scooted in and as soon as the seatbelt sign blinked off, he was out of his seat. And then," Olivia fanned her hands in front of her eyes like she was trying to hold back tears. "The captain came on over the speakers and said one of the passengers had an announcement to make."

Kate reclined back in her cushioned chair and turned the page of her magazine while the other three oozed with eagerness.

Olivia took a deep breath. "Next thing I know Tyler's voice is coming over the speakers and he asks me to marry him. Says I am the rock he wants to stand on when times get tough and that we are made for each other."

The rock he wants to stand on, Kate thought. That didn't sound like a romantic standard for Olivia, but whatever. It probably sounded a lot more romantic at thirty-five thousand feet.

"Everyone was cheering and crying and he made his way back down the aisle to me and gave me the ring."

Olivia showed off the two-caret diamond set in a thin platinum band. She swung her arm toward Kate who lowered her magazine long enough to offer a bland, "Pretty," before raising her magazine again.

"Someone took a video of the whole thing," Olivia went on. "It's on YouTube. Did you see it?"

"Oh yes, I have it right here." Madison whipped out her iPhone and within two button pushes, Kate could hear the sound of tinny recorded voices. Olivia took the phone from Madison.

"Here Kate." She pushed the phone in front of her. "Have you seen this?"

"Um no," Kate replied, setting her magazine aside as the Fierce Four crowded around.

The cosmetic smell of their bodies saturated her non-girly parcel of the waiting area. Kate watched as the video bounced up and down, documenting the proposal. The camera zoomed in on Olivia's flawless features as Tyler knelt in front of her and popped open a blue velvet box. A single tear traced a perfectly choreographed line down Olivia's cheek as the word "Yes," flowed from her lips.

"That's really special," Kate said, wondering if she sounded like she cared at all.

"Let's watch it again," Madison said, taking her phone back and restarting the clip.

Kate slipped out of her chair as the Fierce Four relocated to form a tight circle around Madison. Kate went over to check on Mary who sat grim-faced in the salon chair.

The old warehouse turned salon with its gridded windows was flooded with natural light. The stylist pulled a thin strip of Mary's hair from the clamped mouth of the curling iron and pinned it to the back of her head. Mary's eyes watched the Fierce Four through the mirror, her mouth pulled into a straight thin line.

"Looking good, Miss Mary," Kate said.

Mary's eyes found Kate in the mirror. "Think so?"

"Absolutely." Kate stepped in for a closer look. Mary's strawberry blonde hair was teased to give it a little pouf on top and curls were being pinned one by one to the back of her head. Her bangs were swept and pinned to the side. It was such a soft and elegant look on Mary.

After pinning six more curls into place the masterpiece was complete and Kate stepped back as Mary was engulfed in a fog of hairspray. The zebra striped salon cape was whisked off Mary.

The stylist, in a black plastic apron and tattoo wrapped arms, grabbed the tiara and set it firmly into place on Mary's head. Kate reached for the veil draped over the neighboring chair and passed it off to the stylist. Once the veil was secure under the curls, Mary was handed a mirror and her salon chair was turned in a half-circle. The stylist stepped back awaiting the critique.

"I like it," Mary said, catching her reflection in the hand mirror. This statement got the attention of the Fierce Four and they rushed over.

"Super cute," Brandi offered as she stood next to Mary.

"Classic and elegant," Madison proclaimed.

"Looks good," Michelle chimed in.

Olivia turned Mary in her chair and studied the veil in the back. She ran the ribbon edging through her fingers and tilted her head as she completed her examination. The air was oddly still as everyone waited for her assessment.

Olivia finally spoke. "Is this how long your veil is?"

Duh, dimwit. Luckily, Kate caught the words before they slipped out of her mouth. Did Olivia think the veil would grow between now and the wedding? What a ridiculous question.

"Yes." Mary's smile wavered ever so slightly.

"Hmmm," Olivia responded and dropped the veil with a shrug. "Mine's going to be cathedral length at least and with a good deal more detailing. I'm thinking lace, but we'll see. This is hardly a show piece."

"Oh well," Mary's voice quavered.

"Your dress is going to be the show piece Mary," Kate jumped in. "This veil will be a solid compliment to all the soft layers of the skirt." Kate hoped her words were enough to reassure Mary that her veil was the perfect choice. But her friend didn't look reassured, instead she looked what—frightened?

"You've seen the dress?" Olivia turned a snake eye glare on Kate. A quick look at Mary's panic-stricken face told Kate the answer was "no."

Kate gave her head a little shimmy. "Of course not," she lied. Why was Kate's observation of the dress suddenly a taboo subject?

"But you just said the skirt had soft layers. How did you know that?"

Again a plea from Mary's eyes.

"Oh, well. I just assumed. Mary said our dresses are similar to hers in style and the bridesmaid dresses have long flowing skirts. It's just what I imagine her dress will look like." Kate turned to Mary whose face was relaxing by the second. "Am I right?"

"I'm not telling," she said with a playful shrug. "You all get to see it on the wedding day. I want it to be a surprise. For everyone."

"Oh, I can't wait," Madison chirped from behind Olivia. "I just love weddings."

"Me too," said Olivia, leading her pack back to the cushiony chairs.

A silent thank you trickled off Mary's lips as the stylist removed the veil and tiara.

Kate just nodded, not knowing or needing to know why she was keeping a secret for Mary.

The Fierce Four were armed with their purses when Mary and Kate rejoined them.

"We're going to grab some drinks," Olivia announced. "Do a little celebrating." She waggled the fingers on her left hand. "You guys up for a little pub crawl tonight?"

"Sure," Mary said, lacing her arm through the strap of her purse. "Can we go by Alejandro's? I need to drop off some paperwork there."

Hmmm, a quick pop in to see AJ might be a nice way to round off the day, Kate thought.

"Is *he* going to be there?" Brandi asked. Everyone knew exactly who *he* referred to.

"Of course," Mary said. "He's expecting me."

Abort plan, Kate revised. Watching Alejandro be ogled by this group wasn't worth her time. Besides, she still needed to get to the ranch tonight. Traffic was already going to be terrible leaving the city. She might as well get started.

"Sure," Olivia consented. "I guess we could start there."

Mary glanced at Kate. “You coming?”

“Wish I could,” she lied. “But I’m heading to the ranch tonight. Maybe another time.”

All the girls turned away from her with little disappointment, except for Mary who trailed a few steps behind the group.

Nineteen

Kate pulled up to the side of the restaurant and shut the engine of the old Ford off. She hopped from the truck and knocked on the metal door, hoping to see AJ. Five phone calls and three text messages had passed between the two of them over the last week and she liked the way their banter was ebbing toward an intimate exchange. Their conversations always began with a few test prep questions and then veered toward talk of the wedding and happy customers at the restaurant who were enjoying Michaels Hereford beef.

Kate smiled as she remembered the way the corners of her daddy's mouth turned up last night when he told her today's delivery was an increased order. She already knew it would be. AJ told her about it the day before she left, but to hear it from her daddy's smiling lips was a gift to her heart. Not to mention the increased bottom line that was a gift to her bank account.

Unfortunately, Mr. Dreary-Like-a-Raincloud Earl opened the door instead. Without an acknowledgement, the burly man turned back into the kitchen and rumbled in his deep gravelly voice, "Hey Boss. She's here."

Boss, Kate thought as her heart plummeted to the floor. AJ hadn't said anything about Alejandro being here. If she knew she was meeting the boss today, she would have put a little more effort into her appearance. This faded ball cap and her threadbare jeans were not first impression material for meeting Alejandro. She steeled herself, ready to play nice with the man she was assigned to endure Mary's wedding with, but to her great relief AJ appeared, a slight flush to his cheeks.

"Hey," he said.

"Hi," Kate replied, stuffing her hands in her back pockets and shyly dropping her head. The bill of her cap concealed her face for a moment while she let the blush from her cheeks subside. She took a step back toward the truck and then turned.

She released the latch on the trailer and then froze when AJ clasped his hand around her arm. His touched rendered her motionless.

"We've got this," he said, putting both hands on her shoulders and turning her toward the kitchen door. "You've been up for hours, so go inside. There's a fresh pot of coffee brewing behind the bar. Help yourself and I'll be there in a few minutes."

"But," she started to protest.

"No, buts," AJ said, adding his irresistible smile to the words. "Earl and I can handle this. Right Earl?" He shot the question over her shoulder to the giant man behind her.

"Whatever you say, Boss," Earl replied.

AJ's eyes settled on her again. "Go on."

Kate summoned the use of her legs and did as she was asked, delighted to know AJ would be joining her. A cup of coffee did sound inviting at this early hour. Behind the bar, she found a mug and poured the coffee.

Soon AJ joined her and she wondered how he and Earl had unloaded the increased order of meat in half the time it had taken her, Carly, and Earl to do it. Either Earl sprouted a sudden super-human speed in the presence of his boss or it was all AJ. By the look of those well-shaped biceps, Kate's money was on AJ doing the work of two, while Earl shuffled along at his snail-pace to carry in one box at a time.

AJ handed Kate a check that she quickly folded and stuffed into her pocket, resisting the urge to read the sum and calculate her percentage. She'd have time for that later. Right now, she was getting a rare moment alone with AJ that she didn't want to let slip away.

AJ poured himself a cup of coffee. "Can you stick around or do you have to be somewhere else this morning?" His eyes were hopeful and Kate smiled at him.

"My morning is completely free," Kate said as she wrapped her hands around her mug, wondering what he could possibly have in mind.

AJ smiled. "Great. Follow me." He took her hand and she followed him like a happy puppy to a secluded table at the back of the restaurant. It was the only table covered with a white linen cloth and set with napkins and silverware. AJ produced a lighter and lit the three small votive candles at the center. He pulled out a chair for her and Kate was overwhelmed by the gesture. She couldn't remember a man ever pulling out a chair for her in all the years she'd been dating.

"I'll be right back," he said before disappearing behind her. Kate sipped her coffee, trying to imagine what she was in store for when AJ reappeared with a large tray. He set a plate piled with a full breakfast in front of Kate.

"Wow," she said, mildly impressed by the presentation. "Is Alejandro's now serving breakfast?"

"Only upon request," AJ said, sitting across from her.

"But I didn't request it," Kate said.

"I know. I did." AJ smiled. "Since my schedule hasn't allowed me an available evening to take you to dinner. I thought we could do breakfast instead."

"What an excellent idea," Kate said, draping her napkin over her lap. Taking up her knife and fork, Kate sliced into her poached egg topped with a rich and creamy hollandaise. Her knife pushed through the layers of egg, Canadian bacon, and English muffin. The soft yolk spilled gracefully into the center of her plate, creating a pool of vibrant yellow. The flavors settled over her palette as she took her first bite, and warmed her soul. "My compliments to the chef," she told AJ who'd been watching her this whole time.

"I will pass that on," he said with a smile and cut into his own breakfast.

"He certainly does have a knack for flavor," Kate said after her second bite.

"Yes, he does," AJ agreed. "I'm lucky he came along when he did. I was afraid I was going to have to start manning the grill on a permanent basis after I let Bucky go."

"You cook?" Kate asked with surprise.

"Of course I do," AJ said, a visibly pained look crossing over his face. "You don't grow up in the restaurant business without picking up a thing or two."

"Oh sorry," Kate said. "I didn't realize you had been involved with restaurants for so long. I assumed you joined the industry after college."

AJ smiled. "You assumed wrong," he said and his eyes twinkled with a subtle glint of mischievousness.

Kate pushed her fork into her egg again and gave AJ a sideways look. "So, enlighten me. What can you whip up in the kitchen?"

"Well," AJ said with a slight pause. "Most of my kitchen education happened when I was very young. My dad was a dishwasher at a diner in San Francisco called Smokey's. After school, I'd go there and sit in the backroom. I did my homework and watched TV while he worked. On slow nights Smokey would pull a chair up to the grill and show me how to flip a burger, fry an egg, and sear a steak. My talent is very limited. And I do prefer to leave the cooking to Earl."

"So, you grew up in the bay area?" Kate asked.

AJ nodded.

"What about your mom?"

"She worked all day at a motel in town, cleaning rooms. She picked me up at the end of school, walked me to the diner, and then took the bus to the local college where she took night classes."

"Your parents sound like hard-working people," Kate said.

"They are," AJ agreed with a nod. "They've worked hard to get where they are today and I have a lot of respect for that now."

"Now?"

"Yeah. Once my mom finished school and both my parents got better paying jobs, it was easy to forget about the tiny apartment we lived in. The sacrifices they made to provide for their family."

"Do you have any brothers or sisters?" Kate asked.

"No, it's just me and the parents. That's why I'm such a spoiled brat." He smiled at his own joke.

"I don't think you're a spoiled brat," Kate said, crossing her knife and fork over her plate.

AJ crossed his arms and leaned them onto the table. His eyes, penetrating blue, bore into hers. "I don't know if you know me well enough to make that assessment just yet," he said.

"Well, then I guess I'm going to have to take the time to get to know you better, aren't I?" She leaned in, mimicking his posture.

AJ reached across the table and took her hand in his. Kate felt a shiver of excitement trail down her spine. "I think that can be arranged."

The distant sound of a phone ringing didn't shatter the connection the two of them had formed. They were in a world all their own. A world filled with innuendos and sexual suggestions that promised to be explored in the future. At least, that's how Kate was interpreting all this eye gazing.

Earl's sandpaper filled voice is what finally broke the trance between the two as he called across the restaurant from the kitchen door. "Hey Boss, the phone is for you."

If only Earl had taken the ten seconds to walk across the restaurant he would see that AJ was far too consumed to take any phone call. Kate didn't want to let him go.

"Take a message," AJ said, keeping his eyes locked with Kate and she smiled.

"It's Mr. Silva," Earl called again and the connection was lost. AJ's face changed dramatically and he pulled away from Kate. "He says it's important."

"I'm sorry," AJ said, pulling his hands from Kate's grasp. "I have to take this."

"Of course." The sudden change in AJ's demeanor worried Kate, but clearly, whatever it was it didn't involve her. "I should be going any way. Thanks for breakfast."

AJ stood and reached for her hand as she stood. She followed him back to the kitchen where Earl stood with the phone in hand. AJ took the phone, rested it on his chest, and stared earnestly at Kate, conflict in his eyes.

There was something unsaid between them. Kate could feel it. She wanted to let AJ know that nothing had been spoiled. That he could attend to his business without putting her off. The desire to kiss him, softly, reassuringly tugged at her subconscious. But as she took a step toward AJ, Earl's gigantic voice bellowed, "Excuse me."

Both Kate and AJ stepped out of his way, bringing a great divide of space between them. AJ glanced at the phone he was holding again and Kate stepped toward the door. Earl's grand interruption and his presence right behind AJ had sucked the romantic urges right out of her.

"Thanks again," she said and slipped out the kitchen door.

Twenty

An hour later Kate sent a quick text to AJ.

`Thanks again for breakfast.`

She waited for a reply as she stood in the single rectangle of sunlight coming through the half-sized window in what was shaping up to be her new kitchen—kitchenette was more like it. When no reply came through Kate set her phone on the floor next to the door. It was where her phone received the strongest signal. If AJ called or sent a text back, she didn't want to miss it due to these thick concrete walls.

Kate returned to the kitchenette and the load of plywood she brought back from Hayden Valley. A few weeks ago, she dropped off some measurements at Hardy's and last night she picked up her order of pre-cut plywood from the hardware store. It was only enough for Kate to build one base cabinet right now, the others would be built when she had more money to spare. She decided to start building on the wall where the sink would be plumbed, so today—or maybe over the next week, depending on exactly how complicated this project would be—Kate was going to start constructing the cabinets. One piece at a time just like her handy dandy little printout from the internet told her to.

Kate looked down at step one when her phone chimed with a message and in an instant, she was there reading AJ's reply:

`Same time, same place next week?`

That sounded like a perfect plan to Kate.

`It's a date.` She typed back, wishing she didn't have to wait seven more days to see AJ again. But a date to look forward to in seven days was better than no date at all.

To her surprise, AJ must have been thinking the same thing, because his next text read:

`Can't wait that long. Can you come by tonight and hang at the bar with me? I'll bring the book.`

The book? Oh, that's right. He still had her exam book. She completely forgot to ask him about it this morning. It would be good to get it back, so she could start on her ten exams a day regiment again.

`Yes. See you at 7.`
`Are u coming for me or the book?`
`Good question.`
`Bad answer.`
☺

When had Kate become an emoticon kind of girl? She didn't know, but she loved this new carefree and flirtatious feeling she found herself suffering from. Without question, AJ was the reason she would show up tonight. The book was but a minor conciliation prize.

*   *   *

"So, have you decided how the estate will be divided yet?" AJ asked, leaning over the bar. Kate was already a full page into her essay answer about how Richard's estate would be divided equally between his only child and the charity he had named. AJ's face was less than a foot away from hers, the smell of his cologne wrapped around her like a blanket as she watched the tantalizing movement of his lips. The way they formed the words distracted Kate from her train of thought

. A patron at the other end of the bar raised his empty glass and AJ walked away before she could utter an answer. Kate stared down at the notebook in front of her. The brilliant white page with its blue lines, blue like AJ's eyes... No. Don't think about his eyes. Think about Richard's estate.

Kate began to draw her letters on the page again to form sentences and coherent thoughts all the while keenly in tune to AJ's location. Her body lightened whenever he walked by and she listened to his voice when he served a customer close to her. Somehow, despite the distraction, she filled the pages with her answer and as she lifted the notebook to turn the page, his twinkling eye caught hers and she just about completely gave up her effort to stay focused on her studies, but then the blonde little vixen stepped between them and Kate returned to her essay.

At the end of page three, Kate called it quits on Richard and his estate. She hit all the high points and her hand was beginning to cramp. Not to mention her neck and shoulders too—she shrugged and rolled her shoulders working out the tension. "How'd we do?" AJ asked, leaning into their private conference space.

Kate shrugged. "Okay, I think."

"Well, here you go," AJ handed her the book. "I'd read it for you, but I'm not going to have the first clue about what you've written." He walked off and was replaced by the little blonde.

"What'cha working on?" she asked in a voice that was as high pitched, as it was annoying. Kate looked up to find her occupying AJ's private space and pulled back to give herself a little distance. At this proximity, though, she had finally solved the mystery about the little vixen's name. Kristi was spelled out in red on the left side of her shirt that was gaping with too many open buttonholes.

"Just studying," Kate replied.

"Yeah, ya got a big test coming up or something?" Kristi asked.

"Something like that," Kate replied as AJ stepped next to Kristi and filled a glass from the tap.

"Well, it's so sweet AJ's helping you out," Kristi said, giving AJ a hip bump that sent a shocking jolt of jealousy through Kate's body.

"I'm not really helping her," AJ said as foam reached the top of the glass. "This girl's as smart as they come. She's going to nail this test." AJ flashed his smile to Kate and Kristi's face faltered for a moment.

"Aaaw, AJ you're always so good to everyone with the compliments," Kristi said in an annoying baby-talk way that was almost as off-putting as the arm caress she gave AJ from shoulder to elbow and back again. Kate could read her message loud and clear, it went a little something like this: *Ha, ha. Look at me touching this fine specimen of man while you have to sit all the way over there. Nanny-nanny-poo-poo.*

AJ walked away to deliver the beer and Kate returned her attention to the book trying to assess whether or not her answer was close to what the evaluators might be looking for.

After another hour of watching Kristi brush past AJ behind the bar at every opportunity or grabbing him by the waist to switch places with him as she mixed a martini, Kate called it a night and closed her book.

"You leaving?" AJ asked. The bar had thinned out. The noise finally abating, but Kate had a lot of work to do tomorrow in the duplex and she wanted to try to get some more studying done before she headed to the ranch for her market pickup.

"Yeah," Kate yawned. "I think I'd better get home."

"Okay," AJ said as he picked up the book and set it on the back counter.

"Hey, I'm going to need that now," Kate said.

AJ turned around, a comical look of hurt on his face. "So it *was* the book you came for tonight. Just as I thought," he said, shaking his head remorsefully. "I guess that means I'm going to have to keep it." He leaned forward onto the bar. "So you'll come back and see me."

Oh, that closeness felt so good again. "Don't worry, I'll be back," Kate reassured him. Wild horses couldn't keep her away now.

"Good. Tomorrow night?" AJ stood.

"Can't," she told him. "I have to go to the ranch and get my meat for the market."

"That's right," AJ said with a level of disappointment that made Kate's heart thump with glee.

"I need my book, so I can go over some more test questions before I leave tomorrow afternoon."

"Okay," AJ said and rubbed his five-o'clock shadow, which had appeared closer to eight o'clock, with one hand. "I'll let you take it on one condition."

"What's that?" Kate asked and he leaned forward closing the gap between them again.

"That you come back on Saturday. Day or night. Whatever time you have free. Just promise me I can see you again on Saturday."

"I promise," Kate said, already looking forward to her post-market study session at the bar.

AJ reached for her book and slid it across the bar to her. "Now you promised."

"I always keep my promises," Kate said as her feet touched down to the floor and she gathered her book and notepad.

"Okay," AJ said, his eyes crinkling with his smile. "See you Saturday."

"See you Saturday."

* * *

Kate sat cross-legged on her bed in her flannel plaid pajama shorts and t-shirt when a new text from AJ came in.

Are you up for one more multiple choice tonight?

Kate wondered what kind of question AJ would drum up off the top of his head so she typed back,

Yes.

She waited approximately thirty seconds while he typed the question. Finally, his five lines came through:

When will you see me again?
A.) Tomorrow night
B.) Sat night
C.) In ur dreams
D.) Not sure

Kate sucked in a breath. She immediately knew the answer.

There was no question. AJ
not only haunted her thoughts during the day, but also at night. Their walk at the ranch, their breakfast in the restaurant, all of her memories of him came to her day and night. But C was a very bold answer. Was she ready to give a bold answer? Admit not only to herself, but also to him that she was enamored? Yes, she was.

C, she typed.

Good answer.

Great question.

Twenty-one

Kate was back at the restaurant Saturday night, Sunday, Monday, and Tuesday. She was becoming a permanent fixture on the third stool from the left. Nights that Kristi worked alongside AJ, Kate had to stomach the sight of the girl deliberately touching and caressing AJ. When she went so far as to run her fingers through his hair Kate just about threw her double-digit backside over the bar to drag the puny, little blonde out back by the ponytail. Kate refrained.

But the girl really tipped the scales on Thursday morning when Kate showed up with her weekly delivery. Carly, instead of AJ, was on duty again to help unload the order. Carly, usually a friendly-sort at least with Kate, showed signs of a bad-temper as each box was unloaded. Kate bit her tongue to ask any questions of the fired up waitress, even to know where AJ was.

Stepping into the kitchen Kate hooked her hands in her back pockets and waited. A sniffle and sob came from behind a cracked door along the other wall. Carly came out of the walk-in freezer at about that time and followed Kate's gaze.

"I don't know how he puts up with her," Carly breathed out. With a roll of her eyes and a shake of her head, she marched over and barged through the door, leaving it wide open behind her. The sobs ceased at the abrupt entrance and Kate saw Kristi, puffy-eyed and runny nosed, sitting in a plastic chair. Kristi's eyes darted out to the kitchen and one look at Kate sent the tears flowing again.

Carly returned with Kate's check. "Drama, drama, drama," she sighed as she handed over the check. "AJ said to grab some coffee and he'd meet you at the back table in five minutes."

Kate pocketed the check and went for the coffee, before settling herself into the chair at the table where they'd shared breakfast last week. No tablecloth, silverware, or candles were set out this morning.

Five, or maybe seven, minutes later AJ appeared with his own mug of steaming coffee.

"Sorry about that," he said, sliding into the chair across from her.

"It's no problem. I don't mind waiting for you when you have a beautiful and distraught woman bawling at your feet," she said over her coffee cup and then sipped a drink.

"The girl's cat just died," AJ explained.

Kate nearly spat out her coffee. "She was in there bawling her eyes out to you, because her cat died?"

"Yeah." AJ sipped his coffee. "She got home from work last night and found the old guy struggling for breath. Thoracic tumor, I think she said. She took him to the emergency vet room and they said there was nothing that could be done for him. She held him as he took his last breaths."

Kate stifled the laugh she felt brewing inside her. "Wow. Tough stuff," she finally managed to say. "What kind of cat was he?" He had to be a million dollar Siamese or something spectacular to have evoked those kinds of tears from a girl.

"Gray tabby, I think. Mr. Whiskers was his name."

This time Kate couldn't keep the laugh inside. *Mr. Whiskers. Now that sounded like a made up name for a cat if she'd ever heard one.*

"What?" AJ asked, giving her a sideways glance.

"Nothing," Kate said, putting a lid on her giggles. "I just don't see myself running straight to my boss after losing a pet. She's so transparent."

"Transparent?"

"Um yeah, like she wants to get you in the sack."

"She does not?" AJ said, shifting his posture.

"Yes, she does," Kate said. "Why else does she have her hands all over you when you work behind the bar together? If I were you, I'd be thinking about filing a sexual harassment case against her. It's just wrong." Kate sat back folding her arms over her chest.

A slow smile crept over AJ's lips. "I will definitely take your legal counsel under advisement."

Kate shot him a teasing glare and he returned it with a laugh.

Just then, Carly arrived, carrying two plates of hot breakfast—a vegetarian omelet with a side of hash browns and blueberries and strawberries.

"Thanks Carly," AJ said as she set the plates and silverware down.

Carly nodded and turned to leave.

"Carly," Kate asked and the waitress turned back. "How is your bereaved coworker?"

Carly shrugged. "As soon as AJ left. She dried her eyes and took off."

"Shows over when the audience leaves?" Kate said, her eyes drilling AJ. Carly shifted her gaze from Kate to AJ and back again without a word. "Thanks Carly," Kate said and Carly walked away.

"Point made," AJ said, setting his coffee mug on the table. "Now do you mind if we change the subject?"

"By all means," Kate said with a gloating smile.

"Good, because there's something I want to talk to you about."

"And what is that?" Kate asked, sitting up straighter and wrapping her hands around her mug.

"Are you very familiar with South American art?"

"Not especially."

AJ's head bobbed.

"What exactly do you want to know?"

"Well, when I think of South American art, I think of really bright colors, geometric designs, clay pots. That sort of thing."

Kate nodded. "I guess I would agree with that. But I'm still not sure where you're going with this."

AJ's face brightened with his smile as he continued, "It's all part of my new vision for this place. I want to blend the Pacific Northwest's bounty with South American flavors. I want this place to be more authentic than the restaurants owned in California. They all have a very Baja feel to them and I think this place would thrive with a different beat."

Kate nodded as she listened to his explanation.

"Earl and I are working on a new menu. But, I want to take it a step further and blend the atmosphere too. I want to take this modern, sophisticated Northwest feel and blend it with South American art. And I'm trying to figure out how to do that. Do you have any ideas?"

Kate held her fork, full of the cheese omelet, in midair, caught off guard by his question. She set her fork back down. "Do I have any ideas for what?"

"When I saw you working on those plates at the pottery store it got me thinking that maybe we could change up the plates and cups or something as a way to blend the cultures, but I haven't the first idea how to do it. I thought you might have some ideas."

"Oh." Kate didn't want to disappoint AJ, but she honestly didn't have the first clue. "I don't know off the top of my head. But I could probably do some research. Look at some designs or ask around the shop. Some of the other potters might have some ideas."

AJ brightened. "That'd be great. I'd really value your input."

Kate smiled. Thrilled that he would value her opinion. His vision sounded amazing and she would do whatever she could to help him.

* * *

It was Saturday night, three days away from bar exam attempt number three, and Kate found herself back at Alejandro's. She was finding it hard to stay away. Tonight she was tucked away in AJ's office where Kristi had her little kitty-cat meltdown. It was quieter back here. When AJ noticed her inability to concentrate at the bar, he suggested a change in setting. But it still wasn't working. Her mind was far from the exam and focused squarely on one other subject. AJ.

A soft knock sounded on the door and AJ walked in. "How is it going back here?" he asked, coming up behind her and leaning over the back of Kate. He rested his hands on the edge of his desk, pinning her in her seat. She felt her hair catch on his tiny whiskers as he leaned in closer to look at the blank notebook page.

Kate just shrugged.

AJ moved, so he was next to her, sitting atop his desk. Kate sat back and looked up into those intoxicating blue eyes that scrambled her brain and filled her body with lust. She looked back at her blank page to divert her thoughts. The same thoughts that had already been distracting her from her work all night.

"What's going on?" AJ asked, reaching for her hand. He placed her hand on the center of his thigh and rubbed the back of it, sending a delicious tingle of pleasure down her spine. She stared at her hand there, white skin against black fabric. And all she could think about was how she wanted to feel his skin beneath that cloth. That's all she'd been thinking about the last few days, ripping AJ's clothes off. To see the man underneath the clothes. She could do it now, sweep the desk clean, throw him down and satisfy all the fantasies that had been swirling around in her brain over the last few days. But another knock at the door interrupted any plan she might have been willing to put into action.

"I'm just tired," Kate said, shaking her head as the door swung open and Kristi stepped inside. When she saw Kate at AJ's desk and the handholding going on, she immediately grabbed onto AJ's arm and dragged him off the desk. "Major emergency at the bar. C'mon, Carly's swamped out there."

"I think I'm going to go," Kate said, closing her book.

"Okay," AJ said, but Kate could hear the concern in his voice. "Text me when you get home, so I know you made it and I'll call you in the morning…" AJ trailed off as Kristi dragged him through the door.

Kate picked up her bag, books, and the plate AJ had brought her with Earl's latest beef entrée. With her hands full, she stepped into the bustle of the kitchen. A rushed server pushed through the swinging kitchen door and knocked into the back of her. She dropped her notebook and reached down to retrieve it.

In a half-bent over position, Kate stopped as a pair of black shoes appeared in front of her.

"Can I take that for you?" a man's voice, as smooth as silk, asked her doubled-over figure. Kate's eyes travelled slowly from the shoes to a pair of black pants, a white kitchen jacket, and then into a pair of deep brown eyes. A perfectly chiseled nose sat square in the center of the man's face, highlighted by mountainous cheekbones. He tilted his head toward her and his ponytail made a peekaboo appearance from the back of his head.

Not Alejandro. Please no, Kate thought fumbling for words as he reached out to take the plate that was about to spill a puddle of ketchup onto the floor. "Thank you," Kate mumbled, as she went bottoms-up again to grab her notebook. Another server rushed through the door and crashed into her raised backside, nearly landing her on her nose. Red-faced she stood ready to face Alejandro, but when Kate looked up again he was gone.

Stung that he was uninterested in making an introduction, that he wasn't the least bit curious as to who she was roaming around back here, she made her way to the back door and stepped into the falling night.

Twenty-two

The bell jingled on the front door of the Pottery Shack on Sunday morning when Kate walked in.

"Hello. Welcome to the Pottery Shack," Kitten's disembodied voice yelled from the backroom. "Oh, it's only you," she said as she appeared on the floor, flashing her fully pierced face. And if Kate wasn't mistaken those were two new silver studs coming out of her cheeks.

Kate pointed to her own cheek in a silent question to Kitten.

"Yep, got me some cute new dimples," she said, turning her head side to side to show Kate the matching studs.

"Didn't that hurt?" Kate asked. Kitten seemed to have a ridiculous tolerance to pain, insisting that every new piercing, no matter where it was located, was never that bad. But the thought of some of those piercings through the skin made Kate wince.

"Some," Kitten shrugged as Kate put her bag behind the counter. "Mostly just bled like a sum-bitch, though."

I bet, Kate thought, looking at her cheeks, still a little puffed and swollen.

"Okay, so you got any questions?" Kitten asked, tossing Kate the keys. She was taking care of the place for Kitten for the rest of the day while she took some time off to attend an art show on the coast.

"I think I've got it," Kate said. This wasn't the first time she'd been left in charge of the shop. She knew her way around here pretty well. She glanced at the display case and noticed her teapot and saucers weren't inside yet.

"Hey Kit," Kate called before the girl was out the door.

"Yeah?"

"Is my tea set still in the back?"

"Nope. Already sold it," she said. "Money's in the till for you." And then Kitten was out the door.

Kate was going to have to find the time to make more of those tea sets, if they kept flying off the shelves like this. Maybe she would stay late tonight and work in the back. See if she could throw another set.

She could use it as an excuse to avoid the restaurant. After her near collision with Alejandro last night, she wasn't too keen on making a second appearance. She'd been afraid that AJ's boss might have said something to him about her being in the kitchen last night, but he hadn't mentioned anything in the three texts they'd exchanged over the last fourteen hours. Perhaps, if she didn't see him again right away and put off her next meeting with Alejandro until closer to the wedding he would forget their first introduction. He didn't get a good look at her face, did he?

It didn't matter. The guy's opinion of her really wasn't that important to her. The time she had to spend with him was merely a few hours. But she didn't want to start racking up those hours until it was absolutely necessary.

*   *   *

Kate dodged AJ's calls for the next two days, sending him messages that she was knee-deep in her studies. The bar exam was tomorrow and she was trying to remain focused. A single word from his mouth could easily be her undoing. It had taken her two full days of evasion to reach this level of concentration.

Visions of AJ, and what she had in mind to do with him, had clouded her brain but finally the fog was clear until the last text came through:

`Please, please, please call me.`

She couldn't ignore a triple please and so against her better judgment she dialed his number.

"You're sure you're not avoiding me?" AJ asked for the third time.

"I'm not avoiding you," Kate said. "I just really need to study and get a good night's rest tonight." No tossing and turning all night, lusting after a man. Although, the fantasies were already beginning to take shape in her weak little mind. Kate shook her head trying to clear the images.

"Fair enough," AJ said. "But would you be able to spare a few minutes to come by? I've put something together for you in honor of tomorrow."

Resist, resist, resist, she told herself, but the pull was too strong. She wanted to see AJ, but there was one thing that could still keep her away. "As long as I'm not going to have a run in with your boss if I stop by."

"My boss?"

"Yes, am I going to have to see your boss if I come down there?"

"No, he isn't even in town."

"Really, so he won't just suddenly pop in when I'm there."

"Well, since he lives in southern California and would need to book a flight and make arrangements before he travelled, I'm pretty sure I'd know about it. Why? Have you softened your opinion? Are you ready to meet the guy?"

"No way," Kate said. "I'm steering as far away from him as I can, until it is absolutely necessary to spend time with him. Just promise me you'll give me a heads up the next time he saunters into town."

"Okay, but I'm not expecting the Big Guy until a day or two before Mary's wedding."

"Good. And since the coast is clear tonight, I'll swing by. But I'm only giving you five minutes and then I'm back to the books. Got it?"

"Got it," AJ replied and Kate could hear the sound of victory in his voice. She liked that sound.

A little after four Kate arrived at the restaurant, beating the dinner crowd. She showed herself to the bar and was rewarded with AJ's giant grin.

"I'll be right back," he said, disappearing into the kitchen, only to return a moment later with a to-go style bag.

"What's in there?" Kate asked, rising up on her tiptoes to lean across the bar. She was resisting the urge to take a seat and spend the whole evening in AJ's company.

"Brain food."

"Brain food?"

"Yeah, a tuna and tomato sandwich on wheat. For some good omega-threes and whole grains. A broccoli salad and blueberries for the side. And then, a bag of pumpkin seeds and another bag of almonds for you to snack on during the next couple of days. It's all the best recommended foods to boost brain power."

"And you came by this knowledge how?"

"I googled it."

"Very savvy, aren't you?"

AJ smiled and stuffed his hands in his pockets. "I was hoping I could bring it to you and help you prepare for tomorrow, but duty calls."

"I understand," Kate said, wanting to bend so badly, but fearing what might happen to her concentration if she stuck around.

AJ leaned across the bar. "Promise me something?"

Kate nodded.

"Don't crack the book tonight. Trust yourself. You know this."

Kate nodded and leaned over the counter, hoping AJ would interpret her gesture for what it was, a thank you kiss. A loud clattering of dishes sounded from inside the kitchen, shattering their near embrace to pieces.

* * *

`Go get 'em.`

AJ's words of encouragement greeted Kate in the morning on her phone. She happily sprinkled blueberries leftover from dinner last night on top of her yogurt and took off for the hotel where the test was scheduled.

She walked into the enormous banquet room, where four hundred of the most tense and anxiety-filled bodies waited for the next eight hours of their life to disappear. Kate stepped over the power cord obstacles stretched across the floor, eyeing the faces of her latest competition. The panic-stricken look of a girl who couldn't get her laptop to fire up was something she had seen before. But not Kate, there was no panic today. She wasn't going to let her nerves get the best of her today. She took a seat near the far edge of the room and waited for the word go.

After day two of the mind-numbing tests Kate walked like a zombie to her waiting truck. Once inside she rested her head on her steering wheel and dialed AJ's number. The only person who knew what she had just gone through.

He picked up on the first ring. "Hey, how'd it go?" he asked, the question almost lost under the weight of the background noise.

It was physically painful for Kate to separate his words from the commotion of the kitchen. "It's over," she said, wondering how her brain was even functioning at this moment.

"Hang on, just a second," AJ said, as the noise grew louder. Shouting. Pots banging. Ouch. Ouch. Ouch. Kate's head throbbed and then all was quiet. "There I can hear you better now. How do you think you did?"

"I don't know and right now I don't care. I'm never subjecting myself to that torture again. My brain hurts so bad from thinking." She rubbed at her temple.

"Can you come by?"

"I wish I could," Kate said. "But I've got a pounding headache. I'm going to head home. Take a bath, pack a bag, and then I've got to get out of town. I have a special delivery to make in the morning."

"Then I guess I will have to wait until the morning to see you," AJ said, his smile evident over the phone.

"Okay," she managed to say and attempted a smile of her own, but the pull of the muscles increased the headache. Ibuprofen. Bath. Nap, these were of the highest priority right now. "Tomorrow," she promised.

Twenty-three

Kate spent the next four days driving back and forth from the ranch with her loads of meat and sleeping. She had breakfast with AJ on Thursday, but she couldn't remember a single detail of their conversation. The emotional, physical, and intellectual stress from the bar exam had left her a wasteland. But, today after sleeping until noon, she was possessed with a renewed energy.

Art designs filtered through her mind and when her feet hit the floor, she went straight to her sketchpad. All the designs she saw in the art books at the Pottery Shack from the South American region were bold, in both color and design. Kate started by trying to recreate some of the same designs and color, but nothing grabbed her. The bright blues and gold wouldn't jive with the restaurant at all. Sprawled on her bedroom floor in a puddle of mid-day light she turned the page in her sketchpad and waited for inspiration to strike.

Nothing.

Who was she kidding—she was no artist.

Her phone beeped with a text message from AJ:

`Call me when you can.`

She picked up her phone to dial his number, but then changed her mind. She didn't want to share her sour mood with him. He'd pick up on it in an instant and she didn't want to admit her failure yet. AJ had asked her for help. To provide some inspiration and right now she was coming up dry.

Feeling a pinch of defeat, she took to the shower, resolved to get herself in a better frame of mind before calling AJ back. As the water rained down, her mind started to work overtime. Shapes and patterns came to the surface and she sketched a simple repeating diamond pattern on the steamed up shower door.

This could work, she thought and shut off the water. Wrapped in her robe, Kate twisted her hair up in her towel and headed back to her sketchpad. In no time flat, she sketched out three simple yet distinctively different designs. One a floral pattern, flowing organic shapes to circle the edge of the plate. Another was a bold combination of thick and thin lines with a hexagonal motif threaded through the center. And finally, her personal favorite, a simple series of diamonds in an x-pattern.

Kate finally decided to get dressed and pulled on a pair of jeans and a t-shirt. She ran a comb through her nearly dry hair and applied a touch of makeup. Instead of calling AJ back, she was going to do one better and run down to the restaurant. Give him a little surprise visit, complete with the presentation of her design drawings.

* * *

When Kate walked up to the bar, Carly was busy stacking glasses on the lower shelves.

"Hi, Carly," Kate called down to her and the waitress stood up, blowing a stray curl out of her eyes.

"Hi," she replied. "Are you here to see AJ?"

"Yeah." Kate climbed up into her favorite bar stool.

"Good. I'm glad he called you."

"He didn't call me."

"He didn't?" Carly's face clouded with concern.

Kate didn't like Carly's reaction, an alarm bell sounded from somewhere deep inside of her. "No. He sent me a text earlier, but that was it. What's going on?"

Carly shrugged. "Nobody knows. He called me in to work for him tonight, but didn't say why. Earl made him a sandwich, but when I brought it up to him, he wouldn't answer the door. Said he wasn't hungry."

Kate was off the stool in a nanosecond, "Where is he?"

"Upstairs." Carly pointed to the ceiling. "In his apartment."

Apartment? Upstairs? This was new information to Kate, but she'd process it later.

"Come on," Carly motioned for her to follow and Kate went through the swinging kitchen door, hot on the heels of the waitress. The kitchen was full of staff prepping for the dinner crowd, an odd silence coursed through the slicing and dicing action in the back of the house. Questioning eyes trailed Carly and Kate as they went to the refrigerator and retrieved a cold wrapped sandwich. Carly handed it over and pointed to a set of stairs tucked in the corner that Kate had never noticed before.

At the top of the stairs, Kate found a black door with a brass doorknob and deadbolt. She knocked.

"Who is it?" AJ's voice asked, but it was rough and thick. So unlike his normal easy-going tone.

"It's Kate," she answered and heard the deadbolt disengage.

AJ opened the door slowly and tried to brave a smile. But his worn and tired face gave him away immediately.

"Carly sends a sandwich," she said, handing the wrapped food over to him.

"Thanks." He took the sandwich.

"Can I come in?"

"Oh yeah, yeah," he said and stepped out of the way to open the door wider.

Kate set foot inside the studio size apartment, decorated with smart black furniture and a king size bed along one wall. The opposite wall was draped in drawn floor to ceiling curtains. AJ closed the door behind her and walked to the corner kitchen, separated from the living area by a tall granite covered bar. AJ stowed the sandwich in his barren refrigerator.

"When's the last time you ate?" Kate asked.

"A while ago," he answered with a shrug and then pinched the bridge of his nose.

"Uh-huh," Kate said, setting her design drawings on the bar before pointing at one of the stools. "Sit."

"What?"

"I said, sit down."

AJ complied while she made her way to the fridge and pulled out the sandwich. She unwrapped it and set it in front of him. "Eat."

"I'm not hungry," he said, shaking his head.

Kate folded her arms over her chest. "Fine, then we can just talk. Let's start with what's going on here? You look like hell and haven't eaten all day. Your staff is down there walking on eggshells wondering what's happened to their boss. So why don't you fill in the blanks for me?"

There was a tiny tug to AJ's mouth, but then he looked down at his untouched sandwich and the smile was gone. He turned grim once again. "My grandfather passed away today. I just got the call this afternoon."

Kate's gruff demeanor abated and she filled with compassion as she walked around the bar and into AJ's arms. "I'm so sorry," she whispered.

He tightened his hold around her, resting his head on her shoulder and she could feel his body relax against her.

"Thanks," he breathed out behind a muffled sob. "This feels really good." He rubbed his hands up and down her back and let out another deep, ragged breath.

Kate ran her hands down his shoulders and onto his arms. She leaned back to look into his deep watery blue eyes. "Is that why you texted me this afternoon?"

AJ nodded and Kate slapped his arm. "Why didn't you tell me that's what was going on? I would have dropped what I was working on and rushed down here instead of putting you off because I thought you were suffering from some selfish bout of impatience. Why do men go all stoic in the face of grief? Why do they feel the need to face their grief alone?" she asked, thinking of her father and the way he had enveloped himself around his grief for years.

"Because we think we're a whole lot tougher than we really are?"

"Well, I guess I can't fault you for stupidity now can I?"

AJ's eyes alighted with amusement as he smiled and slid his hands down her back, locking his fingers together at her waist.

"Is there anything you need?" she asked, searching his eyes.

He shook his head. "No, having you here is more than I could ask for."

Kate smiled and ran a hand through his hair. He closed his eyes against her touch.

"When's the funeral?" she asked, enraptured in the way he was taking comfort from her presence.

"Not until this weekend, but I'm flying out early tomorrow. My folks are taking it pretty hard and I feel like I need to be there for them." He lazily opened his eyes and she looked down at him completely understanding how he felt. "I think I'm ready to eat something."

"Yeah?" She smiled.

"Yeah, if you'll sit here next to me," he said, letting her go. "And talk to me about the project that was more important than my selfish bout of impatience." His half-smile teased her fantasies that she had kept at bay since before her exam.

"I didn't really mean that," she said with a little pout.

"I know," he said. "But what were you doing today? I really am interested. It would be a good distraction to listen to you talk."

Kate walked around behind AJ, letting her hands slide across his shoulders as she made her way to the other stool. He reached for his sandwich and took a tentative bite. Kate picked up the drawings she brought and showed them to AJ.

"I've been doing some research on art from South America. And I think I have a few workable ideas. Here I'll show you." She shuffled the papers and laid them out side-by-side, so AJ could compare them. "I was thinking the best way to combine the feel of the restaurant and incorporate these designs is to keep them black and white. I was trying to stay simple, but also in keeping with the lines of the region's art."

AJ squinted as he studied the designs. "These are just some rough ideas," Kate said, suddenly feeling self-conscious by his long strand of silence.

"I think they're incredible," AJ said and she blushed at his approval. "Could you make a prototype of each?"

"Um, me?"

"Yeah. A dinner plate or something with each design. I like them all, so maybe I'd have a better chance of choosing if I saw how they looked on the plate first. I'll pay you of course."

"Sure, I can probably whip something up. But don't you want to go with a distributor?"

"No, I want to work with a local artist to go along with my new mission of supporting the local economy."

"I'm not a local artist. You give me too much credit."

"And you don't give yourself enough credit," AJ said as he took another, more hearty bite of his sandwich.

"Well, I'll make some up and then you can decide."

AJ nodded and finished his sandwich while Kate studied her drawings. Next to her AJ picked up his plastic wrap and rolled it between his hands, making it into a ball, then free throw tossed it into an open wastebasket.

"Feeling better?" Kate asked.

"Much."

"See what a little food will do for you."

“I think it’s more than the food that has me feeling better.” He smiled, but his eyes were still weighted with the emotional fatigue that the loss of a loved one brings.

Kate reached for his hand.

“I think I’d better go inform the staff,” he said, giving her hand a squeeze. “Will you come with me?”

“Of course,” she answered, sliding off her stool.

Downstairs, AJ called for the staff to report to the kitchen. Never letting go of Kate’s hand, much to Kristi’s dislike—the affronted lip curl was hard to miss. AJ announced the passing of his grandfather and that his absence over the next week would be covered by Carly. The waitress nodded her consent. Everyone resumed their duties as Kate and AJ slipped out into the evening.

Pink streaks stretched across the blue-gray sky, gently messaging that the end of the day was near. The streets were mildly crowded on this warm summer evening. Kate and AJ adopted a leisurely pace as they headed for the waterfront.

They found an empty bench along the wide concrete path. A canopy of green leaves above them and a rolling river in front. AJ still held Kate’s hand and she loved the way he had laced his fingers through hers.

“So where is the funeral going to be held? “

“Um, San Francisco,” AJ said. “My grandparents moved there shortly after my folks did. Lived in the same house for the last twenty-five years.”

“Will your grandmother stay there?” Kate asked.

“No, she passed away seven or eight years ago.”

Kate nodded.

AJ looked out toward the water. “I used to come here a lot when I first moved to Portland,” AJ said, not taking his eyes off the river. A seagull landed on the path in front of them and hopped around looking for a morsel before flying away. “It was the first time I’d ever been so far from my family or the ocean. That was back in February and it was cold and dreary and it rained for twelve days straight. I almost packed my bags and left. I didn’t know how I was ever going to survive living here. I hated my job. I hated the rain. Everything looked pretty bleak in those months. But I told myself to just get this restaurant going and then I could head back to California. Closer to home again.”

“I know the feeling,” Kate said, remembering how hard it was to return to school when all she wanted to do was be at home with her father.

AJ smiled at her and then looked down at their fingers laced together. "I didn't realize what an opportunity I'd been given by coming here to help start up this restaurant. It felt more like a huge mistake at the time, but now I see what a gift it has brought me."

Kate sat speechless. His poignant words struck a chord in her heart. AJ leaned toward her and just when Kate thought he was about to plant a kiss on her, an unleashed dog loping behind its bike-mounted master stopped at their bench. It sniffed the leg and then marked its territory, sending Kate and AJ leaping from their seat.

* * *

With the sun tucked beneath the horizon and the first star making its solo appearance, AJ and Kate ended their waterfront walk. Two blocks from the restaurant AJ led Kate to her truck. Kate stood with her back pressed against the door, not wanting to leave AJ. He leaned in, covering her body with his and traced a line down her face with his finger. Kate reached up and placed a hand on either side of his face, the rough sandpapery feel of his cheeks scratched against her skin.

"I don't have to leave just yet," she whispered, her eyes on his lips. "I can stay and help you pack."

AJ shook his head, "I already did that. I'm going to head back and take care of a few things at the restaurant, then head up for a shower and bed."

"I can help you with those things," Kate said, letting a seductress's tone enter her voice. She pressed her hips into his to let him know exactly how the evening would play out if she went back to his place with him.

AJ leaned back, but left his hips attached to hers, making her aware of his arousal. He shook his head and laughed, "You are a temptress, aren't you?" His face came back level to hers and she thought for sure he would lean in to kiss her, but then he hesitated. She was too far gone to let this opportunity pass by, so she circled her arms around his neck and pulled him in, forcing his lips on hers. He resisted at first and Kate was about to pull away when AJ tightened his arms around her back. The way he pulled her closer turned her knees into melted butter.

AJ's hands moved up her sides before he charged them through her hair, massaging her scalp and setting off a round of sexual fireworks below her belt. He moaned with a desire that matched her own and trailed a line of kisses from her chin to her neckline. Their hips were pressed together and rocked against the truck.

"So tempting," AJ said in a heady breath and took a step back, leaving Kate a panting mess. "You have to go home. Now."

Before Kate could sputter out a refusal, AJ put a finger to her lips. "Thank you for coming tonight. I can't tell you how much it has meant to me. And I will call you. Tomorrow. If that's okay?"

Kate nodded. AJ's finger was still pressed to her lips. He reached for the keys inside her pocket and unlocked the door. He held her hand as she climbed inside and handed her the keys. "Good night, Kate," he said as he stepped back and closed the door.

Kate turned the key over in the ignition and then sat there in the dark, stunned. This had never happened to her before. How had a red-blooded, living, breathing member of the male species just closed the door on a sure thing? This made no sense at all to Kate.

Twenty-four

"Why would a guy just walk away like that?" Kate asked as Mary slid the zipper of her dress up the back. Once Kate got past the bright and dazzling shade of the pink dress, she had to admit it wasn't so bad.

"I don't know," Mary replied, pulling the bust tight, since Kate's hips and chest didn't reside in the same dress size. "Maybe he's actually a nice guy with a little self-restraint? Where did you say you were again?"

"In a parking lot."

Mary dropped her arms to her side and locked eyes with Kate in the bathroom's full-length mirror. "A parking lot? Are you serious? And you're wondering why he didn't throw you down on the dirty asphalt? Eeew, that's just gross."

"No. I didn't say I wanted to do it in the parking lot." Okay, maybe she did, a little, but that wasn't the point. "We were two blocks from his place and he wouldn't take me there. He just put me in my truck and told me to go home."

Mary worked out the wrinkles at the bottom of the layered skirt. "Here put these on." Mary pulled the sparkly, glittery silver shoes out of the box. "Maybe it's his religion to wait until he's married. Or maybe he's a virgin? Or one of those born-agains?"

"Born agains?"

"You know the guys that were having rampant sex and then decided to stop and save themselves. One of The Bachelors was getting all kinds of press for it. Maybe that's what this guy is doing." Mary put her hands on her hips. "Look at you," she said, pulling the pink bodice tight again with one hand and finger combed Kate's hair with the other. She twisted the hair into a bun. "How do you want your hair done? Up or down?"

Kate thought of AJ's fingers sliding through her hair, "Down."

"Or maybe like half up?" Mary asked, dropping the bun and sweeping one side of Kate's hair back. "And lots of curls."

"Lots of curls would be great." Kate examined her image and again the vision of her and AJ walking arm in arm into the reception hit full force. If only it was his arm she could hang from that night and not his sleazy boss's arm.

"Do you think Val will be able to get these sides taken in before the wedding?" Mary asked.

"Of course she will," Kate said with confidence. "I'll bring it with me tomorrow and pick it up next weekend. There's plenty of time. Don't worry."

"Okay," Mary agreed. "It's just that all the other girls had their alterations done downtown and it just might be easier. You know to have the dress…not so far away."

"It will be fine," Kate said again, not adding that Aunt Val's services were free as opposed to a local seamstress's fee. "Now help me out of this thing."

Mary reversed the zipper down Kate's back and abandoned her in the bathroom so she could change. Kate replaced the dress on its hanger and pulled the plastic cover over the top of it before slipping back into her jeans and t-shirt. She carefully wrapped her new glitter shoes in tissue paper and tucked them into the box, noticing the tiny puddle of sparkles she left on the floor. With her arms full of her wedding wardrobe, she left the bathroom and carefully draped her new dress over the back of the couch.

"Here's the money for the dress," Kate said, retrieving a check from her pocket. *Good-bye new carpet for my bedroom,* she thought as she handed over the money.

"Thanks," Mary said and tucked the check under the open face of her wedding notebook on the coffee table.

"I'll get you the money for the shoes as soon as I can," Kate said as she sat on the couch next to Mary. It looked like she was studying the seating chart.

"Are you going to bring this guy to the wedding?" Mary asked. "I know you rsvp'd for one, but I'm sure I can talk to Alejandro and add him. We could squeeze him in here," Mary pointed to the top of a round circle. That way he'd be near the front, and close to the bridal table." Mary picked up her pencil ready to add an x to the table.

"That's really sweet of you, but he has to work…"

Mary turned to Kate. "But I want to meet this guy. Give you my approval before I leave. Make sure he's worthy of you, considering your track record."

"Gee, thanks for reminding me," Kate said with a sarcastic smile.

"Then how about the rehearsal? Can you bring him to the dinner? I'll tell the Fishers. One more won't be a problem, trust me. Their inviting half of Portland to the thing already," Mary said with an eye roll.

"Really? You wouldn't mind if I invited him."

"Not at all. It would be perfect."

"He might have to work," Kate said and the look of disappointment on Mary's face surprised her. "But I'll ask him and let you know, okay?"

"Okay," Mary said in full smile mode again. "Yay, I'm so excited," she squealed as the door opened.

"What are you so excited about my darling?" Tony asked, walking into the apartment.

Mary jumped up and dashed to her young groom. Tony's arms held a large box and bags of what Kate could only assume were takeout. He bent down to accept Mary's welcome home kiss. His dark features, the nearly black hair and deep-set brown eyes, gave him an unmistakable family resemblance to Olivia, but it all stopped there.

"Hi Kate," he said, after pulling back from Mary's embrace. See like that he genuinely and un-snobbishly acknowledges other people in the room.

"Hi Tony," she replied as he walked across the room and set the box in the corner amongst a stack of other boxes.

"What's with all the boxes?" Kate asked, realizing that the tower of brown boxes were in the same a place a bookshelf had once stood.

"Presents, presents, presents," Mary answered from the kitchen where she was busy opening the bags of takeout Tony had brought home. "Do you want to stay for dinner?" Mary asked Kate. "We've got plenty," she added as Tony joined her in the tiny kitchen and wrapped his arms around her from behind.

So happy and in love, Kate thought as she witnessed another embrace between the two. "No, thanks," Kate said as she stood and gathered her new dress and shoes. AJ had promised to call tonight and Kate wanted to be somewhere private to take the call. She would leave these two lovebirds to enjoy their meal alone.

Twenty-five

Kate stood in the arched doorway between her living room and kitchen listening to the distant comments of Liz and Todd, potential tenants. So far, the positives were one up on the negatives. The living room and kitchen had gotten a thumbs-up from the couple and so had the bedrooms. But the bathroom and its single sink had produced a frown from Liz. Kate hoped it was still enough to convince this couple to choose her place.

Otherwise, she might have to rent it out to the three guys that looked at it yesterday. Their half-lidded eyes and slowly produced questions left Kate wondering how many joints they had smoked before coming to tour the place. They were not her first pick.

Kate's hope was on this couple. Liz came down the stairs ahead of Todd and crossed the living room to Kate.

"Do you take cats?" she wanted to know and looked back at Todd who had reached the center of the living room.

Todd queried her with his eyes. "We don't have a cat."

"I know. But I was thinking that we might get one after the wedding." Liz turned back to Kate. She learned through a brief introductory conversation with the couple that they would be married in three weeks, right before the start of their senior year at Portland State.

Todd's smile to Liz's back told Kate that this was typical of his fiancée, throwing out some idea she'd been pondering while he was left completely in the dark. His shrug told her that this was one of the things he loved most about her.

Not wanting to jeopardize the couple's interest in her duplex Kate readily agreed that a cat was a definite possibility.

Liz nodded, seemingly satisfied and Todd held out his hand. "Thank you for your time," he said as he shook Kate's hand. His smile and kind eyes behind the wire frames of his glasses had Kate hoping once again that these nice people would be her new tenants. "We'll let you know on Monday."

"That will be perfect," Kate said, following them to the front door and out onto the porch. She watched them pass Jake on the sidewalk and offered a wave as they climbed into their car.

"Who was that?" Jake asked, jerking his head in the direction of the couple as he climbed the front steps.

"New tenants, I hope," she replied, leaving her eyes on the blue sedan.

"You going somewhere?" Jake asked, stepping closer to her, a little too close.

Kate didn't dignify his ignorance with a response. She'd only mentioned the basement renovation to him a hundred times.

The blue sedan pulled away from the curb as Jake jingled his keys, but made no move toward his door. Kate turned away from him and closed her own door behind her, throwing the deadbolt, in case his peanut brain interpreted her actions as an invitation to follow. Jake was out of her system for good and she was going to keep it that way. A much better something was on the horizon.

Her phone bleeped with a text message:

`Thinking of you.`

* * *

"So what do you think?" Kate asked Val as she stood in the middle of Gavin's bedroom. It had been converted into Val's sewing headquarters years ago, but Kate would always think of it as her brother's bedroom.

"It's very pink," Val said through a mouth full of pins. She pulled another one from between her teeth and pinned the side of the dress. "But you will look great."

"Thanks," Kate said, raising her arms to avoid being poked. "Do you think you'll have this done by next weekend?"

"Easily," Val reassured her and switched sides to run the pins up the other seam. "How's your friend?" Val asked after she placed the final pin.

"Good, I think," Kate said with a blush that turned her cheeks the same shade as her dress.

"Hmmm," was all Val had to say.

"Did you get an extra order of puppy meat cakes made up?" Kate had informed all of her regular customers of her absence at the next market for Mary's wedding. Stuart, the only sour one of the bunch about the hiatus, wouldn't be pleased if he ran out of meat treats before her next appearance at the market.

"Yep. Your daddy and I got all the extra orders filled. You should be all set."

"Thanks Val."

"You're welcome sweetie. Now get your beautiful behind out of that thing, so I can start ripping some seams."

* * *

"You look so worn-out," Kate said to AJ a week later from across their breakfast table.

"And you look amazing."

Kate blushed as his smile stirred the attraction inside her. "You look amazingly worn-out," she countered, not letting his charm sway her from her concern.

"Yeah, I'm pretty beat. But it feels good to be home."

"Is there anything you want to talk about?"

"No, I've just got to jump back into everything. Get this place sorted out again." Kate and AJ had talked for only a few minutes last night after he returned home. He didn't divulge the details, but she had definitely gotten the sense that things hadn't run smoothly at the restaurant while he was gone. AJ stood up and reached for her hand.

"I can stick around and help," Kate said as she let him pull her up from her chair.

"You would be too much of a distraction." AJ tightened his grip on her hand.

"Distractions can be good," Kate said.

"Distractions can be very good," AJ said, kissing her palm. "And I will call you when I need one. But today I have to remain focused. I've been gone for too long and there's a lot of havoc I have to sort through. I'm afraid some firing is going to happen today."

“Oh no,” Kate said as AJ raised her hand to his cheek and closed his eyes.

He nodded and she stepped closer to him, leaning in for a satisfying kiss.

“AJ! Guess what…” Kristi’s voice carried through the empty restaurant.

Kate’s eyes popped open, but she didn’t back away. “Mood sucking cow,” she whispered against AJ’s lips and felt him smile.

The cow continued her approach and AJ gave Kate a quick peck instead of the long, luxurious good-bye kiss she had hoped for. “I’ll call you as soon as I get a chance,” he said, turning her by her shoulders.

Her only reward was the scowl Kristi drilled into her.

“Kristi, we can take this up in my office,” AJ said from behind Kate and she saw the fake tears begin to well in Kristi’s eyes. *Here comes the drama*, Kate thought as she pushed through the kitchen door.

Twenty-six

AJ called on Saturday afternoon. His voice was rough and tired as it travelled through the phone. “I could sure use a distraction right now,” he said.

Kate’s heart twisted beneath her white tank top and glittery pink sash that read “Bridesmaid #4” in sparkling silver letters. She’d be there in a heartbeat if she could. “I wish I could. But I’m in the middle of kidnapping someone,” Kate whispered.

AJ laughed, and then stopped when a loud thunderous knock sounded from Kate’s end of the phone.

“Open up,” Olivia shouted. “We know you’re in there.”

“You’re serious, aren’t you?” AJ asked, changing his tone in an instant.

“Yeah. It’s Mary’s bachelorette party,” Kate explained as Mary’s door opened and a riot of squeals broke out in the hallway.

“Just call me tomorrow, okay?”

“Okay,” Kate said as Olivia threw a black silk scarf over Mary’s eyes.

“Oh, my gosh. What are you doing?” Mary squealed. Olivia grabbed Mary’s arms and pulled them behind her back. She looked to Kate who stepped in and secured her friend’s wrists with a half hitch knot.

"By this time next week you're going to be a married woman. This is your last Saturday night of freedom. So, we're taking you out to celebrate."

Madison giggled and clapped her hands.

"Is this my bachelorette party?" Mary's face drained a bit of color.

"You better believe it," Brandi chimed as she placed the bride's white sash over her head. "We've got some wicked plans for you tonight." A little more color drained from Mary's face, her white skin against the black scarf made her look ghostly.

"Tony. Shoes," Olivia barked into the apartment.

A moment later, Tony appeared with a pair of pointy heels and handed them to Olivia, who passed them off to Kate.

"Help her with these," Olivia ordered and started down the hall, three bridesmaids following closely behind her.

"Bye, baby," Tony leaned in to kiss the blinded Mary. "Have fun, okay?"

Mary nodded while also trying to slip her feet into her shoes.

"You'll keep a good eye on her for me won't you Kate?" Tony's eyes followed his sister already turning the corner in the hall, and then returned his attention to his bride.

"Of course, I will," Kate promised and led her restrained friend down the hall to catch up with the others.

A black stretch limo waited outside Mary's building. The uniformed driver opened the door as Kate and Mary approached. The others were already settled inside.

"So, where are you taking me?" Mary asked the moment her backside hit the leather seat.

"Somewhere spectacular," Olivia said as the car went into motion and took them south out of the city.

A scant hour later, the limo pulled up to a rustic lodge-style building, straight green rows of crops stretched behind it. Olivia whipped the scarf off Mary's eyes, "Voilà!"

Mary blinked. As her eyes adjusted to the light she peered through the tinted window. "Oh, my gosh! Are we on a wine-tasting tour?"

Olivia nodded. "Some gals in the office took a tour last summer and said it was great. So I just had to try it and your bachelorette was the perfect excuse to book an afternoon of tastings." Olivia smiled, but not in a gracious I'm-so-happy-we're-celebrating-together kind of way. It was more of a wicked, challenge-me-if-you-dare, kind of smile that crossed her lips.

“Oh,” Mary said. “This will be lovely.”

“Really? You’re okay with this location?”

“Of course,” Mary said, turning in her seat as if she was looking for clues about why this particular winery wouldn’t satisfy her. The green trees, the barrels of potted flowers, the rolling hills of the vineyard were exquisitely beautiful. Kate herself was rather impressed with Olivia’s selection.

“Because Tony warned me you might not like this. Is there anything you want to tell us before we get out?” Olivia pursed her glossy lips and squinted at Mary.

This was a set up. Kate could see it now. The way Olivia leveled her gaze on Mary, invisible steam wafting from her ears. The girl was still convinced Mary was knocked up and dragging her brother unwillingly into marriage. *Of all the low-life, despicable things for a maid of honor to do…*

“It’s a gorgeous location,” Kate said, grabbing Mary’s hand and dragging her out of the open limo door before she had a chance to answer Olivia’s ridiculous questions.

“What was that all about?” Mary whispered to Kate as they approached the wood-planked stairs leading to the tasting room.

“Just Olivia being Olivia,” Kate sighed.

* * *

Four wineries later, complete with a gourmet meal in the country, the five-some were headed back to the city and up to Olivia’s condo. Inside each tasting room, Olivia had watched Mary like a hawk, counting and mentally measuring each sip of pinot or chardonnay that passed her lips. It would have been annoying, if not for the fact that Kate knew the truth which made watching Olivia rather comical.

The current topic of conversation was the list of nightclubs and dancing that was yet to come this evening. Kate and Mary would be hitting the clubs in their jeans alongside their fashionably fabulous four companions, who had the forethought to bring along a change of clothes.

In the middle of Olivia’s living room was a wrapped package. Brandi pounced on it.

“This is from all of us,” she said, holding the gift out to Mary. “Open it. Open it.”

Mary tore at the pink wrapping and tossed away the ribbon. She lifted the shiny silver lid off the box and pulled out a twisted pile of black lace.

"I got to pick it out," Brandi said, grabbing the lingerie from Mary's hand and turning it right side up. "Isn't it the best? Look at this lace and the deep v-neckline. Tony will love it on your wedding night. What man wouldn't?" Brandi held the scrappy frock up to herself to model how the scraps would cover the essential parts of her body.

"Oooh, it's great," Mary said, stuffing it back into the box.

"Time for act two," Olivia announced and headed for her closet. Madison, Michelle and Brandi followed. In what had to be a record time for their costume change, the Fierce Four paraded from Olivia's bedroom in tight stretchy dresses.

Olivia went to her refrigerator and pulled out a small tray of pink filled cups. Everyone, including Mary and Kate gathered around the tiled island bar in the kitchen.

"Who's ready to get this party started?" Olivia asked, passing around the shooters.

"Oh, me. Me. Me." Madison clapped and bounced her curls. "I'm not ovulating until next week, so I'm going to party it up tonight."

Kate passed Mary the "too much information" look. Mary just smiled.

"Here's to you and a very long and happy marriage with my brother," Olivia said, raising her cup in Mary's direction. They all clinked their little plastic cups and tipped back the strawberry gelatin shooters, all except Mary that is who looked at her cup with a slight tinge of green on her face.

"What's wrong Mary?" Olivia quickly asked. "Is there something wrong with my shooters?" The innocence on Olivia's face didn't hide the now-I've-gotcha tone to her voice.

"No, I've just never liked doing shots," Mary replied, setting her cup on the granite tile.

"Since when?" Olivia asked. Her eyes widened as she played up that fake innocent face even more.

"Do we not all remember the Flaming Beaver shots of Freshman Year?" Mary asked.

The eyes of Mary's sorority sisters all looked at her blankly. They didn't remember—what a surprise—but, Kate did. It was the first sorority function Mary attended right after she pledged Delta Gamma and everyone was doing shots. Long-story short Mary didn't have much experience with alcohol and when that whiskey and hard cider combo hit her belly, it didn't stay there for long. Kate received a phone call and went to pick up her affected friend. Ever since then, Mary had more or less sworn off the hard stuff. Why these so-called sisters of Mary's didn't remember this was beyond Kate.

The shots were probably part of Olivia's benefit prenatal probe plan. The pregnancy sonar that pulsated from her devious scowl bordered on the realm of childish. Kate knew with just one word, one easily placed comment, she could clear the whole thing up, but it was way more fun to see Olivia play this aloof person.

Kate reached for Mary's shot and downed it.

"You can't do that," Olivia gasped at her.

"Looks like I just did," Kate said. "Now, let's get this party started." Kate grabbed Mary's arm for a little stability after doubling up her shot and then headed for the door.

* * *

Kate sat at a booth with Mary in the raunchiest dance club she had ever visited in Portland. The club was in full swing with their '90's theme night. Marky Mark and his Funky Bunch were rapping out a tune as hundreds of people crowded the dance floor.

A few feet away, Olivia, Madison, and Michelle in their short, clingy dresses and heels stood in a tight circle and danced. Brandi had taken up a position at one of the strategically placed poles in the joint, near a table of drooling drunk men. She had just initiated some ponytail swirling move that had the men cheering.

"Why does she have to do that?" Kate asked, leaning close to Mary so her voice could be heard above the rap song. She sat back and squeezed the lemon into her fizzy water. All night Kate had kept the water coming for Mary and herself. At the first club stop of the night Olivia refused to put Mary on her tab unless she was drinking from the top shelf. Rather than letting Mary duke it out with Olivia, Kate had simply produced her own plastic card to cover the club soda for the non-pregnant bride-to-be.

Mary circled the straw in her drink and shrugged. "That's just who she is."

"Just like how Olivia is a top-notch bitch." Kate took a drink.

Mary smiled, but didn't reply.

"You know she is still convinced you're pregnant, don't you?"

Mary whipped her head in Kate's direction, their noses almost coming into contact. "Are you serious?"

"Why else do you think she's been dropping all those questions about you not drinking?"

Mary shook her head. "I'm not drinking because I never drink. Alcohol doesn't mix well with anyone with the Goodwich name, especially my mom. I never want to be the spectacle of the party like her. Ever."

Kate just smiled at her friend. She'd never thought of Mrs. Goodwich as a spectacle at any party, but she wasn't her daughter and that changed the perspective dramatically.

"I think I want to go home now," Mary said as the music transitioned to another song.

Kate turned to her, "I hope it's not because of what I said. You know, about Olivia. I was just…"

"No," Mary said and tugged on her sash. "I'd just rather be at home with Tony than here. He was gone most of the week."

"Are you sure? I mean this is your bachelorette party. I'll get out there and dance with you if you want."

Mary shot Kate a look that told her she probably wanted to be here even less than Kate did. "I was hoping we could skip the whole bachelorette thing. I knew it'd be a booze fest, but Olivia was bent on throwing this whole thing together, wasn't she?"

Kate shrugged, saving herself from having to yell a response over the Spice Girls who were singing about what they really, really wanted.

"She can't get Tyler to set a date for their wedding, yet," Mary said, looking a tad guilty for sharing the gossip.

"Really? Why do you think that is?"

Mary just shrugged and stirred her drink again.

"Tony likes working in the L.A. office." Mary's eyes became distant and then she smiled. "He saw Alejandro while he was down there on his last trip. They spent some time together too, you know like the old college days."

"Oh that's great," Kate shouted, hoping "like the old college days" didn't mean he was out with Alejandro, the alleged Mr. Hot-Pants, scoring with the women of Southern California while Mary pined away for him at home. Tony was a good person and she hoped his friend, Alejandro, hadn't been a bad influence.

Kate and Mary scooted out of their booth and threw Olivia a distant wave before sneaking out into the night and hailing two separate cabs.

Twenty-seven

Kate didn't see AJ again until her early morning delivery on Thursday. He quickly shooed Kate inside to get some coffee when she arrived. Two plates and a paper bag sat on the bar.

"Can I show you something before we eat?" AJ asked when he joined her.

"Of course," Kate said, putting down her coffee cup and following AJ. He took her hand and led her up a set of stairs. The second level provided additional seating when the restaurant was busy. AJ unlocked a door. Through the door was the hallway leading to his apartment.

Yeah, she thought, *he's taking me to his place!* A shiver of excitement bolted through her, but AJ didn't stop at his door. He kept walking to what looked like a fire exit door, but turned just in front of it to another tucked away staircase. This one led to the rooftop. On the top of the building, Kate saw a dozen planters sprouting crops.

"What's this?" Kate asked.

"Another part of my vision." AJ pulled on her hand, leading her toward a pot full of lettuce. "Organic greens," he said. "Parsley, basil, rosemary, cilantro." He pointed to the other containers lined against the wall. "I've been reading about rooftop gardens and decided to see what I could pull off. A couple of other places in town are doing it, so I thought I'd give it a try."

"So now you're turning into a farmer?" Kate laughed as she teased him.

"Yeah, I guess I am." AJ smiled.

"And what does the man in charge think of your rooftop farming idea?" Kate was curious to know how AJ's vision was playing out with his boss.

"I haven't told him yet," AJ said, wrapping his arms around Kate's waist. "I'm waiting for his next trip up here to throw out the whole idea."

Kate nodded, letting her body attach to AJ's. He leaned in and kissed her. When he pulled back, his eyes left hers and jumped to a planter.

"Hey, look," AJ said, plucking a red tomato from the vine. "My first tomato. Come on let's go cut this baby open and see how she tastes!"

Back at the bar, AJ carefully sliced the tomato and laid it on the plate next to Kate's cinnamon roll. "Sorry. I had to run out for breakfast this morning. Earl's a little swamped with the wedding coming up this weekend."

"It's no problem," Kate assured him, reaching for her pastry. She took a bite and then gazed across the bar at him, drinking in the sight of all his perfection.

"What is it?" AJ asked under her scrutinizing gaze. "Is something wrong?"

"No," Kate replied, looking away. "It just feels like I haven't seen you in a while. That's all."

"It hasn't been that long," AJ said, lowering his voice and leaning across the bar toward her. Kate was taken back to the first time she met him. Here. At this bar. Just like this.

"A week can feel like a long time," she said before bashfully dropping her eyes to the tomato slices.

"So what do you think? Will my boss be impressed or what?"

With a turn of her stomach, Kate was reminded again of her impending date with Alejandro. "That's right. Your boss will be here soon, won't he?"

"Yes and I've told him a lot about you." AJ smiled. "He can't wait to meet you."

Great. Kate let out a discomforting sigh. "When will your boss be here?"

"He gets in tomorrow afternoon." AJ stepped back, crossing his arms and legs as he leaned against the counter behind him.

Kate forced a sarcastic smile, "Super."

"Are you still set on disliking the guy?"

"Yeah, I guess so?"

A look of dismay came into AJ's eyes and Kate wondered what she had said that bothered him so much.

"I promise to be on my best behavior around him. I won't embarrass you, I promise," she said.

"I'm not worried about that at all," AJ said, his face relaxing. "Is there anything I can say or do to change your mind about the guy you're going to meet tomorrow? Is there anything he can do to win you over?"

"Hmmm, I'll have to think about that," Kate said, playfully. "What could a womanizing, self-centered jerk do to appeal to me?"

AJ shook his head.

Carly pushed through the swinging kitchen door. "Harried Bride on line one for you," she said, passing a cordless phone to AJ.

"Oooh, harried brides. My favorite," AJ said with a look of apprehension.

Kate slipped off her bar stool. "I assume that's Mary," she said in a hushed voice.

AJ nodded.

"Just tell her everything is set and everything is going to be perfect. Because it will. You make everything perfect, AJ," she said and blew him a kiss before she walked out of the restaurant.

* * *

AJ's perfection swirled in Kate's mind all day as she went about her daily tasks and picked up the plates she'd thrown and designed for the restaurant. Even now sitting ankle deep in warm water with a back issue of *People* in her hands, she couldn't force herself into the present. The spa treatments had started with a one-hour massage for everyone and now they were onto the pedicure portion of the afternoon.

As Kate grazed over the latest celebrity gossip Mary chattered on about what was going to happen over the next couple of days. It wasn't until Alejandro's name was mentioned that Kate actually started to pay attention.

"I talked to Alejandro this morning," Mary said. "His staff at the restaurant will be taking care of all the decorating." Mary must have made that call before she phoned AJ at the restaurant. Kate could just imagine Alejandro being awakened at the early hour among a bed of silk sheets and a California beauty in his arms. He probably rolled over and groaned when he saw Mary's number. And that's probably why he immediately passed her off to AJ, insisting she make direct contact with his staff, so he didn't have to be bothered. What a jerk.

"I was planning to drop all the decorations off at the restaurant first thing in the morning," Mary continued to say. "But Rose has me scheduled to be in court and now I can't do it. Would any of you be able to come by my place and pick up the boxes for me?" Mary looked around the circle of women as each of them dropped their gaze to avoid her eye contact.

"I would, except I have a client meeting tomorrow morning," Olivia said, feigning regret. Kate wasn't surprised when none of the others volunteered.

"I can do it," Kate said. She had to bring the plates to AJ tomorrow too, so it was no big deal. It just would have been nice to see someone else shed their selfishness for once for Mary's sake.

"That'd be great," Mary said. "I'll let Alejandro know. Can you be at my place at seven?"

"Absolutely," Kate said and returned to the pages of the magazine. A luxuriously soft towel dried her right foot after it was pulled from the tub of warm water.

"Zak told me the other night," Madison blurted out. "That Alejandro, dumped his last girlfriend—a swimsuit model or something like that—after she'd been in some disfiguring accident. Is that true?" Her mouth dropped opened as she waited for an answer.

"Pig," Kate muttered under her breath, thinking how Alejandro had a long ways to go to get into her good graces.

"What was that?" Madison turned to look at Kate.

"Nothing," Kate said with a shake of her head, but the subtle smile of the girl painting pink polish on her toes let her know her assessment of the man hadn't gone unheard by everyone.

"That sounds pretty harsh," Michelle said.

"Doesn't change my opinion of him," Brandi said. "He's hotter than hot. I'd still sleep with him. The girl was probably a cow anyway."

"Oh, I don't think it happened like that," Mary said from her chair, but no one looked her way, because Olivia had taken the floor once again.

"That's exactly what happened," Olivia confirmed. "Her modeling career is over and he just walked away. My Tyler would never do a thing like that." She pressed her hand to her chest, the one featuring her gigantic engagement ring. "He'd find me the best plastic surgeon on the west coast and turn me right as rain again." She laughed at her own joke and Kate felt Mary's body stiffen from all the way across the room, but she couldn't see her friend's face because she'd shielded it behind her own copy of *People* magazine.

Twenty-eight

At seven o'clock sharp Kate met Mary on the front stoop of her apartment building. Three cardboard boxes sat at her feet.

"Good morning." Kate waved as she came around the front of her truck, idling in a no parking zone.

"Good morning," Mary called back as she lifted the top box and handed it to Kate. "This should probably go up front, since it's open."

Tony appeared on the porch with another box, a smaller flatter one, and a small suitcase. He met Mary on the steps and leaned down to kiss her goodbye. "Have a great last day as Miss Goodwich," he said with a smile. "Tomorrow you become Mrs. Fisher." He kissed her again, a deep riveting kiss that had Mary gripping his arms for balance.

"Mrs. Anthony Fisher," she reminded him when he pulled his lips from hers.

Tony nodded and stepped away from her with a quick glance to Kate. "See you tonight Kate."

"See you then," Kate said. "Speaking of tonight." Kate turned to Mary. "Is it still okay if I bring someone to dinner?"

"Of course," Mary said, her eyes as bright as stars. "I'm counting on it." She reached out to hug Kate, holding on a moment longer than usual before releasing her. "I've got to get to work. Thanks again for your help."

"What are friends for?" Kate asked as she rounded the truck again and pulled the door open.

Mary gave her a wave as she drove away and in a matter of minutes, Kate was pulling up beside the restaurant. She knocked on the hollow metal door. AJ opened it, greeting her with a heart-melting smile.

"What a great way to start my day," he said and she boldly reached up and kissed him. She pulled back at the sound of his staff approaching from behind. Carly and Earl unloaded the boxes from the back while Kate retrieved the box from the front seat for AJ to carry. Tucked under her arm Kate carried the three plates she wanted to show AJ.

In AJ's office, Kate set the plates down on the desk, but before she unwrapped them from their newsprint. She looked at AJ. "I have a message for Alejandro," she said.

AJ's brow furrowed in surprise, "And what is that?"

"The florist will be here at nine tomorrow morning and the band will be here to set up at eleven. Can you remember that or should I deliver the message personally? Has he arrived yet?" Kate looked toward the door.

"I can remember that and Alejandro will be arriving on a plane later today. Look Kate…" AJ trailed off, his eyes finding the wrapped plates. He pulled back the top layer of newsprint with his finger. Only the edge of the diamond-trimmed plate was exposed. He looked back to Kate and she pulled the plate out of the wrapping.

"This is incredible," he said, glossing his hand over the design while Kate pulled the other two plates from the wrapping.

"These turned out better than I imagined," AJ said, inspecting the floral pattern.

Kate beamed at his praise. "So, are you going to show them to your boss today?"

"First chance I get," AJ said, his smile and eyes lost a bit of their luster as he wrapped the plates up again.

"So," Kate hesitated. "I know this is probably a long shot, but I'd love it if you could join me for the rehearsal dinner tonight."

AJ's eyes focused on her.

"It's at six-thirty, at the Portland City Grill." Kate waited. Why wasn't AJ answering her? "Do you know where that is?"

"Yes. I do know where that is."

"Good. So, do you think you could be my date tonight?" She knew he probably had to work and couldn't ask for time off with his boss waltzing into town today, but she had to ask. The thought of being there with AJ made the whole soirée feel more bearable.

"Your date, huh?" AJ pulled her closer to him. "You'd really want to show up with the likes of me? A lowly restaurant manager, who lives in a tiny apartment above his place of employment and doesn't even own a car? A guy who can't even drive himself out of the city when he wants to. Who works around the clock? Because that's who I am Kate. Just a guy who works in a restaurant owned by someone else. Is that good enough for you?"

"Yes, you most certainly are good enough for me." She smiled.

"Then, I would love to be your date."

"Thank goodness. You'll save me from having to spend the whole night with your ego-maniac boss."

A shadow crossed over AJ's face, as his eyes went somber. "Please give him a chance? Promise me you'll be open-minded."

"I'm not giving him or any other guy a chance. Only you," she said, reaching up to kiss him. There was a hesitation in his reception of the kiss, but then he relented and kissed her with passion.

When he pulled back as breathless as she was he gasped as words came tumbling out of his mouth. "There's something I have to tell you…"

"AJ," Carly called. "Come quick. Broken tap line. Quick."

He was out the door in a flash, leaving Kate in a stunned silence. She left him a quick note before she left—*See you tonight. ~K*

Twenty-nine

"Where the fuzz is he?" Mary asked Tony for the seventh time in ten minutes. Tony shrugged with his phone pressed to his ear. The back of the church was quiet, hushed conversations hid behind Mary's keyed up energy.

The wedding coordinator tiptoed across the floor and sat next to Mrs. Goodwich and Mrs. Fisher in a padded wooden pew. She whispered out the details about how the mothers would be escorted down the aisle. The rehearsal was due to start in two minutes and they were all awaiting the appearance of the ponytail-sporting, swimsuit-model-dumping groomsman.

Tony walked away from the group, a hand pressed to his ear and talked into the phone. Kate stepped in to stand next to Mary who looked like she might come undone. She wrapped an arm around her friend.

When Tony returned Mary's expectant face asked the question for her.

Tony shrugged. "I could hardly hear him."

"Well, where is he? When will he get here?" Mary wanted to know.

Tony shook his head. "He's not going to make it. I think he's still at the airport. I don't know." He turned to Kate, maybe looking to recruit her for support. "He said he'll make it to the dinner, okay?"

Kate nodded and Mary's face paled.

Stupid, selfish jerk. Ruining my friend's wedding, Kate thought. Mr. Alejandro was not scoring any points with her yet.

"Okay," Mary finally said slowly, then turned up the wattage on her smile as she brushed the kink in her master plan aside. "Well, I'm sure he can figure out what to do, right? I mean he's been in plenty of weddings before."

"Absolutely," Tony said, leaning in to kiss her on the cheek. "Everything will be fine. I'll go tell the minister we're ready."

Mary nodded and turned to Kate when Tony was gone. "So, Alejandro has been detained," she reported to Kate as if she hadn't just witnessed the entire conversation between her and Tony. "But you'll help him tomorrow, won't you? Show him where to stand and everything."

"Of course," Kate said, even though she couldn't imagine it would be that hard for Alejandro to figure out the logistics of walking down the aisle. But then again, she could be wrong—the guy couldn't even get to the rehearsal on time. Kate squeezed Mary's shoulder for extra reassurance and then handed her the lame ribbon bouquet when the minister approached.

* * *

Kate walked to the huge windows of the privately rented room on the thirtieth floor of the U.S. Bancorp Tower. The Fisher family went all out for the rehearsal dinner—they couldn't have chosen a place with a more spectacular skyline view of the city. Kate tipped back the cocktail she snagged at the open bar, jumping in line right behind Mrs. Goodwich. She looked down at the sidewalk below, wondering if one of those tiny ant-people was AJ.

Mary was right that the Fishers had invited nearly everyone they knew. The stream of people coming through the door continued for a good half hour, but AJ wasn't among them.

Dinner was served and Kate kept her wine glass full as the night progressed and both chairs next to her remained open. The pity-filled looks from the Fierce Four had ruined her appetite and her pork tenderloin was returned to the kitchen scarcely touched.

By the time the champagne toast came around, Kate had lost count of her drink total and silently clinked glasses with the imaginary glasses of the men not sitting beside her. Neither AJ nor Alejandro had the courtesy of making an appearance.

Kate pulled her phone from the clutch she purchased to match her navy beaded dress, sparing no expense just this once for her date with AJ. There were no messages. Kate shoved it back in her purse as Mary sat down next to her.

"You doing okay?" Mary asked.

"Absolutely," Kate answered but it came out more like *abs-a-hooty.*

"Sorry he didn't show," Mary said and Kate wasn't sure which guy she was talking about, and at this point she didn't care. Kate just shrugged and grabbed the full glass of champagne sitting untouched at Alejandro's seat.

"I think you've had enough, sweetie," Mary said, taking the glass from her hand. "I've called you a cab and Anthony's going to take you downstairs." Kate swung her head to the right a little faster than she intended and saw Tony approaching. She swayed in her drunken state. He reached out to help steady her to her feet. Mary handed over her purse.

"I thought he was different," she breathed out to Mary.

"I know you did." Mary's eyes were sad and Kate didn't want to further dampen her happy occasion with her lack of choosing respectful men, so she leaned into Tony and let him take her away from the party.

In the elevator, Tony propped her in the corner. The downward motion made Kate's head spin and her stomach flip. The sick feeling left Kate wishing she'd done more than poke at her dinner. At the main floor, Tony helped steady her steps again as they walked out to the awaiting cab. Kate leaned into his chest.

"Be good to her," Kate said with the randomness that an alcohol-induced message could bring. "She's soooo goooood." Kate patted his chest, "So, be good to her."

They reached the car and Tony opened the door. "I will," he said, understanding what she was talking about. Kate nodded her head, dropping it like a weight before she got into the car.

Tony gave the driver the address and passed him some cash saying, "This should cover it." Kate vaguely remembered thinking he was a good man before the door closed and the car pulled away.

In front of her duplex the driver turned, "Do you need some help, Miss?" The words jogged Kate from her foggy state and she looked up at the blackened windows of her half of the duplex. She had secretly hoped she wouldn't be returning here tonight, she'd planned a much different ending to the evening, but here she was, back home and all alone.

“No,” she said, pushing the door open and stretching one foot out to the sidewalk. She staggered up the sidewalk and stood at her front door. The car behind her still idled and she wondered if it was written in the taxi driver’s code of conduct to make sure all drunken women get inside their homes safely. She riffled for her keys, listening for their jingle at the bottom, but the only noise she heard was the TV coming from Jake’s side of the duplex. She dropped her purse to her side and knocked.

Jake with his stubble-filled chin opened the door a crack and with one look at Kate, he opened the door all the way, letting her inside. The sound of the cab pulling back onto the street went unnoticed.

Thirty

Jake's arm felt like a careless weight pinning Kate to the wrinkled sheets. She slid out from under it and sat up on the edge of the bed. Morning light streamed through the paned window, lighting the untidy bedroom. Kate found her shoes and purse piled inside a rectangle of light next to an overflowing basket of laundry. She zipped up her dress. The unmistakable throb of a headache, leftover from a night of too much drinking, escorted her out of Jake's bedroom. She had an insatiable need for water.

Successfully finding her keys this morning she transferred herself from one side of the duplex to the other. Through her sparsely decorated living room, she stepped around the piles of boxes and packing material that she had gathered for her imminent move to the basement.

Still carrying her sandals in her hand she went upstairs and straight for the shower. Using her soft white shower sponge she scrubbed at her skin until it was raw and tingly. She had to rid herself of Jake's smell and the animal sex they performed the night before. The sad thing was she couldn't even remember their horizontal jig. Not that it really mattered. She and Jake had done it so many times before she could easily piece together the sequence of events. Beginning with his short pudgy fingers reaching for the hem of her dress, and ending with their final collapse into a few hours of sleep.

Self-pity. No, self-pity and inebriation had driven her into his bed. What a mistake. The alternative of being alone in her bed last night had seemed like a far less desirable scenario, but now it had more appeal. If she went to bed alone last night, she wouldn't be in the shower heartbroken and ashamed, just heartbroken.

Kate wouldn't allow the image of AJ to come into her mind as she scrubbed. Motion. She needed to keep moving. No thinking. Blatantly going against Mary's wedding morning list of do's and don'ts Kate washed her hair. She couldn't let any of Jake's smoke tainted aroma interfere with her day. The first thing she wanted to do this morning was forget about last night.

Out of the shower, Kate wrapped her hair in a towel and tied her robe around her waist. She popped some pills for the killer headache she was sporting before heading back to her bedroom. Kate slipped into a pair of shorts and a black button down shirt. Her phone rang from her purse on the bed. Kate lifted it to see a multitude of missed calls and voicemails.

"Hello,' Kate answered.

"Finally." Mary's voice was in near-panic mode. "Why haven't you returned my calls?"

"I just got out of the shower," she said.

"Don't you lie to me on my wedding day Kathryn Michaels. I left you a million messages and you never returned any of my calls. And I really need your help right now." A giant sniff followed her stream of words. Mary was near full tear mode now.

"What is it? What's going on?" Kate asked, hoping she could keep Mary from prying too deeply into last night's happenings for a very long time, like forever.

"I need to borrow something."

"Okay," Kate said, sitting on her bed. She held her throbbing head in one hand. "What do you need to borrow?"

"I don't know," she breathed out. "I don't know. I can't believe this is happening. I had everything planned. Everything was supposed to go perfectly. Then there was the whole thing with Alejandro last night and now the bracelet. It's all falling apart."

Kate tried to ignore the way Alejandro's name and his unanticipated absence conjured the image of AJ and his failure to appear last night too. What a pair of ill-mannered jerks. "Nothing is going to fall apart and nothing has been ruined yet." Kate should have left that last word off, because it immediately evoked another sniffle from Mary. Kate carried on as quickly as she could, trying to grasp the situation. "So, tell me about the bracelet. What's going on with the bracelet?"

"I was supposed to borrow Muriel's diamond bracelet, but now Olivia has taken it. She says she needs it to balance out the weight of the diamond on her other hand. I have nothing borrowed. I *need* something to borrow."

"Okay," Kate said, pulling open a drawer on her side table. She riffled through some papers and pens, but nothing bridal stuck out. She closed the drawer and moved into her bathroom.

"Does lipstick count?" Kate asked.

"I don't think so," Mary sniffled.

"What about your mom?"

"She only has a pearl necklace. No diamonds. And I can't wear pearls."

"Of course not," Kate agreed. "Did you try asking Olivia for the bracelet back? I mean it is your wedding day after all."

"Yeah, I did." Another sniffle. "But she just laughed at me and told me it was a silly tradition that didn't mean anything. But it means something to me." Mary's voice wavered on the verge of tears again.

"I know it does," Kate told her and turned to look at her closet. Anything wardrobe related was out. She and Mary never shared a closet. Her friend's petite frame was too small for any of her clothes. "Okay," Kate said. "I'm going to find something for you. Don't give this one more second of worry. I'll take care of it. I won't let you down. I promise."

"Okay," Mary said, sounding somewhat soothed. "Thanks."

"You're welcome. I'll see you in about an hour at the salon."

Kate disconnected the call with Mary and set out on her new mission. Her home was void of anything appropriate for a wedding, so Kate had to come up with a Plan B and quickly.

* * *

After downing three glasses of water, Kate was set to head out the door. With her garment bag in hand and another packed bag slung over her shoulder Kate left the duplex and walked up the street. She made a quick detour into a costume jewelry boutique and found an antique-looking set of crystal bobby pins. She grabbed the pack and paid for them before catching the bus at the corner.

Kate met Mary and the other bridesmaids at Shabby Chic right on time.

Mary broke away from the group when she saw Kate enter. "Did you find anything?" Mary asked.

Kate nodded and pulled out her makeup case, handing over the half dozen loose bobby pins to her friend. On the bus ride over Kate had the sense to dump the packaging, otherwise Mary might have had a breakdown about them being new and not meeting the borrowed criteria. Kate wanted to remove any potential for a bridal breakdown if she could help it. "Will these work?"

Mary's mouth dropped open and then turned into a smile. "These are gorgeous Kate. Just gorgeous. I didn't know you owned anything like this."

"Oh yeah," Kate lied. "I just found them in the back of a drawer. I think they'll go perfectly with the beading on your dress."

"She's seen your dress?" Olivia asked with a lip curl. Why did that girl seem to have radar hearing whenever the subject of Mary's dress came up? "I thought you wouldn't let anyone see your dress."

"Of course I haven't seen her dress," Kate said. She could handle this lie-train far better than Mary who would chug around in a circle to avoid telling an actual lie while clumsily evading the truth. Deception, this was Kate's domain. "I had to get some sort of a description out of her to find something that matched better than a run of the mill diamond bracelet. I think these will be a far better solution, don't you?"

Kate watched the blood drain from Mary's face and rise up in Olivia's. She waited for the overbearing maid of honor to voice her comeback. Kate was ready for it, even if it meant tainting Mary's wedding day with a little discord. Kate was a highflying funnel cloud right now fueled with regret and ready to touch down. She was prepared to rip through Olivia's frozen and bewildered stare like an F4 tornado, leaving behind a twisted path of destruction. All she had to do was open those pretty pink lips one more time.

But before Olivia's comeback could escape Mary dragged Kate to the waiting salon chairs for round one of the morning's prep work.

* * *

Kate lost track of time as her hair was curled and re-curled and then piled whimsically on top of her head, she no longer cared about it being free flowing for AJ's fingers to comb through. She would avoid him at all costs today. Maybe she could even attach herself to his pretentious boss. That would serve AJ right for his unexcused absence last night.

Kate moved from one chair to the next and let the cool brush of the technician paint a layer of foundation, and then blush onto her cheekbones. When the entire process was complete, Kate could barely see the shame of her actions from the night before in her face and for some reason she thought that would make it easier if she did run into AJ at the reception.

All looking like a herd of beauty queens ready to hit the stage, Mary and her wedding party arrived at the church. Kate kept herself a safe distance away from Olivia, in case another funnel cloud stirred inside her.

A lovely sampling of small tea sandwiches along with a fruit and vegetable platter and bottled waters waited in the bridal suite at the back of the church. While the girls munched and gabbed Kate sequestered herself in a chair, keeping her interactions with the Fierce Four to a bare minimum. She pulled her phone out of her bag.

Kate dialed up her voicemail, figuring she'd clear it of Mary's messages.

First message: "Hi Kathryn. It's me. Just checking on you. Call me when you get this." *Delete.*

Second message: "Are you home yet? Call me." *Delete.*

Third message: "Hey, Kathryn where are you? Please call me, so I know you made it home. I talked to Alejandro he was so sorry he missed you tonight. See sweetie there are still some decent guys out there. Don't give up hope. And CALL ME!" *Delete.*

Fourth message: "Serious trouble now. Call me. I have to talk to you." *Delete.*

Fifth message: "Hi," this was a man's voice. A very tired man's voice. "I'm so sorry about dinner. I wish I could have called sooner. Hope you got my message. We'll talk later. Sweet dreams." *AJ?* AJ had called. Kate restarted the message and listened to the automated voice tell her the call came in at two-seventeen this morning. Then, his voice, slow and coarse streamed into her ear, bringing his apology.

Oh, how the sound of his words soothed the torment in her soul. To hear him speak was like a salve to the pain she'd been under. But, really it came too late, by two-seventeen this morning she was sacked in another man's bed. The damage had been done, but then as she listened again he said he left a message. Kate listened to the following messages.

Sixth message: "Hi…" Mary. *Delete.*

Seventh message: "It's me…" Mary. *Delete.*

Eighth message: "Call me…" Mary. *Delete.*

That was it. That was every message on her phone. Kate checked her text log. Nothing. No messages from AJ there either. Had technology failed her in her time of need last night? That didn't seem right since Mary's seven messages all came through. Was a message left with the wait staff last night, had some idiot waiter failed to give her a message that could have led her away from Jake's door? *Eeeew Jake's door.* Kate had ruined it. How could she ask AJ to forgive her very deep, very drunken lapse in judgment last night? She thought about calling him now, to uncover when this message was supposed to have reached her and if there was any way to move forward from her unfaithfulness.

Was it considered unfaithfulness…when had she and AJ committed to a full-blown relationship? They weren't even sleeping together. A few stolen kisses. One passionate night of kissing in a parking lot. Was that grounds for a committed relationship?

Unfortunately, the answer was all too clear to Kate in her post-slipup frame of mind. If the tables were turned there's no way she would forgive AJ. She was responsible for ruining the best thing that had ever walked into her life.

Thirty-one

With less than an hour until show time, the church's wedding coordinator and entourage entered the bridal suite.

"It's time to get dressed," she announced as her assistants cleared the room of all the leftover food and water. When the room was free of strangers, the bridesmaids disrobed down to their thongs and strapless bras, and slipped into their pink dresses.

Then Mary unveiled her dress. She stepped into her oversized ball gown. Michelle zipped her up and they all stood back to admire the bride.

"What do you think?" Mary asked, clasping her hands together.

"As pretty as a princess," Kate offered when no one else said anything. Olivia leaned in closer to examine the beading.

"Are these real?" she asked, reaching out for one of the appliques, but Kate stepped in front of her to adjust Mary's skirt.

"Of course, they're real," Kate insisted. "Mary has the finest taste I know and she'd select nothing but the best quality for her wedding day." Kate looked over the dress as if this was her first inspection too. "Wow, Mary the handiwork on this is exquisite. You can't find a dress like this just anywhere. You struck gold."

Olivia's jaw sprang open. Kate kept up her praise, not allowing Olivia's words to breathe. "My Aunt Val used to make wedding dresses. Like twenty a year when she lived in the city." Lie. "And she said you can spot a custom gown by the stitching." Kate leaned in close to the applique. "See here. These stitches are tight like a machine's, but there is the slightest variation to the length of each one. You wouldn't use a machine on real crystal." More lies, but she had caught the interest of the three other bridesmaids. Michelle, Brandi, and Madison all leaned in, while Olivia stood back with her arms crossed.

"Oooh yeah," Madison squealed. "I see it. It's beautiful Mary."

Michelle and Brandi nodded and gave their appraisals too. *Score one for the deceptive diva,* Kate thought. Olivia, without sharing in the assessment process, joined the other girls as they fluffed her skirt. Mary caught Kate's eye and mouthed a "thank you."

Mary's nerves were on edge and Kate didn't want the nit-picky critiques of her soon-to-be sister-in-law to ruin the day. Kate was happy to do a little lie-dropping if it spared Mary any more scathe from Olivia.

It only took a moment for the limelight-seeker to take over the leading role again. "For my wedding we're thinking of doing a vintage theme. Dee's already shown me some fabulous dresses in vintage lace. Something classic and iconic for our wedding. And white is so outdated. I'm definitely going to have an ivory dress."

Mrs. Goodwich couldn't have chosen a better moment to burst through the door to announce it was time for pictures, because Kate was just about ready to dropkick Olivia out the door. With a pasted on smile Kate took the small bouquet of pink roses Madison passed her and fell in step behind Mary. Mrs. Goodwich waved them out the door with her free hand, the other one already held a glass of champagne—*where had she scored that*?

Olivia continued her report on how all the details of her wedding would unfold. Starting with pictures, they were to be done ahead of time. The silly tradition of not seeing the groom before the wedding was a time waster in Olivia's mind. She was going to be with Tyler every minute before the ceremony until they had to part. Kate caught up to Mary and walked beside her as they entered the sanctuary.

The photographer, a tall man, clean-shaven and young looking—the perfect object for Brandi to set her sights on—waited for them. "Over here ladies," he called and waved the pink parade to the curved step in front of the alter.

"We're going to start with pictures outside," Olivia said as she stepped into place beside Mary.

Mary acknowledged her with a tiny nod before turning and trying to straighten her skirt for the first shot. Kate stepped in and lifted the train, spreading it out behind Mary while the delinquent maid of honor continued to gab about her special day, which still did not have a confirmed date.

"When are you getting married?" Kate asked and Olivia shut her trap long enough to shoot a drop-dead glare at Kate.

"We haven't set a date yet," Olivia huffed. "And how is that special someone in your life? Showing up for dates now, is he?"

Well played, Kate thought, *hit me back right where it hurts.* "He's wonderful," Kate lied with sigh-driven words and a warm glowing smile that she hoped could pass for a woman in love rather than a woman who screwed the wrong man last night.

Olivia flashed a wry smile before turning back to the camera and throwing an arm over Mary's shoulders to pose for the look-at-us-we're-best-friends picture. A hundred or so pictures of the bride and her party were snapped inside the church.

After every click of the camera, Olivia shared another wedding detail. They wanted to be married here at the same church, but the reception would have to be held at the country club. The men would wear gray suits, not tuxedos…again so out of style. The group moved outside for more shots. Brandi lagged behind drenching the young photographer with her silly little girl laughs that had Michelle raising her hackles.

Another hundred plus pictures were snapped outside and finally the bridal bunch returned to their suite. Mary paced across the floor, unable to sit down, and afraid she would wrinkle her dress. Brandi had somehow found a bottle of champagne and was already drinking it, perhaps with the help of Mrs. Goodwich. Kate couldn't help but notice the way Michelle deliberately stayed on the opposite end of the room as Brandi whenever possible.

Madison was talking with Olivia who'd finally shut up about her own wedding long enough to listen to Madison for a brief second. She was stressed about missing her period this week and afraid to drink champagne tonight.

"Well, you'd better not be knocked up for my wedding," was Olivia's compassionate response. "I'm not having a basketball protrusion on any of my bridesmaids. You'll all be wearing black sheaths. Not very forgiving on the figure."

Kate checked her phone one more time and thought about how she would love the distraction of texting AJ right now. He'd appreciate the selfishness playing out behind these closed doors, but then she was reminded of her own misconduct and that sent the phone plunging back into her bag. Before the phone clunked to the bottom Mary's little fists balled up at her sides and she stopped dead in her tracks, clapping the heel of her shoe on the floor for emphasis.

"Would you all just stop it," she screamed in a voice that Kate could honestly say she had never-ever heard from Mary. "This is my wedding day." She looked at Michelle. "Forget about Leo. He's a louse. We've all known it since law school. He hooks up with a different girl at every wedding, you know that. At Madison's wedding it was you, this time it's Brandi and at the next wedding it will be someone else, so get over it and move on." Michelle's big round eyes stared back at Mary who now turned her attention to Miss Champagne-Sipping Brandi.

"And maybe you should try thinking about your friends before you going kissing on some guy. A little self-restraint every now and again isn't going to hurt you." Brandi's glass stopped mid-tip as she received her reprimand.

"Madison," Mary shouted. "Go get a stick to pee on if you're so worried about being pregnant, otherwise shut up about it." The doe-eyed look from Madison told Kate she was still processing Mary's words, probably wondering how she could find a stick outside to pee on and how that would help her solve the pregnancy question. It would take some time, but eventually the words would make sense to her.

And now Mary's eyes were on Kate. "Turn your phone off. I don't want to see you look at it again, because I know exactly what went down last night."

Kate tilted her head toward her friend, like she had no idea what she was talking about. How could Mary know about her and Jake?

Mary received Kate's unasked question and nodded. "Yeah, I know, because I called him when you didn't answer any of my calls last night and he told me exactly where you were. Just because one loser leaves you high and dry doesn't mean you should go running to another one. Now turn that phone off."

Kate did as she was told. Mary's shoulders heaved as she filled her lungs with air and blew it out, calming the winds inside her. Olivia's smirking face scanned the room, giving them all a look of shame for ruining Mary's day, but it was wiped away the moment the bride turned to face her future-sister-in-law.

"If I hear one more word about how you're going to do things at your wedding I swear I will throw you out of this church by your hair. Do you understand me? This is my day and I want all of you to quit ruining it for me." The room was speechless. Mary fanned her eyes that were ready to produce buckets of tears.

"Water," she said. "I need water." Everyone jumped into action, but Kate was the closest to the door and escaped the room first. She found a stash of bottled waters in the vestibule and started back to the bridal room when she caught sight of AJ entering the church through the giant wood doors.

He looked tired, but his smile was such a welcomed sight to her day. He stopped in front of her and she couldn't hold back the shy smile that surfaced on her lips.

"Hi," she said.

"Hi," he said back and watched her, like he was trying to read her reaction.

"What are you doing here?" she asked and then noticed the garment bag he carried. "Oh, you're boss has you running his errands, I see."

AJ just smiled, throwing the bag over his shoulder. "About last night…"

Kate waved her hand at him. Last night had no good meaning for her. It was best if she just forgot it altogether. "I got your message. We'll talk later," she said and looked at his face. The faint marks of a bruise on his lower left jaw seemed drastically out of place on his perfectly designed face. She reached up to touch it and he pressed his cheek into her palm.

Kate instantly felt reconnected to him. Whatever had kept him away last night and her misguided reaction could all be worked through. She was sure of it. She was meant to be with this man and he was meant to be with her. "What happened?" she asked.

AJ's lips parted about to say something when Zak approached. "Hey, AJ," he said, slapping him on the back and Kate dropped her hand. "'Bout time you got here."

AJ nodded in his direction.

"I told you those strippers would be a hit, didn't I?" Zak asked, draping an arm over AJ's shoulder like they were the best of buds.

"These guys pulled together a bachelor party at the restaurant last night," AJ told Kate.

"What was that gal's name? Garnet? She liked you, man," Zak said with a wink and AJ only got a half smile out before Zak started to walk away. "Hey, you better get your ass and that tux down to the room ASAP. This shin-dig's about to start." Zak disappeared around the corner and Kate went to step around AJ.

So, that's why AJ's call hadn't come in until so late. He chose a stripper stampede over her last night, huh? Well, looks like she was much lower on his list of priorities than she first thought. Maybe AJ wasn't the man she thought he was.

"Kate wait," he called, but she was already on her way.

"Gotta go," she said, holding the water in the air. "Bride in meltdown. Duty calls." She turned and left him standing there with his boss's tux hanging over his shoulder.

* * *

Being the last bridesmaid in line meant Kate was the first of the pink ladies to grace the grand aisle of the old-fashioned church. The organ played beautifully and Kate looked to Tony as she made her way to the front. He smiled at her. Kate only hoped he could make Mary as happy as she deserved and that he could protect her from the nastiness of his sister. She prayed Mary wouldn't be tainted by her ugly behavior.

As she reached the alter she scanned the line of groomsmen. Gabe nervously fidgeted with the cuffs of his tux. Zak and Leo both looked disinterested and tired. Zak's wide-mouthed yawn and Leo's bloodshot eyes were dead giveaways of their late night capers. Kate couldn't see Tyler's face. He was turned away from her with a hand over his mouth talking to the final groomsman, Alejandro. When Tyler straightened his body, Kate got a full look at the last man in line. *What the f...*

The photograph held his hand out to her. "Stop there," he said. Kate froze as the camera snapped a shot of her staring at AJ standing in for his boss.

Thirty-two

Why was AJ giving Mary a thumbs-up? And why was she not freaking out?

The light bulb finally flickered on in Kate's brain. *Holy crap! AJ was Alejandro. Alejandro was AJ. But how?*

Kate silently screamed the question at him, but he looked away. She resisted every urge in her body to throw down her pink bouquet, to march over there and get some well-deserved answers from the fourth groomsman in line.

He lied to her. For months, he had kept his identity a secret from her, parading around as a friend instead of a skirt-chaser.

Kate dropped her eyes to the floor where her silvery shoes sparkled against the warm honey glow of the hardwood floor. She thought of every single conversation she'd had with AJ, or was it Alejandro? It didn't matter.

Kate searched her memory for any clues she might have missed. But there were none. The guy had referred to his boss as Alejandro the first time she met him. He said he wanted to buy the restaurant from Alejandro. These were his words.

Why the charade? What sick game had he been playing with her?

Kate shook the despicable thought of how she had almost fallen for his genuine nice guy trick from her body.

"Are you cold?" Brandi whispered.

Kate shook her head. "Just excited for Mary," she said with a sugary smile.

Brandi nodded and cheesed a smile for the photographer.

For the rest of the ceremony Kate kept her eyes off the man she'd believed to be a friend—a very good friend—and focused on the only friend she had left. Mary. Dear, sweet Mary who was standing before God and a church full of witnesses, pledging her life to a man for all eternity. It was a beautiful union as long as Kate didn't take too many points away from Tony for his family or certain people that he referred to as good friends.

The church erupted in applause as the minister introduced the newly wedded couple. Mr. and Mrs. Anthony Fisher, bright with smiles, marched down the aisle to the back of the church. Kate followed Brandi and reluctantly accepted AJ's arm as they joined in the procession.

"So, you're Alejandro?" Kate whispered from beneath the shield of her plastered bridesmaid-y smile.

"I prefer for my friends to call me AJ," he whispered back.

"And I prefer not to be lied to, Alejandro," Kate said before she dropped his arm and walked away.

As the guests left the church and stepped into the afternoon sunshine, the bridal party was ushered back inside to the alter where they took a series of "time-consuming pictures"—Olivia's words. Thankfully, Kate and AJ were posed on opposite ends for most of the shots. Kate found herself able to relax only when she was a safe distance away from him, which equated to anytime she couldn't make visual contact with him.

Two white limousines waited in front of the gray stone church. Olivia pulled Tyler into the front one with Mary and Tony, before it sped away. Madison and Zak climbed into the second limo followed by Michelle who possessively grabbed onto Leo's hand and pulled him in.

The distance to the restaurant from the church hardly warranted the need for transportation and Kate thought walking off her anger might be a good idea before reporting to the reception, but the gigantic heels she wore fizzled that idea fast. Occupying a limo for a few dreadful minutes with three-fourths of the Fierce Four and a lying groomsman was going to have to work.

"Let's go," Kate said, taking a hold of Gabe's arm, and leaving AJ to deal with Brandi who was already running her hand down his arm.

*   *   *

"They're going to announce us and we have to be in order," Olivia said, corralling the party as soon as they were through the door of the restaurant. She stole Gabe away from Kate and dragged him to the front of the line. Kate made her way to the back where AJ waited and offered his arm. She refused to take it.

A techno beat came from the central hub of the restaurant and Olivia and Gabe's names were announced like they were part of a starting lineup. Thunderous applause followed their entrance. Olivia, Kate could imagine, was probably soaking up the attention.

As each couple stepped through the curtain it brought Kate one-step closer to having to accept AJ's arm and finally it was their turn. With a deep breath, Kate mustered all her fake happiness and reached for AJ's arm, stepping into the reception in her pink dress. Déjà vu rained down on her. Hundreds of eyes witnessed her entrance on the arm of the one man she wished to be here with until about twelve hours ago.

Maintaining her role as a happy-happy bridesmaid, Kate let AJ lead her to the group standing in front of the bridal table. Her eyes swept the interior of the restaurant. It had been transformed. The hip urban styling was gone and in its place was a soft whimsical feel, perfect for Mary's wedding. The tall brick walls were covered with soft white satin curtains. The subtle shade of the pink tablecloths was paired beautifully with white slip covered chairs. At the center of each table was a small bowl of floating pink flowers. Kate immediately recognized the centerpieces from a marked page in Mary's wedding notebook. White lights wrapped the second story railing.

A voice boomed over the microphone and introduced Mr. and Mrs. Anthony Fisher as Mary and Tony miraculously appeared at the top of the stairs. It all took Kate's breath away. Mary in the fairytale setting of this restaurant in disguise was simply beautiful.

"What are you thinking?" AJ asked, leaning in close to her ear. She stiffened and dropped her hand out of the crook of his arm, shaking the warmth of his breath from her neck.

"Honestly," she said, letting go of her grudge for a moment. "The place looks beautiful. It's exactly what Mary wanted." And then she turned away from him and headed for the bar.

*   *   *

Kate looked across the room at AJ talking to a couple of young, peppy college girls. He caught her eye and smiled. She turned away as Carly slid her drink across the bar.

Kate climbed up onto a stool and took a drink of her margarita. A crash, only loud enough for those closest to the kitchen to hear, sounded from behind the scenes. Kate saw Carly make eye contact with someone in the crowd and gave a slight nod toward the kitchen door. Soon enough, AJ was bursting into his kitchen.

Maybe he'll stay there for a while, Kate secretly wished.

A figure that Kate would recognize anywhere came out of the kitchen balancing a tray on his flat palm. Her automatic reaction was to turn away, but then she remembered her assumption of this tall, ponytail-sporting man's identity was all wrong.

"Who is that?" Kate asked Carly, as the man disappeared into the crowd offering up hors d'oeuvres.

"That's Marco, he works here part-time as a dishwasher. AJ thinks it's good experience for him to serve, so he lets him play both roles at these kinds of events."

Right, Kate thought, taking a swig of her drink. *Marco the dishwasher, not Alejandro the hot-bodied owner.* She couldn't even begin to describe the level of foolishness she felt.

After what seemed like hours, the bridal party was finally asked to take their seats for dinner. Kate took her place at the end of the bride's side of the table next to Brandi.

From out of nowhere, AJ approached and asked Brandi to switch seats with him.

"Leo said he wants to sit by you," he whispered in her ear. Brandi jumped up and left a steaming Michelle behind.

"You're breaching protocol," Kate said as he sat next to her.

"No, I'm not," he said. "Look Madison and Tyler switched sides, so why can't I?"

"Because," Kate started to say, but she couldn't find the steam to finish with *I don't want you to*.

Why did AJ want to sit by her? To rub it in that he was too busy with strippers last night, but now had the time for her.

I don't think so, Kate thought, squaring her shoulders. But then she turned and the sight of AJ's achingly familiar face, those deep blue eyes and gap-tooth smile begged her heart to erase all that had happened and start again. If only it were that easy.

Marco set Kate's plate of chicken in front of her and she unrolled her silverware from the white linen napkin. "Why aren't you serving beef?" she asked as she picked up her knife and fork.

"Because, when the overly efficient bride selected her menu I didn't have a beef supplier lined up. Once I did the menu cards were already printed and there was no changing her mind after that."

Kate forked a piece of the stuffed chicken breast into her mouth. *Mmmm, it was good.*

"Do you like it?" AJ asked and Kate realized he had been watching her this whole time.

Kate shrugged indifferently. "It's all right."

"I'm sorry about last night…" AJ started to say.

"Don't ruin my meal by trying to talk to me about last night." Kate reached for her water glass.

"But…"

Kate threw her hand up like a stop sign. "Stop talking," she said.

"I'm sorry…"

Again, Kate gave him the hand. He turned away from her and sliced into his herbed halibut.

The toasts began and Kate raised her glass after Olivia's speech where she more or less took all the credit for uniting Tony and Mary. And again after Gabe and Mr. Goodwich gave their short and sweet toasts.

Tony stood and tapped his glass with his fork, gaining the attention of the guests to give the final toast. "I would like to thank everyone for being here to share in this special day. Mary has been an angel in my life since the day I met her and I know we are in for a great ride together." He paused as his emotions surfaced on his words. "I would like to thank our parents and families for their support and love as we have planned for this day. I also especially want to thank my good friend AJ for making this place sparkle for my Mary. I highly recommend his services and those of his staff for any event you're planning." Tony raised his glass in AJ's direction, who gave a gracious nod back to his friend. "AJ has also been a godsend in helping Mary and I prepare for the next phase of our life."

Kate heard the loud whisper of, "I knew it," from Olivia four chairs down.

She's not pregnant, Kate wanted to shout, but Tony kept up his momentum.

"When Mary and I return from our honeymoon we will be moving…to Los Angeles." Tony paused as the room took a collective gasp. "I've taken a position at the firm down there and AJ has helped us to secure a beautiful beachside bungalow. So please raise your glasses with me in a toast to my new wife and our new adventure."

A mix of applause and shock circled the room. AJ clapped and turned to Kate when she didn't join in. His smile faded and his hands froze when he saw the icy stare Kate had fixed on him.

Thirty-Three

"What's wrong?" AJ asked.

Kate jumped up as Mary and Tony scooted past, leaving their seats at the head table.

"You're moving?" Kate asked as she enveloped Mary into a hug. Kate felt Mary's chin press into her shoulder as she nodded. "Why didn't you tell me?" Kate stepped out of the hug and searched her friend's eyes for an answer.

Mary looked back at her new sister-in-law who attached herself to Tony's hand when Kate blockaded their escape. "Um, it wasn't all final until recently." Mary's eyes shifted left and right and then landed on Tony.

"I can't believe you did this without consulting us," Olivia said to her brother with a noxious flare. "Mom and Dad are going to be furious."

Tony gave her an unaffected shrug before turning back to Mary, "Come on honey, we have to cut the cake now."

AJ stood next to Kate and slapped Tony on the shoulder. "I'm glad it's all working out for you," he said to Tony.

"Thanks man. You've been a major help." He showed his gratitude with a man-hug, complete with the single back slap, before passing Kate.

Mary went to follow Tony, but turned back for one more quick hug with Kate. "We'll talk later. Just be happy for me, okay?" Mary whispered in her ear.

Kate reached out to pull Mary back to her. She had questions and didn't want to wait for the answers.

"Let her go," AJ said, from a proximity that used to be comfortable, but now felt unnerving. "She has a lot of people to talk to today."

Kate turned on him with a glare that rivaled the intensity of the look Olivia was projecting on the newlyweds. "Easy for you to say, since you've been in the loop on this whole scheme. Why didn't you tell me? Why didn't you tell me my best friend was planning to up and move away?"

AJ shot a look in Olivia's direction, "Can you blame them for wanting a little distance?" His voice was low and Kate strained to hear him. "And they asked me not to tell anyone. They weren't sure if the position was going to work out until just a week ago."

"But, why you? Why did you know all about this when no one else did?"

AJ shrugged. "Convenience, I guess. Tony needed a place to stay while he was in L.A. So, he stayed with my parents. And when he needed to find a house fast, I hooked him up with a family friend who owns property down there. Otherwise, I think I would have been in the dark too." Somehow, AJ's hand had found its way to the small of Kate's back and he gently guided her toward the cake table.

A tearful Mrs. Goodwich hugged Mary with one arm and held her champagne aloft in the other. She pulled back to dab at her eyes and then sipped her drink. Tony on the other side of his bride was getting an earful from Muriel.

AJ left Kate's side for a moment to intervene between Tony and his mother. At the end of his whispered words, Muriel looked up, slightly bewildered by the number of eyes that had turned on the cake table, and graciously smiled. The woman could have won an Oscar for her skilled actions in suddenly portraying an overjoyed mother of the groom. She planted a kiss on Tony's cheek before stepping to the side. AJ pointed to the knife on the table, reminding Tony and Mary to move forward with cutting the cake. He passed a boohooing Mrs. Goodwich on his way back to stand next to Kate.

"What did you say to her?" Kate whispered.

"I just reminded her it was time to cut the cake." AJ applauded with the rest of the guests as Mary and Tony carefully fed each other a slice of white cake. Muriel and Olivia stood behind Tony and viciously traded whispered words. Kate watched as the mother-daughter pair scowled at Mary.

The music started and the DJ announced the first dance as the staff of Alejandro's stepped in and served the cake. Tony and Mary took to the open floor and shared their first dance as husband and wife while Elvis Presley sang *Love Me Tender.* It was a Mary Goodwich favorite—make that a Mary Fisher favorite, now.

AJ took Kate's hand and led her to the dance floor as the other members of the bridal party joined the bride and groom. Kate let AJ lift her arm into hold and slide the other arm around her waist. Kate wished her body didn't respond to his when he pulled her closer, but it did.

This was it, she told herself. Here she was in her one official dance with thee Alejandro and after this, she'd be done—obligation fulfilled. She kept her head turned away from him and as the music ended she tried to break away, but another slow song followed and he didn't let go of her hand.

"Are you ever going to talk to me again?" he asked in her ear, his breath sent an unwanted tingle down her spine.

She leaned back from him. "No."

"Why not?"

"Because you led me to believe you were someone else?"

"Who did I lead you to believe I was?"

"It's not who I thought you were. It's who I thought you weren't."

"Okay," AJ's smile reached his eyes. Tired eyes. "Who did you not think I was?"

"Alejandro."

"I'm not Alejandro. I'm AJ."

Kate sighed in exasperation. "But, Mary called you Alejandro."

"Mary is the only person I know who doesn't use people's nicknames. Isn't that right Kathryn?" Kate opened her mouth to rebut him, but he was right.

"But you still knew you were leading me on."

"How was I leading you on?" AJ's lips quirked into an adorable half-smile—no not adorable—conniving, scheming, false, deceptive, anything but adorable was a better description of that smile he'd been using on her.

Kate rolled her eyes. "Did you enjoy listening to me talk about Alejandro? Was it just some big joke to you?" her voice was sharp enough to invoke a sideways glance from Olivia and Tyler who danced near them. AJ smiled back for the both of them.

"Nothing about you has been a joke to me, Kate." His blue eyes turned serious. Kate wanted to look away but couldn't.

"When were you planning on setting the record straight for me?" she asked him.

Kate watched as AJ swallowed, likely choosing his words carefully. Before he could answer, the song ended and Kate dropped his hold. Brandi was quick to take advantage of the opportunity to snatch up AJ as the next song began.

Kate left them on the dance floor and went to the bar. Sitting on the same stool Kate had studied from was Dennis, a former classmate of Mary's from Lewis and Clark. He'd been to many study groups at the duplex and Kate had gotten to know him.

"Hi Dennis," Kate said, saddling up in the stool next to him. She had always liked Dennis with his mild-mannerisms and genuinely nice-guy attitude. He was the real deal. He worked for a firm downtown, and rumor had it his boss was a tyrant.

"Hey Kate," he said with a smile. His kind eyes shined from behind dark-framed glasses. "How've you been?"

"Good," she replied and then ordered a beer from Carly. "How's corporate law?"

Dennis shrugged. "It's fine. What are you up to these days?"

Kate gave her own shrug as Carly passed her a foam-topped stein. "Not much."

Kate took a drink of beer and turned to look over her shoulder. Brandi was out on the dance floor doing her thing with AJ. She looked away from the spectacle as quickly as she could. That was an image she didn't need burned into her brain.

"How are you holding up?" Kate asked Carly when she wiped down the bar next to her. The dark circles under the woman's eyes spoke volumes about the toll this wedding was taking on the staff.

"Let's just say between last night and this morning, I'm ready for a little time off," Carly replied.

"Well, the place looks incredible," Kate said. "You did a fantastic job with the decorations."

"It does look good, but AJ did all of this. Not me."

Kate looked around the large space again. "What do you mean AJ did all of this?"

Carly tossed her rag on the counter behind her and rested her hands on her hips. "As soon as the doors were locked last night AJ sent the staff home. When I showed up at ten this morning all the decorating was done. I don't know how he managed it, after all the mayhem from last night. But the place was spotless."

"I'm sure he must have had some help." *Like his new little friend, Garnet.*

She looked over her shoulder again and saw AJ untangling himself from Brandi. When he was free, he started to move toward Kate.

"So, Dennis does your firm have any positions available?" Kate asked, trying to engage herself in a conversation before AJ arrived.

Dennis shook his head, "Not that I know of."

"Well, keep me in mind if they do, okay?" Kate said with a flirtatious laugh and patted Dennis's arm. *Hope AJ saw that*, she thought.

Dennis nodded and Kate wished he would join in her flirting game in front of AJ, but he didn't.

"Water please," AJ ordered as soon as he reached the bar. Carly quickly set a glass with ice and water in front of him. AJ took a drink and set his glass down. He reached for Kate's hand. "Come on, there's someone I'd like you to meet."

"Can't," Kate said, pulling against his grip. "Dennis and I were about to dance."

Dennis looked up from his beer in surprise. Kate smiled at him, hoping to change his bewildered look into one of irresistible desire, but it didn't work.

AJ put a hand on Dennis's back, "I'm sure Dennis won't mind if I steal you away for a minute now, will he? I promise to bring her right back."

Dennis, of course, didn't protest so Kate followed AJ up the stairs where Mary and Tony had made their grand entrance. A couple sat at a table along the railing where they had a grand view of the scene below. The man was vaguely familiar—tall, broad shouldered and a sprinkling of salt in his dark pepper hair. She had seen him before. But where?

The woman in his company smiled when she saw them approach. She reached out and hugged AJ. "Oh, everything looks beautiful. You did a fantastic job."

"And the food was excellent." The man smiled proudly down at AJ and Kate suddenly remembered where she'd seen him. At the bridal shower, he was the one sampling the food in the kitchen. Why would AJ invite the health inspector to the wedding?

"Thanks." AJ smiled and wrapped an arm around Kate's waist. "I'd like you to meet Kate. Kate this is my mom, Juanita." The woman held out her hand to Kate. "And this is my dad and boss, Alejandro Silva Senior."

Holy crap, Kate's knees nearly buckled under her. AJ was introducing her to his parents. She felt amazingly unprepared for the event. The moment was surreal.

AJ followed up the introduction with, "She's our new beef girl."

Beef girl? Kate crashed back into reality at the unflattering introduction. That's all she was to him, the meat supplier. Kate summoned her composure, refusing to let him see the affect his comment had on her. Instead, she turned her charms on his parents and chatted with them about their satisfaction with her family's product.

AJ smiled at her, probably thinking he was slithering his way back into her heart.

"AJ tells me you've been the inspiration behind some of his new ideas for the restaurant," AJ's father said.

"Oh I don't think there's anything very inspiring about me," Kate said. "AJ came up with these ideas all on his own. He's completely running on his own agenda here." Kate let her syrupy smile and bubbly giggles disguise her jab at AJ.

"AJ says you are an artist," Juanita said when the conversation paused.

"I'm a hobby artist, really," Kate said.

"But you love what you do?" his mother asked.

"Very much so," Kate replied.

"I haven't had a chance to show them you're plate designs yet, but we'll be discussing my grand plan tomorrow."

"Would you be able to join us, dear?" Juanita asked. "Maybe over a light breakfast before we head back to California?"

"I wish I could," Kate said. "But I have a meeting with my tenant tomorrow morning." AJ's arm stiffened around her waist. Dropping Jake into the conversation had done its job to rile him.

"On a Sunday morning?" AJ asked.

"Yes," Kate lied, turning to look at him for a moment. She put the most serious look she could muster into her eyes, deflecting the hurt she saw in his beautiful blues. Kate glanced away and returned her attention to his parents. "It was nice meeting you both. Have a safe trip back home."

"It was lovely meeting you too." Juanita reached out and gave Kate an unexpected motherly embrace. The woman was far from a size two and wore it with such grace and beauty. Kate suddenly felt a pang of regret that she wouldn't have the chance to get to know this woman better.

Kate offered a quick smile to the senior Alejandro and then turned for the stairs. AJ was right behind her.

"What are you meeting with your ex-boyfriend about tomorrow? Are you finally kicking him out?" he asked before they reached the bottom step.

Kate spun around when she reached the first floor, coming nose to nose with AJ. "No, I'm not kicking him out. And he's not an ex anymore. We're back together."

AJ's eyebrows shot up and he grabbed Kate by the elbow, pulling her through a short hallway and into the kitchen. He didn't stop until they were in his office behind a closed door.

"When did this happen?" he asked.

"Last night."

"Huh?" AJ leaned against his desk and rubbed his chin. "So is he here? I'd love to meet this amazing barely-employed guy that you can't stay away from."

His voice was cocky and Kate didn't like the way he was trying to call her bluff. "Well, maybe I've decided to stand by him while he gets his life in order. Instead of being the kind of person who dumps a girl, because she isn't pretty enough anymore."

"What are you talking about?" AJ asked with a shake of his head.

"The swimsuit model you were dating that got into a car accident." Kate nodded. "Yeah, I heard about it. How you dumped her after her disfiguring accident, instead of standing by her." Kate crossed her arms over her chest. "What was the deal there? Girl loses her looks and you're out the door, huh?"

AJ dropped his head and shook it. "I told you about her. I broke up with her because she stole my car while intoxicated and totaled it. Yeah, she was probably going to have a scar on her forehead where the glass from the windshield cut her, but I'd hardly call that a disfiguring accident."

"Well, she couldn't model anymore."

AJ shrugged. "Maybe. But I wasn't dating her because she was a model." AJ took a step toward Kate. "Why are we talking about this anyway?"

Kate took a step backward, maintaining their distance. "Because I'm still trying to figure out who you are?"

AJ didn't come any closer. "You know exactly who I am Kate."

"No," Kate shook her head and reached for the door handle. "No, I don't. The AJ I knew would never stand me up for a stripper party. That's something Alejandro would do. And my opinion of him has not changed."

Thirty-Four

"Kate, wait." AJ chased after her, but she was quick to get out the door and through the kitchen. Gathered just beyond the bottom of the stairs were all the single women waiting for Mary to toss her bouquet from the second story.

"Kathryn," Mary screamed from above. "Hurry up and get over there."

Kate moved into the group, burying herself in the middle, so AJ couldn't get to her easily. Mary turned around and tossed the bouquet over her head. Kate stepped back as a flock of women dove for the flowers. Brandi was the first to make contact with it, but Michelle was quick to get a hand on it too. The two wrestled with it for a bit before Michelle's relentless yank freed it from Brandi's grasp and sent it flying right into Kate's hands.

"Yay," Mary called from the balcony and clapped. "Yay, Kathryn you caught it!"

Kate looked down at the white flowers. *Now this was a stupid tradition. There was no way Kate was the next in line for marriage.*

With her new prize, Kate walked to the bar and sat next to Dennis again. "This still mine?" she asked him, pointing to the beer.

He nodded and she took a drink.

"Here you go Carly," Kate said, tossing her the bouquet. "You want this?"

"Not really, but I'll keep it back here for you."

Kate shrugged and took another drink. From the corner of her eye, she saw AJ making his approach. She set her glass back down. "Hey, Carly can you call me a cab?"

"Sure," she agreed, but then made eye contact with AJ.

"And my stuff?" Kate inquired. "Do you know where the limo driver stashed my bag? I'll be needing that."

Again, Carly made eye contact with AJ.

"It's in the back," AJ said. "I'll get it for you whenever you want it."

"I'd like it now, please." Kate didn't bother to give AJ her full attention. "And the cab too please, Carly."

Carly turned and reached for the phone.

"My bag," she reminded AJ with an impatient clip.

"Come on Kate. Can't we finish talking?"

"My bag," she said again.

With a shake of his head, AJ turned to leave and returned with her bag.

"Thank you," she said, taking all measures to avoid looking at him full in the face. "I'll wait outside."

"I'll go with you," AJ said. "I don't want you waiting out there by yourself."

"I'll be fine," Kate said.

"I really don't want you waiting out there alone." AJ's voice was tight.

"I'm really not your concern, now am I?" Kate said matching his tone.

"Kate, please," AJ begged, quietly, but Kate would not bend.

"I'll wait with you," Dennis said, standing from his seat. AJ's face showed defeat, but he nodded.

"Thank you Dennis."

"Kate," AJ said, putting a hand on her shoulder before she could leave. "I left a message with Tony last night. I'm sorry he didn't tell you I wasn't going to make it."

Kate thought back to last night. "Tony gave me a message," she said and stepped away to free her shoulder from his touch. "But it was from Alejandro, not AJ." Kate spun and hooked her arm into Dennis's, walking into the twilight without a look back at AJ's forlorn face.

Thirty-five

Kate cried herself to sleep that night and every other night for the next five days. She didn't answer AJ's calls and she didn't reply to his text messages. The morning of her next delivery to the restaurant Kate showed up and unloaded the boxes herself. Leaving the stacks against the wall, she pounded on the door and hopped in her truck. When AJ came outside, she drove away, tears filling her eyes at the sight of him in her rearview mirror.

For the next week, Kate kept herself busy packing and cleaning out her side of the duplex. The dungeon-like basement could now pass for a living space and starting next week she would call it home and collect rent from Todd and Liz for the space above.

The mail delivered her bar exam results right before she left the city on her way to the ranch to bring the restaurant their next order. The passing score sent a flood of joy over her that was quickly replaced by sorrow. She had no one to share the good news with.

The three-hour drive gave Kate more than enough time to remember all the people in her life that were gone. Her mother, her brother, AJ, and now Mary who was going to move across the state line.

When she pulled into the driveway of the Michaels Hereford Ranch, crossing under the aged threshold, she felt a temporary respite from her loneliness. She still had her daddy and Aunt Val. The front fields, having given their final cutting to the hay trucks weeks ago, were now populated with their beautiful Hereford cows. This group of red and white females would start calving in mid-October.

Kate arrived as Val and her daddy were sitting down to dinner.

"Hey," Val called. "Grab a plate and join us."

Kate sat at the table and dished up a fried chicken wing and a helping of the garden fresh salad.

"Miss Virginia had a bull calf this week," her daddy reported.

"Really?" Miss Virginia was Kate's old show heifer who had turned into a real pet over the years. Her gentle disposition made her a favorite among everyone at the ranch. She had excellent bloodlines and for years, Daddy had been hoping for a bull calf out of the old girl that he could sell for a premium at the purebred auction, but so far, Miss Virginia had calved nothing but heifers.

"He's a beauty too." The smile on her Daddy's face was a rare treasure.

"The restaurant increased their order again," Aunt Val shared. "Seems your friend has recruited us a few new buyers. A deli and another restaurant are sending some folks out next week to take the tour. If these people buy, we're thinking we'll hire Mac to haul the orders for us. That way you'll have more time for the work you're doing at the restaurant."

"My work?" Kate asked.

"Yeah, your friend told you're daddy all about the work you've been helping him with at the restaurant and your plans to do the new plates and everything. It sounds very exciting."

"You called AJ?" Kate asked, switching her attention to her father.

He shook his head.

"No, the young man calls him," Aunt Val reported. "Once a week like clockwork to place his next week's order. Your daddy says he's always polite and always well spoken."

Kate turned to look at her father. "He's a good fella, Kate." The endorsement from her daddy was almost more than she could take. If only they knew, what she knew.

Without hardly touching her dinner Kate pushed back from the table, "I think I'd like to go meet our new little guy in the barn."

Her daddy nodded and Kate went out into the evening. Inside the barn, she found Miss Virginia locked in her pen. The cow pulled her head from the hay trough when Kate stepped into the straw-padded pen, but turned back to her supper when Kate knelt beside the newborn calf.

Kate stroked the bull calf's silky white head and he lifted his chin as she scratched the underside of his neck.

Before long, she wasn't alone in the barn. Her daddy stood with one foot on the bottom rail of the fence and watched Kate. Miss Virginia left her feeder and came to check on her new baby boy. She licked his nose and he hopped up to latch onto the udder for his meal. Kate leaned against rail next to her daddy.

"Best mothering cows there ever were," he said. "That's what your mama said she always liked the best about them. They were good mama cows." He dropped his foot to the ground, but didn't walk away just yet. "I'm real proud of you Kate and I know your mom would be too."

"Thanks," she whispered as he pushed off the rail and moved onto the next pen, inspecting the cattle.

Kate left the barn and found herself on the dusk lit path leading to the family graveyard. She stepped inside the crooked hanging gate and sat down between the headstones of her mom and brother's graves.

"Hey, Mom," she whispered. "I passed the bar. Finally." She laughed as the tears welled in her eyes. "And I fell for the completely wrong guy. Again." Kate propped her elbows on her knees and rested her forehead on her arms.

The scent of lavender wafted gently on the breeze and Kate looked around, feeling the presence of her mother descend upon her. "You're doing great. Just try again," she heard from somewhere deep in heart.

"I don't know how," Kate whispered to the silent voice.

Thirty-six

Kate met Todd and Liz on the front steps of the duplex. She handed over the key and watched as the young man carried his new bride over the threshold of their new home. Kate smiled.

Jake's door opened and he poked his scruffy head out. He looked at Kate through sleep-squinted eyes—for goodness sake it was late afternoon and he was just getting up? Not much of a go-getter, was he?

"What are you doing out here?" he asked.

"Just giving the keys to the new tenants," she said, turning for the stairs.

"You want to come over for a little bit?" Jake asked, opening his door wider.

Kate dropped her head back and closed her eyes against the September sun. "No, Jake. I don't want to come over right now."

"Come on," he said, turning on that smile that he must of thought was sexy. "We didn't exactly get it off the ground last time. Let's not leave things like that between us." Jake's eyes brightened as he leaned one arm against the doorjamb.

"What do you mean we didn't get it off the ground?" Kate asked, stepping toward his open door. "What happened the last time I came over?"

"Nothing."

"Nothing?" Kate couldn't believe her ears.

"Nah, you said you couldn't find your keys. We headed for the bedroom. But you told me to stop. You said you wanted AJ, not me. That pretty much made my dick go limp, and then you passed out. End of story."

Kate's jaw dropped to the ground, "Really I said that. We didn't do anything."

Jake shrugged—clearly communicating he didn't want to remember being snubbed for another guy, "Yeah so?"

Kate threw her arms over her head and went around back to her new home, dragging this new information with her. She had resisted. She had resisted Jake, overcome the pull. Even in a drunken stupor, she had resisted him. And wanted AJ, instead? Well, why wouldn't she have wanted AJ, he was a dream—the too good to be true kind. Too bad, he came equipped with an alter ego Alejandro Junior that was deceptive and despicable.

Well, at least she could cease with the self-loathing. She wasn't as weak as she thought.

Nothing. Happened.

Kate stepped into the cool, dark interior of her basement apartment. The smell was somewhat less foul than when she first began the renovations, but it still looked like a half-finished project.

AJ's deception still tinkered in the back of her mind. If only…

Her phone rang.

"Hello. Hello," came Mary's overly cheery, fresh-from-a-honeymoon voice.

"Hi Mary. How was the honeymoon?" Kate asked as she sprawled across her double bed.

"Perfect," Mary replied, her sunshine-filled voice reinforcing her sentiment. "I'm calling to remind you about the brunch at the Fisher's tomorrow."

"Oh, yeah," Kate said, regretting that there was one more wedding event she had to attend. "I'm not sure I can make it."

"You have to come," Mary pleaded. "We're moving by the end of the week and I want to see you before we go."

Kate heaved a deep sigh, "But I don't want you to move. I want everything to go back to the way it was." A*t least back to when Mary wasn't moving away and when AJ wasn't Alejandro.*

"Hey, hey, hey," Mary piped her happy tune. "I won't be that far away. We'll see each other again soon. And now there is an opening at The Law Office of Rose Patterson. Don't worry I'm going to put a good word in for you."

"Thanks." Kate pressed her fingertips to her forehead.

"So, I have to ask, whatever happened to the guy who didn't show up at the rehearsal?"

"Um. He's history."

"Good. And Jake?"

Kate rolled her eyes. "Still living here. But I'm so over him."

"Glad to hear you're making progress in the relationship department. Those guys weren't good enough for you. You deserve the very best."

"Yeah, okay," Kate said.

"I had the perfect guy picked out for you, but I think he's off the market now."

"Who was that?" Kate asked, with mild interest.

"Alejandro."

"You mean, AJ?" Kate asked with a shake of her head.

"I prefer Alejandro. It is so much more rich sounding. Don't you think?"

"Sure," Kate agreed. "And what do you mean off the market?" Not that it mattered, Kate just wanted clarification.

"Well, Tony talked to him before I called you. It seems that while we were gone he has found someone special. I think he's bringing her to the brunch tomorrow. I can't wait to meet the girl who has stolen his heart. He's pretty great, didn't you think so?"

Kate was still hung up on the fact that AJ was involved with someone. Just goes to show he was a prowling man handler, always on the lookout for the next available girl. "He's definitely something to look at," Kate said, keeping the rest of assessment to herself.

"Oh, he's more than that and you'd know it if you got to spend any real time with him."

It sounded like AJ had worked the same deceptive magic on Mary as he had on her. Playing his nice guy routine to a tee. "I'll just have to take your word for it."

"Okay, well I've got to get going, but we'll see you tomorrow morning at the Fisher's, right?"

"Yeah, I'll be there."

* * *

The next morning Kate promised herself she wouldn't dress carefully. She wasn't going to put any effort into herself whatsoever. She picked out a pair of jeans knowing she would be terribly underdressed, but didn't care. She threw on a white eyelet lace tank top and slipped into her flimsy flip-flops.

Stomp. She eliminated a spider, the first of many that were making their way back into her dwelling.

Kate pulled her hair across the back of her head and into a braid that draped down her left shoulder. She climbed into her old truck and barreled through the city to the high-society end of town, where giant suburban houses looked down on the city.

The extra wide driveway was full of BMWs and Mercedes. Kate set the e-brake just in case the slight incline of the driveway was enough to roll her old Ford into the taillights of a luxury car.

Inside Kate found Mary and the others on the back patio with the late morning sun beating down on them all. Michelle stood snuggly close to Leo. Kate wondered briefly when and how that switch had taken place. Brandi sat all alone, perched on the end of a lounge chair with a mimosa in her hand.

AJ was nowhere to be found and Kate breathed a relaxing breath. The brunch was informal. Everyone ate from the offerings at the tables along the railing. When Kate was halfway through her croissant and grapes, AJ finally made his appearance.

"AJ, always the late-comer, aren't you?" Tony said, greeting him at the door.

Kate ducked behind Madison, even though, the tiny girl was hardly a shield that could conceal her, but at least it was something to block her view of AJ and whoever might follow him through that door. But he was alone. Brandi jumped up immediately offering him her company.

He spied Kate, but didn't make a move toward her. Soon the party moved inside.

Mountains of gifts were stacked in the living room. Mary and Tony ripped through the packages one by one. The lush bath towels Kate had ordered from the registry were met with great appreciation as was the waffle maker and espresso machine from other guests.

AJ worked his way across the room and stopped next to Kate.

"Hi," he whispered over her shoulder.

She turned back looking more at his shoes than his face with a quarter smile.

"Oooh," Mary squealed, tucking a card back into its envelope. "This one's from Alejandro." She looked up and smiled at him before she ripped into the white paper of the square box. Kate tried to subtly step away, but AJ's hand caught her on the hip.

Kate was about to ask him to remove his hand when Mary gasped.

"It's beautiful," Mary said.

Kate froze. It was her teapot. The one with the tiny pink flowers AJ saw her working on at the Pottery Shack.

Mary drew out the matching teacups and saucers. Her eyes lit up. "I love these. Don't you love these, Anthony?" Her husband nodded.

"They are handcrafted and painted by a local artisan," AJ explained. "She's a very gifted woman. They are one of a kind pieces. She's even doing some work at the restaurant for us, crafting new plate designs."

"Really?" Kate said, entering the exchange. "I thought she quit."

"No," AJ said. "Someone made her another offer, but I'm hoping I can convince her to stick with me."

"I hope you do keep her," Mary said, turning the pot over. "These are beautiful and…" Mary stopped and looked up at Kate. "Do you know this artist? Her signature looks familiar." Kate signed all of her pieces with her initials a K and M overlapping. Mary had probably seen it somewhere in all the time they'd lived together.

Kate barely shook her head as she tried to think of the best way to answer. But Olivia silenced any words she was about to speak.

"Let me see." Olivia reached for the box Mary had set the tea set back into. Kate felt her stomach turn. She didn't want to hear Olivia's catty put-downs right now. This was all getting out of hand. Why did AJ buy the set for Mary? She told him they wouldn't pass the inspection of Mary's friends.

"They really are lovely." Olivia handed the box back to Mary and turned to AJ. "Where did you say you got them?"

"A little shop downtown," he said. "I'd be happy to put you in touch with the owner if you're interested in some of the artist's work."

"Oh yes," Olivia said.

"Me too. Me too." Madison said from her seat where she was drinking a cup of decaf. The focus shifted when Tony opened the next gift and pulled out a giant crystal vase. Kate slipped out of the room, needing air.

AJ was only a moment behind her. "Kate," he called.

She stopped, spinning around to face him. "Are you done making fun of me?"

"When did I make fun of you?"

"Just now, with that whole 'very gifted woman thing'. I'm not hanging around for your amusement. You've humiliated me enough."

"I have never tried to humiliate you?"

"So, leading me on. Failing to tell me your real name. And watching me swoon over you like every other dim-witted girl on the west coast isn't your idea of humiliation. You deceived me." Her voice shook and she felt stupid tears filling her eyes.

AJ stepped closer, his eyes were kind. "It was wrong of me to deceive you, but I was afraid." AJ reached a hand to her cheek and brushed a tiny tear away with his thumb.

"Afraid of what?"

"I was afraid you'd never give me the time of day if I corrected your assumption. I didn't want to risk that. I wanted the chance to prove to you who I was."

"Well, you certainly proved something, that's for sure," Kate said, wanting to believe him, but she wasn't about to be fooled twice. She remembered what Mary had said. He wasn't supposed to be here alone. "Where is your new little girlfriend? The one you've been telling everyone about. Just because you show up here alone, doesn't mean I don't know there's someone else in your life."

"Well, where's Jake? Didn't you say you two were back together?" AJ planted a smirk on his lips.

Kate rolled her eyes.

"Aaah," he said, stepping closer. "Was that just a deception to get me to back off?" He searched her eyes.

"Yes and no. I thought we…well…never mind. It doesn't matter. Jake and I are not together and never will be together."

AJ smiled. "Come on Kate, can't we be friends again? I really liked it better when we were friends."

"Sorry." Kate shook her head. "I'm not going to be your little thing on the side while you're dating some hot chick."

"I'm not dating anyone."

"That's not what I hear."

"Didn't you also hear that I dumped a girl who'd had a disfiguring accident?"

"Yeah." Kate thought about it. That information had come from Madison and Olivia. Maybe not the most reliable sources. "But you still threw together a stripper party, instead showing up for a date with me."

"That's not exactly what happened."

Kate crossed her arms. "Then what did happen that night?"

"My parent's flight was late getting in, so I missed the rehearsal. After I took them to their hotel, I went back to my place. I was on my way out the door when a fight broke out, which I got caught in the middle of, trying to break it up. The police were called. Reports were filed. I was passing out free drinks like crazy to keep customers from fleeing the place and then Tony and the guys showed up for a little impromptu bachelor party. Tyler called in the strippers. I spent maybe two minutes in the back room with the guys."

"And then you stayed up decorating the whole place for the reception," Kate added, remembering what Carly had told her.

He nodded. "Kate, I'm so sorry. If I'd known you were going to be this upset I would have left to go find you, but Tony said you went home early."

Kate nodded and dropped her chin, keeping her tears at bay.

"Kate," AJ said, taking her by both elbows. "I've thought of you every minute since you climbed up on that stool at my bar."

"I thought you only dated hot models," she said, a pitiful sound in her voice.

"Maybe I did. But I'd like to date hot cowgirls now."

Kate tried not to smile.

"Look Kate, I think part of the reason I didn't correct your assumption about me is because I was that guy or at least on my way to becoming that self-centered person. I have never had to work hard for anything in my life. My parents have been very successful and made sure I had everything they lacked growing up, including responsibility. I was cruising on Easy Street. After my car was totaled, I took stock of where my life was going and who I was spending my time with. I wanted a change. So Tony suggested I move up here for a while. My dad opened the restaurant just so I could have a job. He didn't even let me find a job for myself. I wanted you to see the man I was trying to become. The man I want to be, not the man I was."

Kate nodded, shaming herself for letting gossip taint her impression of him.

AJ took another step closer, locking his blue eyes with hers. "I fell in love with you the moment you poured ice cold water into your lap. You're as real as they come Kate. And I'll be damned if I'm going to let you go that easily. Please give me a second chance."

AJ waited for her to speak. "I passed the bar," she said, finally sharing the news with the one person she had wanted to share it with all along.

"I knew you would," he said, smiling at her. "You're a smart girl."

"Not smart enough to trust my own heart, though. I'm sorry I doubted you."

He pulled her close and kissed her. Kate surrendered to his hold and melted against his body. The exaggerated gasp that belonged to none other than Mary Goodwich, or rather Mary Fisher, made them pull apart.

AJ turned to look at Mary, holding Kate's hand. "Mary," he said, "I'd like you to meet the girl I've been talking about. This is Kate. My girlfriend." He entwined his fingers in hers as Mary's face changed from surprise to happiness.

Author Biography

Meg grew up in the Pacific Northwest where she still lives today with her husband, children and crazy dog. She splits her time between homeschooling her children and writing in the hours after she's put her husband and children to bed. Writing is a passion that she is excited to share with her readers. To learn more visit: www.megcgray.com

Other books by the author:

The Teacher

Made in the USA
Lexington, KY
12 January 2014